VICTIM

VICTIM

M. R. HENDERSON

Five Star • Waterville, Maine

Copyright © 2002 by M. R. Henderson

This novel is a work of fiction. Names, characters, places, and incidents are either the product of the author's imagination, or, if real, used fictitiously.

Five Star First Edition Mystery Series.

Published in 2002 in conjunction with Tekno Books and Ed Gorman.

Set in 11 pt. Plantin by Minnie B. Raven.

Printed in the United States on permanent paper.

Library of Congress Cataloging-in-Publication Data

Henderson, M. R.
    Victim / M. R. Henderson.
        p. cm.—(Five Star first edition mystery series)
    ISBN 0-7862-3930-1 (hc : alk. paper)
    1. Murder victims' families—Fiction.   2. Mothers and daughters—Fiction.   3. Missing children—Fiction.
    4. Journalists—Fiction.   5. California—Fiction.
    6. Widows—Fiction.   I. Title.   II. Series.
    PS3558.E487 V53 2002
    813'.54—dc21   2001059220

There is no such thing as justice in or out of court.

—Clarence Darrow

PROLOGUE

There was no horizon, only the sharp rise of the mountain beyond the scrub oak and pine. A hundred miles east, dawn came with a crimson flush that paled as the sun climbed over the Ruby Mountains in Nevada and crept across the Great Basin before it crested the High Sierra and eventually spilled down into the California foothills.

Liz lay watching the faint outline of trees emerge from the darkness outside the bedroom window. Her head ached and her eyes were puffy from crying herself to sleep. She wanted to get out of bed and throw herself into the day's activities and drive away the confusing, frightening dreams she'd had all night, but the digital clock showed 6:25. Gil would turn on the light as if she were robbing him of precious sleep, even though the alarm would go off in a few minutes.

She shouldn't have argued with him last night. She seemed to tell herself that a lot lately. Their marriage had become a battleground on which she had no armor. Gil was always the winner in the war of words, a paragon who never raised his voice, a strategist whose weapons were put-downs and piercing sarcasm. It was bad enough when she was the only target, but Jenny had become one as well. Cracks had already begun to show in the child's sunny disposition: the desperate attempts to please her father, the hurt expression when she knew she had failed, again. Last night when Gil had called Jenny a baby for crying about a scraped knee, Liz's heart broke. Jenny was too young to understand that it was really Mommy that Daddy didn't love.

The fight had begun over, of all things, a bedtime story. Knowing it would ease the pain of the knee incident, Liz asked Gil to read one to Jenny before she went to sleep. It was a special treat for Jenny when Daddy was home from work before her bedtime. Any time with him was precious to her. But last night Gil said he was too tired. He worked hard all day. Did Liz have any idea what it meant to be out selling and trying to convince people to invest in Tustman and Husby Construction Company's proposed shopping mall? When Liz said his family deserved some time too, Gil retreated behind his newspaper and a wall of silence. Liz turned away and saw Jenny standing in the doorway, her storybook under her arm and tears in her eyes.

Liz read her a story and tucked her in. Neither of them mentioned Daddy. When she returned to the living room, Gil's jaw was still set stubbornly. She tried to make him see how five minutes of his time would have meant so much to Jenny, but he turned the blame back on her for mentioning it in front of Jenny without asking him first. As she did more often than not the past months, Liz wound up crying and pleading and eventually raising her voice in frustration. Smug because he had not lost his temper, Gil turned away, the battle won. But nothing was resolved.

When the alarm rang, Gil turned it off. Liz reached for her robe. Gil's rigid back told her she was still being punished for her outburst. She would be ignored until she "cooled down and came to her senses." She went to shower, telling herself this time she wouldn't apologize. She wouldn't say she was sorry and wanted to make up. Not this time.

As she turned on the shower, Liz heard the tape recorder start the music that set the rhythm and timed Gil's morning workout. When she was dressed and went through the bedroom, Gil was doing energetic body twists. Liz went to wake Jenny.

"Time to get up, honey."

Jenny came awake full of the delight with which she greeted each day. "Is it school today?" she asked, bouncing up. The novelty of first grade, "real school," hadn't worn off in the two months since Labor Day.

Liz nuzzled her warm cheek. "It sure is. Get dressed. Breakfast will be ready in ten minutes."

Jenny jumped out of bed and pulled off her pajama top as she ran to her pink and white bathroom. How like Gil she was in her morning energy level. How unlike him in other ways.

As Liz got breakfast on the table, cereal for Jenny, juice and coffee for Gil, she wondered if she could have said things differently last night. All she wanted to do was make Gil see the effect his broken promises and constant criticism were having. Their identity as a family was being undermined. Gil had laughed at her and said she was paranoid. But she had tried so many times she knew that nothing she ever said would make any difference. In Gil's eyes, he wasn't doing anything wrong. She was at fault for getting angry. She was at fault for expecting too much. If anyone should change, she should. There was nothing wrong with the playful teasing she called criticism. She had no sense of humor; that was her trouble. No one else took offense, so why did she?

Because they don't live with you, the hurt child within her said. Gil Husby, the eternal glad-hander, irresistible charmer of women of any age. Gil, the philandering husband. She knew he was seeing another woman again. The signs were unmistakable: hours away from the office when he couldn't be reached, sudden lunch or dinner plans that took him out of town, the self satisfied way he turned his back on her if she brought up any subject he didn't want to discuss. And most of all, his offhanded distraction, guilt perhaps, when Jenny tried to claim his attention.

She wondered who the woman was this time, but it didn't matter. He'd never change, and she couldn't live this way anymore. She had been overwhelmed by his attention and marriage proposal seven years ago, eager to escape her miserable home life and flattered enough to brush aside the rumors of wild escapades that had followed Gil home from college. *Boys will be boys. He'll settle down now that he's going into business,* the men said. The women would have killed to be in Liz's place when she walked down the aisle.

Gil's parents had accepted their son's decision unhappily. Liz Husby, daughter of a ne'er-do-well carpenter who drew more drunken breaths than sober ones, was a far cry from what they had envisioned as a daughter-in-law. She wasn't born in Pine Lake. The family were interlopers, undesirables, the California foothills equivalent of poor white trash. Liz's own father had said Gil was more than she deserved.

He was right about that, she thought. No one deserved being treated this way.

Jenny climbed onto her chair and thrust out a foot clad in an untied shoe. "It won't stay," she said. As Liz knelt to tie the lace, Gil came in.

" 'Morning, Daddy!" Jenny stretched up for a kiss.

Gil tweaked her ponytail. "Aren't you big enough to tie your own shoes?"

Jenny pulled her foot away, and the bow Liz was tying slipped loose. Jenny struggled with the shoelace again as Liz got up without looking at Gil. She poured his coffee.

"Eat your cereal, Jenny," she said quietly.

"I have to tie my bow."

"The bus will be here in a few minutes." She prayed that Gil would leave before then.

Glancing at her father, Jenny swung her untied shoes under the table and picked up her spoon.

She tries so hard, Liz thought. *She wants to be perfect for him, to win his hugs and kisses. One hint of disappointment on his part and she's crushed.*

Gil put down his cup. "Don't wait dinner for me. I'll be late. Those preliminary sketches you did won't work. I'm checking with another artist tonight to see if he can fix them."

Liz didn't trust her voice. Jack Tustman had asked her to do the sketches. Granted she wasn't an architect, but the renderings of the proposed shopping center were good! Jack liked them, and Gil had too, until now. Knowing his criticism now was retaliation for last night didn't take the sting out of his words.

Jenny smiled hesitantly as Gil got up from the table. "You promised to take me to the farm after school to ride the pony."

"I didn't promise. I said we'd see."

The smile wavered. "Can we?"

"I don't know, Jenny. I'm going to be pretty busy today. We'll see."

Jenny blinked and stared at her cereal bowl. Liz moved her coffee cup around on the flowered place mat as if finding the right spot would ease her daughter's disappointment. She struggled with the lump in her throat as Gil walked out.

"Finish your cereal, honey. The bus will be here any minute."

Jenny ate another spoonful and pushed the bowl away. She swung her feet toward her mother.

"I can't learn to tie," she said. Liz's heart broke at the discouraged tone.

"Sure you can, honey. It just takes practice." She bent over the shoes.

"Sharie can tie."

"Billy can't," Liz said, remembering the little boy's frequently undone laces. "Lots of kids your age can't tie yet. I'll bet you'll be the best bow-tier in your class by Christmas."

"Will I?" Jenny's eyes glimmered with a spark of hope.

"Sure. I'll help you practice. There. Now what do you say I pick you up at school and take you out to Happy Farm to ride the pony?"

Jenny hesitated. "Daddy said maybe—"

Liz swallowed painfully. "We'll stop at his office first and find out if he can go."

Jenny nodded and slid from her chair as the yellow school bus came around the curve beyond the fence. She ran for her jacket and lunch box. Liz kissed her good-bye and stood at the door until the tiny figure disappeared into the bus and it rumbled off.

So small to be off on her own for the day. So vulnerable. Leaving Gil and Pine Lake would be hard on her, but there was no other way. Gil and his parents would make life miserable for her if they stayed here. Even now, Liz was certain they discussed her shortcomings, real and imagined, in Jenny's presence. They were good to Jenny and she'd miss them, but she would survive. They both would survive a lot better than if they stayed here.

"I don't love you anymore, Gil," she said aloud to the quiet house. "Maybe I never did." She made up her mind to tell him she wanted a divorce.

12

At quarter to three, Liz was waiting in the station wagon outside the school. When she honked the horn, Jenny ran to the car and climbed in, putting the paper she was holding on her lap so she could fasten her seat belt.

"Did you call Daddy? Can he take me?"

Liz forced a smile. "He wasn't back from lunch, but Wanda said he'd probably be there soon. We'll stop and see." If she didn't, Gil would swear he'd been waiting.

Jenny nodded. "I made a picture for him!" She held up the construction paper. A man in blue stood beside a little girl with a ponytail and a sweater the color Jenny had on. The girl was holding out an apple to a brown pony. They were not stick figures, but carefully drawn shapes that were realistic and identifiable. Since the time she could hold a crayon, Jenny had displayed artistic talent that would blossom with encouragement and training.

Liz pulled into the parking space in front of the old livery stable Jack and Gil had converted to offices. The construction division of the company occupied the lower floor, the sales and promotion the upper. In addition to an inside stairway at the back, an exposed outer stairway opened off a walkway along the side of the building.

"I'm going to run in and see Uncle Jack for a minute," Liz told Jenny as they got out. "Come down and tell me what Daddy says, okay?"

"Okay." Jenny was already running around the walkway.

Liz went into the ground floor offices and greeted the gray-haired woman behind the desk. "Hi, Wanda. Can I see Jack for a minute?"

"Hi, Liz." She glanced at the lighted button on her multi-line phone. "He's on the phone. He asked me not to interrupt, so it may be a while. Is it something I can take care of?"

Liz hesitated. "No, it's not important. I was just wondering if he wants me to make any changes on the sketches."

"I don't think so," Wanda said. "He said they were great."

"You're sure?"

"Of course I am. You did a wonderful job. Everybody loves them."

Liz kept her smile with difficulty. "Thanks. Well, that's it then. Is Gil in?"

"I think I heard him go upstairs a little while ago." Wanda's gaze dropped to the papers on her desk.

She knows, Liz thought. "I have to go. Thanks," she said as feet clattered on the outside stairs. Waving at Wanda, she hurried out, ready to scold Jenny about running on the steep steps. As she reached the corner of the building, a man leaped down the last steps and collided with her. She staggered and tripped over the bricks around the flower bed, then sat down hard among the zinnia and mum plants. The man looked back over his shoulder as he raced toward the back of the building. For a moment she was too stunned to react and sat staring after him. She knew him—Rick March. She hadn't seen him since their sophomore year in high school. What in the world was he doing back in town? From the expression on his face, any business he'd had with Gil hadn't been pleasant, which meant Gil would be in a rotten mood. She got up to go rescue Jenny.

The door to Gil's office was open. Jenny was standing in the middle of the room, the drawing she'd come to give her father still clutched in her hand. Her face was chalk white, her eyes as huge as those of a startled owl.

"Jenny?" Liz got right up to her before she saw what was riveting the child's attention. Gil . . . on the floor . . . blood

. . . Instinctively she grabbed Jenny and ran, down the stairs, into Jack's office.

"Liz, what's the matter?" Wanda jumped up and came to put her arm around Liz and Jenny and lead them to a chair.

Liz shuddered. "Gil—" She felt violently ill.

The door of Jack's office opened and he looked out. "What's the matter?"

Wanda pointed upward and shrugged. "Maybe you'd better go see," she whispered.

Jack hurried out. Moments later he rushed back and into his office. Liz heard him dial the phone and even though he lowered his voice, his words carried clearly.

"Doc? There's been an accident. Get over here as fast as you can. And have your girl call the sheriff."

CHAPTER ONE

There are some things you can never escape. The past is one of them.

Beth glanced along the walkway of the apartment complex to see if someone had spoken, but she was alone with her own ghosts. She was suddenly cold despite the flat, scorching heat of an early summer as she stared at the picture on the front page of the *Los Angeles Times*. Not a ghost. Not a trick of the light filtering through the overgrown oleander. It was Rick March.

She jumped as something brushed against her leg, then leaned down quickly to capture the tabby cat that tried to slip outside before she closed the door. In the kitchen, her hands shook as she filled a mug from the electric coffee maker and sat down at the table. When the cat rubbed against her, she petted it absently, unable to look away from the newspaper photograph of the wild-eyed man being led off in handcuffs as the camera caught his expression of rage. In the sea of faces behind him, she recognized her own blurred image in the crowded courthouse hall. Cameras and microphones had been everywhere that day, impossible to escape. She felt a rush of fear, like a sudden blast of frigid air. She sipped coffee and steeled herself to read the brief paragraph under the picture.

"Richard March, shown here being led from a Bakersfield courtroom after being sentenced to life imprisonment for the brutal slaying of real estate developer Gil Husby last year, is being released today from Folsom Prison. His conviction was overturned by the California Supreme Court after March filed an appeal presenting evidence that the alleged murder weapon had been left in an unguarded police car for several hours during the investigation, thus breaking the chain of custody necessary for its admission as evidence at the trial. Story on page 6."

The paper rustled as she turned the pages. When she finished the first few paragraphs, the coffee turned to acid in her stomach. The all too familiar terror she had thought banished forever was once again battering at her defenses. *He was out. Free. How could they—?* She read again, skimming the portion that recapped the details of the crime she already knew. A choking breath escaped when she saw her name.

"One of the key witnesses against March was Elizabeth Husby, the slain man's wife, who now lives in Los Angeles. Mrs. Husby positively identified March as the man who ran from the murder scene shortly before her husband's body was discovered."

"Mom, can I wear my new shirt?"

Beth folded the front page to the inside and closed the paper quickly. Jenny came in wearing a blue T-shirt emblazoned with the Vista Elementary School logo. The PTA was selling the shirts as a fund raiser, and it was the first time since they'd moved to L.A. that Jenny showed any sense of wanting to belong. Beth had happily bought the shirt for her.

"Sure," she said, forcing a quick smile. The blue intensified Jenny's blondeness and the color of her eyes and banished some of her pallor, but she still looked frail and vulnerable. Instead of a lively, happy eight-year-old, she was still skirting the edges of the childhood that had been suddenly snatched away from her. Beth ached to hear her laughter ring the way it used to. She made up her mind that when school was out, they'd go to the beach every weekend. It was time for Jenny to come back into the world of joy.

The cat circled the table waiting for Jenny to sit, then with a smooth leap, settled itself in her lap. Jenny nuzzled it lovingly. "Pretty Sasha. Pretty kitty."

Beth put the paper on top of the refrigerator. "Better eat now, honey. It's getting late." She poured orange juice and put it on the table. Jenny shook cornflakes into a bowl, poured milk over them and stirred carefully.

"We have to leave in fifteen minutes, okay?" Beth said.

Jenny nodded, her mouth full. Beth retreated to her bedroom and looked at herself in the mirror above the dresser. She had escaped the past. This wasn't Pine Lake, and she was no longer the frightened woman named Elizabeth in the newspaper photo. She'd even gone so far as to change her name.

"Beth Davies," she whispered to the image in the glass, then more firmly, *"Beth Davies of Los Angeles."* Liz Husby was buried with all her insecurities in Pine Lake, miles from here. She'd only gone back twice in the past year and stayed just long enough for brief visits to her mother in the nursing home. Duty visits to assuage her conscience. Visits to a stranger who didn't recognize her own daughter and grandchild or even remember her own name anymore. Quick, furtive trips when she didn't let Gil's parents know she was in town for fear they'd find a way to make good their threat to take Jenny away from her.

The Husbys had never liked her, but they adored Jenny.

They wanted Jenny to take the place of their dead son, a possession to have and to hold, to nurture and to mold into a living memorial to the family name. They couldn't admit they had failed with Gil. Gil achieved instant sainthood when he died, his shortcomings erased, the perfect son. Shortly before the murder trial, they filed suit for custody of Jenny, claiming that Liz was unable to care for her properly. If it hadn't been for Gil's partner finding her a sharp lawyer from Bakersfield, they might have succeeded in taking Jenny away.

The law was on her side, the lawyer had told her. The Husbys would have to present convincing evidence that she was an unfit mother or they wouldn't be granted a custody hearing. Instead of reassuring Liz, that frightened her more. Glen Husby had run the town of Pine Lake so long, there were few people who wouldn't bow to the pressure he could apply one way or another and swear to whatever he wanted them to say. As soon as the trial was over, Liz left Pine Lake and except for her mother, erased her trail behind her.

But now Rick March was out of prison and the newspaper story announced to the world that she had moved to Los Angeles. Why in the world had they resurrected the photo, and how had they found out where she lived? Would anyone recognize her from the picture? It wasn't very good. The camera had been focused on March, not the milling, shoving crowd behind him. In the photo, her eyes were swollen almost shut from tears and the sleepless nights she'd spent worrying about the Husbys taking Jenny away. With her long hair hanging straight, she looked like a frightened child.

Glancing at the clock, she turned on the makeup mirror and began applying eye shadow and liner that accented her green eyes. She worked with the quick, sure strokes of an artist. She added a touch of blush to her cheeks and a soft pink lipstick to her bloodless lips to disguise her paleness. The short wedge cut made her blonde hair fuller and rounded her face. She looked like, was, a different person. *Liz Husby is gone forever,* she reminded herself. *I'm Beth Davies now.*

On her way down the hall, she glanced into Jenny's room. The bed was made neatly, Jenny's menagerie of stuffed animals lined up across the pillows. The closet door was closed, but Beth knew that behind it her daughter's pajamas and robe were neatly hung and slippers placed side by side on the shoe rack. On the desk, Jenny's schoolbooks were already in the bright purple knapsack, ready to go.

A need for order in her life after so much chaos, the psychologist explained. *It's not anything to worry about at this stage. She'll outgrow a lot of it.*

They had both grown a lot the past year. The move to L.A. had been good for them. She had taken back her maiden name and changed Jenny's as well in an effort to cut all the ties to her marriage and the horrible tragedy that ended it. She had distanced herself from Gil's parents and their attempts to lay claim to Jenny. Their anger hurt, but Beth had her own life to live, and Jenny to think about. After months of counseling, Jenny was finally beginning to come out of the dark corner into which she'd retreated when her father was killed. She was doing better in school, and she was learning to play and make friends with kids her own age. Her periods of depression were rare now and not as severe as when they'd first left Pine Lake.

The past, Beth told herself. *We're here now, and we're happy. I won't let anything change that.*

Jenny hadn't finished eating yet. Her precise deliberation in everything she did was time-consuming and maddening.

Beth tried hard to sound uncritically cheerful.

"Finish up and go brush your teeth, kiddo, and we're out of here." Pulling the plug on the coffee pot, Beth dumped the grounds and rinsed the pot. Jenny carried her dishes to the sink, rinsed them and put them in the dishwasher. Beth took a bag of dry cat food from the cupboard and filled Sasha's dish, then checked the level of water in the automatic dispenser.

She made a quick tour of the apartment to check the locks on the windows before she picked up her purse and the portfolio of freelance work she brought home every night. The number of projects she did outside of regular working hours was building steadily. In another year, maybe she'd be able to buy a house. The money she had from the sale of the place in Pine Lake and what she could save should be enough for a down payment on a small house with a yard. Real estate in Los Angeles was a good investment. It was foolish to keep paying rent when she could build equity for the future.

Jenny came out of her room with her knapsack. Sasha trailed behind her already complaining softly about being left alone. Jenny ran her hand along the cat's back as it moved toward the kitchen, still meowing. Outside, Jenny waited like a toy soldier on the walkway while Beth double-locked the door.

It was impossible to get around Los Angeles without a car, and sometimes it was impossible with one. Jenny's school was six blocks from the apartment. Beth dropped her off each morning before she went to work. It meant doubling back into the heart of Hollywood in rush hour traffic, but the few minutes of extra time it gave them together helped make up for Jenny having to stay at a sitter's after school until Beth got out of work.

When the light turned green, the driver behind Beth honked. She was a nervous driver. She had explored all the possible routes to the printing shop before settling on Fountain Avenue. It meant going a few blocks out of her way, but it was better than the daredevil darting in and out of side streets she'd have to do otherwise.

Creative Color Graphics was a few blocks east of La Brea on Sunset. Its corner location gave it the rare luxury of an employee parking lot in back in addition to the off-street parking for customers in front of the strip mall. Beth pulled into an empty space in the corner of the lot and eased her door open so it wouldn't hit the wall.

The shop was crowded. She waved to Zane and Frank behind the counter as she went up the open stairway to the art department. CCG's business was a pleasant mix of composites, business cards, stationery and small print runs. Many customers brought their work in camera ready, but those who needed artwork or special layouts came to Beth. She had been hired as an assistant to a woman who'd been there five years. Her work at first was cut-and-paste and a bit of original designing, but gradually she began dealing with customers as well. Her confidence grew as she discovered she enjoyed making suggestions and discussing designs. She enjoyed the variety of people who came in, especially the refreshing show business hopefuls who were always so enthusiastic and eager, so charged with life. When her boss retired three months ago, the owner of the shop, Zane Black, had asked her to run the department. The shop downstairs opened at eight, but Zane let her open the art department at nine so she'd have time to drop Jenny off each morning. She had accepted the offer gladly, and so far it had worked well. She had an assistant, an easy-to-get-along-with boss, and an exciting variety of work.

Kim looked up from the drawing board as Beth came in.

"You're in early," Beth commented.

"I thought I'd finish up some of this stuff so you can get at those rush orders that came in yesterday," Kim said.

"Thanks." Kim was not only a talented artist but, at twenty-two, she already had a good head for business and the ambition to use it.

They were unusually busy for June. With the fall television shows being cast, the flow of actors and actresses who wanted new composites or a change of design on their resumes was at its peak. Everyone wanted something different in the way of layout or artwork. And there were the regular customers as well. She looked at the orders marked *RUSH*. Both were from local businesses that placed frequent orders. Both wanted new artwork for special promotions. Ideas began to sketch themselves in Beth's head as she picked up her pencil.

"I almost forgot," Kim said. "Some guy called a few minutes ago. Said I couldn't help him; he wanted to talk to you personally."

"Did he leave a number?"

"No, he said he'd call back."

"It couldn't have been too important."

"Maybe it was personal," Kim suggested with a grin.

"More likely he wanted me to join a health club or bring my car in for an oil change," Beth joked. The highlights of her social life were PTA meetings or taking Jenny to a Disney movie. Men asked her out, but when she suggested Sunday trips to the park or zoo, they didn't ask again. The only real date she'd had was when Zane Black took her to dinner to celebrate her promotion to manager of the art department. For the evening outing, he insisted on paying for a sitter from a licensed agency to stay with Jenny, something Beth had never been tempted to do on her own for any of the glossy-surfaced men who asked for dates. Zane was interesting and fun, and she was a little disappointed that he hadn't asked her out again.

Footsteps on the stairs cued her to the day's first customer. She went to wait on a young actress who was a regular on *General Hospital*. By the time she finished, the day began in earnest, with her work on the rush orders continually interrupted by customers at the desk. Yet surprisingly, by noon she was caught up. When Kim left for lunch, Beth closed the door and hung the hand lettered sign, "Doing lunch—back at one," on the chain across the stairs. Carrying her portfolio, she walked the four blocks to the electronics shop for which she did freelance work. Thirty-five minutes later she was headed back, the check for the work in her purse along with two new assignments for other projects. She decided to skip lunch in favor of the peach and apple she'd brought from home, which she and Jenny had bought on their Saturday excursion to the Farmers' Market. Maybe she'd take Jenny to that Mexican restaurant she liked so much tonight. If they went early, it wouldn't be crowded and they'd be home in plenty of time for her to start work on one of the new assignments.

A lunch-hour rush of customers crowded around the downstairs counter, and all the copy machines were humming and clicking. Upstairs she put aside her portfolio and munched an apple as she got to work. Kim came in breathlessly a few minutes later.

"Sorry I'm late. Some guy stopped me as I was coming in and asked if I work with you."

Beth looked up. "Oh?"

"I asked why he wanted to know. You'll never guess what he said."

Suddenly apprehensive, Beth said, "What?"

"He said he thinks you're cute and wants to get to know you."

Beth tried to tell herself it didn't mean anything. Hollywood was full of weirdos. "He doesn't sound very sure of himself if he has to ask you to introduce us."

"That was the funny part," Kim said. "He didn't. He just said 'thanks' and walked away."

Uneasiness cramped Beth's stomach. She wrapped the apple core in a napkin. "What did he look like?"

"Tall, dark brown hair, not bad looking." Kim gave her a conspiratorial wink. Rick March's hair had been sunbleached at the trial, but it could have darkened behind prison walls. Beth realized she was clutching the apple core. She threw it into the wastebasket. "If he talks to you again, tell him I said 'no thanks.' " She turned back to her work to hide her concern.

First the phone call, now this. Had Rick March already found her?

CHAPTER TWO

From the shade of the roof overhang, Rick March watched the bus pull away from the diner and be swallowed up in the shimmering heat above the highway. He thought about going inside for a cold drink but in the long run, it would only make him hotter. Besides, the fewer people who got a good look at him the better.

He started walking back toward the town he'd already forgotten the name of. It had no more identity than the sign on the highway that said it had a population of 2,138. It was the kind of town without a newspaper of its own and where not many people would subscribe to the big city dailies. A town where no one knew he was just out of prison or gave a damn.

The bus ticket had taken a bite out of the few bucks the state of California gave him when he walked out. His stop at a big, anonymous hardware store in Sacramento had taken another bite. He had considered stealing a car from the acre of store parking lot but decided that close to the Joint, the cops would start looking for him just to stay in practice. Bastards. It was a lot smarter to hot wire some old clunker in a burg like this where it wouldn't be missed right away. If he changed the plates, he could drive it for a while.

The highway was the main street of town and four blocks long. In spite of the searing heat, cars were angle-parked along the curbs, their open windows tempting, but people were coming and going from the hick stores like trained fleas in a circus—people with nothing better to do than notice a stranger.

He turned the corner and headed for a back street. *The* back street. There was only one. A sign said it was "West Street." Beyond it, the block ended in a flat, still, open field. He measured his stride so to move at a pace that looked as if he were headed somewhere but not fast enough so he seemed to be hurrying. The town was so damned quiet, he felt like a goldfish in a bowl the cat was watching.

Living under the watchful eyes of prison guards had sharpened his ability to see in all directions without moving his head. He checked both sides of the street for driveways and garages. The first few he saw were empty. In the middle of the next block, he spotted an old pickup on cinder blocks in the back yard of a yellow, two-story house that needed a coat of paint. The cab and bed of the truck were covered by a dirty tarp that didn't come down far enough to cover the license plates.

The cart before the horse, but what the hell. You took gifts where you found them.

Glancing along the street, he veered up the driveway, scanning the houses on either side for signs of life. When he spotted a woman moving around behind the flowered kitchen curtains, he ducked and slid past and around the back corner of the house. Pressed against the siding, he counted to twenty. When the broad didn't come out to check, he decided she hadn't seen him. His breath sounded like a spurt of wind in the trees when he let it out. How did people keep from going crazy with all the damned quiet?

A thick hedge with shiny green leaves formed a wall around the house next door, where the shades were down on the upstairs windows. Nothing stirred anywhere.

The window where he'd seen the woman was close to the

back of the house. There was another window on the rear wall a few feet from him. It was the small, high kind to let light into a dark space like a pantry or a stairway. The back door had a pane of glass in the top half. If the broad inside looked out, the pickup was in plain sight. Maybe he should go in and take care of her first, but there was no telling if she was alone or how long she would be. First things first. If she spotted him, he could change his mind fast enough.

Crossing the stiff grass, he knelt in front of the truck and used the screwdriver on the new Swiss Army knife to loosen the screws on the license plate. He let them fall into the overgrown grass. The rear plate was rusted tight. He swore silently until he finally got it off. The tag was six months out of date, but he could doctor it so no one would notice. He stood up and slid the plates under his T-shirt and wedged them into the top of his jeans. Despite the heat, he put on his windbreaker and zipped it up to hide the bulge before he made his way back to the street, ducking again as he passed the windows.

At the next corner, he turned onto a short street that dead-ended against a rail fence. There were only three houses on one side, two on the other. One had a pile of old lumber and two broken kids' bicycles in front of the garage. Across the street, a car engine started up. A few seconds later an '89 Honda Accord backed out of the driveway. A kid's head poked above a car seat on the passenger side. The woman behind the wheel didn't slow down as she crossed the deserted intersection.

He waited until the car turned on the main street, then crossed to the driveway. In a two-car garage at the back of the lot was a beat-up Chevy. He glanced down the empty street, then walked to the fence at the dead end. He followed a path in the dry grass around the house to the back yard. The windows were open and the shades up, but when he didn't see or hear anyone, he sprinted across the yard and tried the back door. It opened. No dog came lunging out, so he went in.

He was in a big, old-fashioned kitchen. There were dishes in the sink and a cup with lipstick on the rim on the table. He went through to a dining room that had a round table with four chairs pushed under it and a huge sideboard with one door missing. The living room was crammed, with shabby furniture and cheap ornaments. His glance registered everything as he headed for the stairs across from the front door.

The two bedrooms upstairs were empty and messy. A kid's room had clothes and toys scattered everywhere. He picked up a bank shaped like rocket ship and shook it, then unscrewed the bottom. He pocketed two dollars and forty cents in change. He left the seven pennies.

The parents' room was more of the same. The dresser top was littered with cosmetics, half of which had spilled or oozed out of tubes without caps. He didn't find any money. He opened the dresser drawers. Two of them were filled with a jumble of the woman's panties and bras, the other one with men's underwear. He held a pair of jockey shorts to his waist. The guy had ten or twenty pounds on him. He tossed the shorts back and checked out a laundry basket of clothes on a chair that looked as if they'd just come from the line. He found some socks and a couple of T-shirts that would fit well enough.

Downstairs again, he went through drawers and cupboards. In the living room, he found a ten-dollar bill under a cheap figurine on the mantel of the fake fireplace. The dining room was a washout. In the kitchen, he took some crackers and a jar of peanut butter from a cupboard and two cans of beer from the refrigerator. Along with the clothes from upstairs, he crammed everything into a plastic grocery sack he found under the sink. As an afterthought, he dropped in his windbreaker and the license plates from the pickup. He went out the way he'd come in and crossed to the garage.

The Chevy's tires didn't have a lot of rubber, but they weren't quite bald. The car wasn't locked. Putting down the bag, he opened the driver's door and yanked the hood latch so he could have a look at the engine. The hoses and fan belt were okay; so was the oil. He lowered the hood and got behind the wheel. Glancing in the rearview mirror at the empty, quiet house and street behind him, he reached under the dash and yanked the ignition wires. A moment later the engine turned over. He cocked his head to listen to the rough idle. The carburetor needed cleaning, spark plugs too. Either the clown who owned the heap didn't give a damn or didn't have the time and money to work on it. The fuel gauge showed almost three-quarters of a tank. He leaned out to retrieve the plastic bag before he shut the door. With another glance in the mirror, he backed out of the driveway.

He followed West Street until it dead-ended not far past the diner where he'd gotten off the bus. He cut back to the highway and headed south. Steering with one hand, he opened the glove compartment and pulled the accumulation of junk to the seat. He pawed through it for a map, but there wasn't any. It didn't matter. The route was stamped on his brain like an old tattoo.

After about twenty miles, he spotted a weedy, overgrown side road in a thinly wooded area. He turned in and drove until he came to a clearing where there was room to pull off. He worked quickly to put on the license plates from the pickup. Done, he sailed the car plates one at a time into the scrubby woods. Then, squatting behind the car, he opened a can of beer and poured some into the dust to make a puddle of mud so he could smear the expired tag and spatter the plate. He did the same with the front one, then drank the rest of the beer.

With both doors open for air, he went through the junk from the glove box again. The only potentially useful thing he found was a gasoline credit card that had expired two years ago. He put it in his pocket.

Under the back seat he found a beat-up Los Angeles Angels baseball cap. He thumped it against the fender until it stopped sending off clouds of dust, then pulled it on. He looked at himself in the rearview mirror. Not bad. He'd pass for a jerk farmer at a glance. He got back in the car and U-turned toward the highway.

He saw the sign shortly before noon. PINE LAKE 22 MILES. Overhead, the sun blanched the sky and dulled the distant mountains in smoky haze. Despite the open windows, the inside of the car was an oven. Every few minutes, he leaned forward to let the hot wind dry his back where it was sweaty from leaning against the plastic upholstery.

He didn't like going through town in the middle of the day when people were around. Pine Lake didn't have a newspaper except for the weekly rag that told who had a birthday party and who was visiting from Kansas, but he'd bet money everyone in town knew he was out. It was probably already the hot gossip in Stella's Cafe and the barber shop. Anyone who caught sight of him would call that stupid, trigger-happy sheriff who almost blew his head off a year ago. He wondered if he should hole up until dark, but the longer he hung around the riskier it was. He'd wait until lunch hour was over and the yokels went back to whatever the hell they did all day. The streets would be empty then.

He dredged his memory for a place to pull off before he came to the town. When he saw the gravel road a few miles out, he turned on to it. Unless he was mistaken, it was the road to the lake where he used to go when he played hooky or ran away. It used to be the only place where he felt good about being alone. *Safe*.

A cloud of dust followed the car like a shadow. About a mile in, it rolled over him as he stopped when he saw the driveway that climbed steeply and disappeared among the trees. It was overgrown with weeds, and there were no tire tracks in the dust. He twisted the wheel and put the car in low gear. It strained and jerked, but he coaxed it to the top of the drive.

It was the place he remembered. It looked empty. All the shades were pulled at the windows, and the yard had a neglected look, with tall grass and no flowers. There was a carport he didn't remember. He pulled into it.

He walked across the clearing to the little summerhouse perched on the edge of the bank and looked down. The steep bank had grown wild with scrubby brush. The steps down to the dock were weathered and cracked. They didn't look strong enough to hold much. He went back to the cabin and tried the doors. Locked. Windows too, he discovered when he made a circuit of the cabin. One of the bedroom ones was only about six feet from the ground, an easy climb once he got the window open. In the carport, he found a metal milk crate and set it below the window. Then he wrapped his hand in his windbreaker and picked up a rock to smash the glass above the window latch. He brushed away the sharp pieces before he reached in to undo the lock and push the window up.

Inside, he prowled the rooms with a sense of being

home. Not much had changed. It might even be the same furniture. He didn't really remember. He walked through the rooms a second time, this time stopping in the bedroom to pull a chair into the closet and look into the hot, musty crawl space above a trap door. Son of a bitch, nothing had changed! He climbed down and put the chair back by the dresser. He went out through the front door and left it open behind him.

He went behind the car to relieve himself, then did a couple of deep knee bends to stretch out his muscles. He had done a hundred push-ups in his cell this morning while he was waiting for the guard to come with his release order. He was in better shape than he'd ever been, lean and hard from his daily workouts the past year. He wasn't used to sitting still the way he had all morning. Pent-up energy pulled at his muscles.

He went back to the steps in front of the house and sat with his feet on the dusty grass. He took the expired credit card from his pocket and went to work on it with the Swiss Army knife. He wouldn't use the card unless he had to, but it could come in handy. Ten minutes later, the expiration date was mutilated enough so it wouldn't print clearly. He rubbed it with the carbon from an old receipt until the fresh scrapes looked as beat up as the rest of the card.

Excitement stirred in his belly when he finally closed the cabin doors and got back in the car. A year was a long time to wait, but it was going to be worth it. He was going to make the whole damned town of Pine Lake pay for every minute of the time he'd done. He drove down the steep driveway and headed back toward town.

Pine Lake was the same crummy little place it had always been, one of those less than zero towns that dotted the Sierra foothills off Highway 99 between L.A. and Sacramento. Like a lot of others, it died when Interstate 5 was cut through the San Joaquin Valley. It was the kind of place you got out of as fast as you could if you were unlucky enough to be born here or dumped in, like he was when he was fifteen. His big mistake was ever coming through this way again.

He drove at a sedate fifteen miles an hour just like the sign said, his guts knotted. The sheriff's office looked closed. There wasn't a soul on the street. He drove past the feed store, the bank, the market, the converted livery stable . . .

At the other end of town, there was a Dairy Queen, then nothing but scraggly live oaks and dusty, barbed-wired fields. Beyond the town limits, the land began to rise into the foothills. The road twisted among stunted pines. Funny the way everything looked as familiar as if he'd been here yesterday. When he came to the blacktop road he was watching for, he turned in and drove until he spotted the mailbox.

The pines along the driveway were tall and straight like those at higher elevations. These had been planted and tended to make the house invisible from the road. When you had enough money, you could buy privacy. He thought about driving up, but the sound of the car would carry a long way in the hot, still air. Instead, he drove on until he found a spot wide enough to turn the car around. He parked near the foot of the drive and waited for the faint haze of dust to settle before he got out and walked up.

The house sparkled white in the slashing rays of the sun. It was an old farmhouse, restored and modernized. The wide front porch had been enclosed with screens and glass, and a screened breezeway connected the back of the house to a two-car garage. The garage was open. A red convertible was parked in it. Not the one he remembered. A later model, but the same color. His guts tingled.

He made his way around the garage, past the breezeway, to the back of the house. He stood behind a clutch of birch trees to study the kitchen window. Nothing moved inside. That didn't surprise him. She wouldn't be in the kitchen. The closed windows meant the air conditioning was on. He listened for its soft hum when there was a break in the high-pitched drone of cicadas. As he walked to the back steps, he reached into his pocket for the knife.

People in small towns had the convenient habit of not locking their doors. In the kitchen, he listened for some sound to indicate where she was. There was nothing but the steady hum of the air conditioning. But she was here. She gave off a scent like a bitch in heat. Smiling, he used the knife blade to cut the cord of the wall phone before he walked softly through the living room to the stairs.

She was lying on the bed, her bronzed body almost naked in brief shorts and a halter that made the fire inside him flare. Her eyes were closed, but she wasn't asleep. From time to time she lifted one arm to brush her hand across her forehead. The movement made the tight cloth strain across her breasts. He sucked air through his teeth with a low whistling sound.

Her eyes opened and she bolted upright.

Grinning, he said, "Hi, Suzie. Remember me?"

CHAPTER THREE

Jenny folded her napkin and put it beside her empty plate.

"Will there be anything else, Senora?" the waitress in the colorful skirt and peasant blouse asked.

Beth smiled at Jenny. "Would you like some ice cream?"

Jenny shook her head. "No, thank you."

Beth asked for the check. Jenny had been pleased with the idea of eating in the cool, garden patio of the Mexican restaurant. She had munched taco chips and ordered her favorite burrito, but halfway through the meal, her excitement began to fade. She slipped back into her quiet mood despite Beth's attempts to keep up a lively conversation that was partly for Jenny's benefit, but also a feeble try at driving off the uncomfortable feeling that had settled over her since Kim mentioned the man who'd questioned her outside the shop. Beth kept telling herself Rick March absolutely could *not* have found her that fast. He'd only been let out today. There wasn't time. She was overreacting to Jenny's somber mood.

Jenny had been a rambunctious, exuberant preschooler, and her hesitancy about life since Gil's death worried Beth. It was as if she were carrying a heavy burden she could only escape for brief flashes. Beth missed the laughter and bubbling enthusiasm. Could Jenny ever forget the murder and go back to being a happy little girl again?

They needed to get out more, be with people. With summer coming, Beth vowed she'd do more fun things with Jenny: Disneyland, picnics, maybe a trip to San Francisco or San Diego. It was time for both of them to start living again. And Jenny needed to play more with children her own age. She seemed to shy away from playmates. Beth had suggested camp, but Jenny seemed terrified by the prospect, so Beth hesitated to bring up the subject again.

When they got home, several neighbors were sitting in an oasis of shade in the courtyard. A woman Beth had met several times in the laundry room waved. Beth returned the greeting as a little boy raced to Jenny and tugged at her jeans.

"Play with me!"

Jenny said, "I can't, Tommy. I have too much homework."

Beth knew it was only an excuse, but she didn't coax. The therapist said she had to be patient and not push Jenny into social contacts faster than she was ready to move. Patience was the key, Beth reminded herself again.

She unlocked the door and blocked it with her foot when Sasha tried to slip out. Jenny caught the cat and carried it to her room. When Beth walked by the open door a few minutes later, Jenny was already at her desk bent over a school book. The cat was on her lap, purring.

"Do you have a lot of homework, honey?" Beth asked.

"Arithmetic, and I have to study my spelling."

"It's so warm in here. You're sure you don't want to play outside for a little while?"

Jenny shook her head. Sighing, Beth turned on the air conditioners. By the time she'd changed to shorts and a T-shirt, the apartment was cool. She settled herself at the card table in the living room and spread out her sketch pad, pencils and the information for the new electronics ads. Electronics equipment didn't stir her creative juices immensely, but she began to sketch, hoping for inspiration to strike.

She had filled a page with snippets of ideas before one took her fancy and she began to work it out. Jenny, already showered and in her pajamas, came out for a glass of lemonade.

"Want one, Mom?"

"Not right now, sweetie. Thanks."

The doorbell rang, startling them both. Jenny froze with the pitcher in her hand. She looked so terrified, Beth gave her a reassuring smile as she went to the intercom.

"Yes?"

"Ms. Davies? Elizabeth Davies?"

Hesitating, Beth said, "Yes?"

"My name is Vince Norris. I'm with the *L.A. Times.*"

"I already subscribe."

"I'm not selling subscriptions. I'd like to talk to you."

Beth glanced over her shoulder at Jenny. "What about?"

"I think it would be better if I didn't say anymore here. My guess is that your neighbors can hear me better than you can."

Beth's heart skipped a peculiar half beat at his strange explanation. But he was right about the people sitting outside. The front gate was close enough for anything to be overheard easily. With a nervous glance at Jenny, she buzzed the front gate. Jenny hurried to her room with the lemonade.

Beth opened the door and made sure the screen was latched as she watched the man come along the walkway. He was tall, about thirty, with dark brown hair, and dressed in gray slacks and a plaid sport shirt. He fit Kim's description of the man who had asked about her. Beth's pulse was too fast when he stopped outside the screen.

"Ms. Davies?"

Beth's mouth was dry. She nodded.

He lowered his voice. "I'm a reporter for the *L.A. Times.* I'm doing a follow-up story on Rick March."

Her stomach cramped in a vicious spasm. She started to close the door, but he spoke urgently.

"Wait. At least listen to me a minute."

She barely recognized her own voice. "Go away, please!" The couples on the patio were momentarily quiet, and her voice sounded too loud. She bit her lip.

The reporter's voice dropped to a near whisper. "You know he's out? He may be tried again, but right now he's a free man."

"How—how did you find me?" The air conditioning slid over her flesh like a frigid wind.

He looked a little bit smug. "It wasn't hard. You went to art school here in L.A. The court records showed your maiden name was Davies. I checked with Light and Power. Your address and place of employment were listed."

Her shock was giving way to anger. "Are you—did you do that story in this morning's paper?"

"Yes, but I picked most of it up from the wire services. Now I want to do an in-depth piece." He glanced over his shoulder as the conversation resumed on the patio. "Look, give me five minutes."

She wanted to slam the door, but one of the women sitting on the patio was watching her curiously. Her hand shook as she unlocked the screen and opened it. When Vince Norris stepped inside, she closed both doors and motioned him to a chair.

"Just a second," she said. She went down the hall to close Jenny's door. Jenny was on the bed, her head on two pillows and her reading book propped on her stomach. Beth kissed her.

"Good night, sweetie, in case you fall asleep before I'm

done. Don't forget to brush your teeth when you finish your lemonade."

Jenny still looked frightened. "Who is he, Mom?"

Beth kissed her cheek. "Just someone who wants to talk to me. About a job." She smoothed the edge of the pillow case. "See you in the morning, okay?"

"Where's Sasha?"

"On the windowsill in the living room where it's cool. I'll let her in when she gets tired of watching the birds. Good night, honey."

" 'Night . . ." It was nervous, tentative.

Beth blew a kiss as she closed the door. She'd get rid of Vince Norris in a hurry. How dare he search her out? In the living room, Norris was standing by the card table studying her work.

"You're good," he said.

She was too nervous to answer. She was sorry she had let him in. She waited until he sat down, then seated herself on a chair close enough so their voices wouldn't carry to Jenny's room.

"All right, Mr. Norris. Your five minutes are running." She tried to keep her voice from shaking but was only partly successful.

"I wasn't at the trial, Ms. Davies, but according to what I've read, March created quite a sensation when he was convicted. He made threats against the people who claimed railroaded him, isn't that right?"

Beth's stomach went from icy to fiery hot as memory replayed that terrible last day in the courtroom. It had taken two bailiffs to subdue March and lead him away. She nodded numbly, willing both the memory and Vince Norris away. That was a lifetime ago . . . another world . . .

Norris ran his hand across his sandy hair and watched

her. "How do you feel about his being released, Ms. Davies?"

How did she feel? Norris had to be kidding. Rick March had killed her husband, her child's father, torn her life apart so that after eighteen months she was just beginning to get it back together. How did Vince Norris expect her to feel? She was terrified. Did he care that he was dragging out all the fear she had managed to suppress all day since she read the story in the morning paper?

She said, "I don't feel anything. I don't know anything. I don't want to know anything. I beg you, please don't print anything about me or my daughter. Let us get on with our lives. It hasn't been easy starting over, but we're doing it. No one here knows about—" She faltered. "About the past. I want to keep it that way. If you drag it all up again, think what it will do to my child. She's only eight—" Beth blinked back tears of frustration. "Please go away, Mr. Norris."

The tabby cat jumped from the windowsill and walked through the room, tail high. When it went down the hall meowing, Beth got up to let it into Jenny's room, then closed the door. When she came back, she stood by the front door, her hand on the knob.

"I want you to leave now, Mr. Norris." She opened the door as a burst of laughter erupted on the patio. Norris got up reluctantly.

"Believe me, Ms. Davies, I'm just trying to do my job. If I found you, other reporters will too. You can count on it. I may not be as bad as you think. I don't want to hurt you," he said. "I just want the story. I'd like to stay in touch. If March comes looking for you, you're going to need a friend." He reached into his shirt pocket and held out a card. "If you want to talk—about anything—call me."

41

When he went out, Beth locked the screen and the inside door, then leaned against it and stared at the darkening room. *If Rick March came looking for her . . .*

What was she going to do?

CHAPTER FOUR

Vince rolled down the window while he waited for the climate control to cool the oven-like car. Beth Davies was scared, plenty scared. He should have leaned on her a little harder to make her talk.

He stared at the motionless fronds of a half-dead fan palm in front of the apartment complex. Did she really think she was safe? If she wanted to hide, she should have been more creative about a new identity and location. Her maiden name, for crissake, and the only place she'd ever lived other than Pine Lake. Well, she had time to think about it now. When the shock wore off, she'd be up against the reality of March stalking her. She'd need a friend then. She'd need all the help she could get. In the meantime, he'd find ways to keep the story alive with what he had. He intended to read everything there was on March and get to know him inside out so he could predict what he'd do next. Cons like March were all alike. They thought big, but they always forgot little things that eventually tripped them up. Rolling up the window, he headed for the freeway and downtown.

In his office, he took out the file of articles on March he'd retrieved and printed from Nexis. The folder was thick. Murders in small towns outside L.A. didn't usually rate many inches, but March's trial had caught the attention of a *Times* crime reporter who had done profiles on him and squeezed the story for all it was worth. The reporter won the Scully Award for the coverage. It was no Pulitzer, but the story had made him. He was working for the *Washington Post* now and had two true crime books out. He was almost as well known as Ann Rule, and it all started with Rick March. Now the sequel was Vince's. He opened the file.

March was born in Bakersfield. From the chronicle of his early life there, it was unlikely he'd ever want to go back. Abandoned by her boyfriend before Rick was born, his mother drank her way through welfare checks in one small town after another along the inner spine of San Joaquin Valley. By the time he was four, March had lived in a succession of foster homes where he didn't fare much better than he had with his birth mother, who disappeared from the system and his life before he started school.

He had a long history of running away by the time he was eight, and a growing juvenile record by the time he was ten. Psychiatrists and social workers tagged him an antisocial personality, but Vince knew that was a cop-out term for anything from slightly schizo to an out-and-out psycho Hitchcock would have found too scary to put on the screen. One psychiatrist who was interviewed at the time of the trial said it was highly unusual for an antisocial personality like March to alter his patterns. Another said it was not uncommon for a sociopath to a build up rage over a period of years and commit a violent act as the result. Judging from March's outburst when he was sentenced, Vince's vote was with the second theory. March was perfectly capable of carrying out his vow of revenge. And more than likely, he'd go after the easiest targets first: the two women who had testified against him, Liz Husby and Suzie Tustman.

March had been farmed out to a foster family in Pine Lake when he was fifteen. His school record was heavy with truancies and failures. He was there less than a year when he got himself shipped off to a juvenile facility for breaking into cabins a few miles out of town and helping himself to whatever wasn't nailed down, including several hunting rifles which he used for target practice on neighbors' windows.

From Pine Lake on, March spent half his life behind bars in correctional schools, local jails and state prisons, for everything from breaking and entering to armed robbery. More recently he'd done five years on a felony murder charge that had been plea bargained down to manslaughter two after a supermarket holdup, during which an elderly customer in the store died of a heart attack after being hit with a gun butt by March. Less than a year after his parole, March was convicted of killing Gil Husby. He got twenty to life.

Jeez, they never learn, Vince thought.

With the civil rights and library access inmates had these days, March used his time in Folsum to become his own jailhouse lawyer and file an appeal challenging the chain of custody of the murder weapon. The idiot Pine Lake sheriff had left the tire iron in an unattended police car while March was being questioned. Enough time, according to the appeal, for the evidence to be tampered with. A California Supreme Court Justice agreed. The technicality opened the gates and let March walk out a free man.

Vince drummed his fingers on the desk. Beth Davies had every reason to be scared. March didn't have much to lose. Sure as hell he'd be back inside as soon as the Kings County district attorney who had tried the original case found a way to get around the hick cop's stupid mistake. March was damned lucky. Cops in L.A. would have wrapped the evidence in a chain of custody tied with Boy Scout knots. Vince made a note to check out the sheriff in

Pine Lake if he was still around.

Leafing through the clippings, Vince's certainty grew that March was crazy enough to go after the people he blamed for putting him behind bars. He'd threatened the sheriff, the D.A., the judge, jury, Liz Husby and the other witness, Suzie Tustman, the wife of Husby's partner.

March's story of what happened the day of the murder was as thin as High Sierra air. He claimed he pulled off the road to change a flat only to find there was no tire iron in the trunk of the car. It turned out the car had been stolen in Reno that morning. March was ready to abandon the car when Gil Husby drove up and stopped. Husby recognized him from ten years earlier in high school. Instead of a ride, he loaned March a tire iron and said he could drop it off on his way through town when he was finished.

March changed the tire and was tightening the last lug when Suzie Tustman drove up in a red convertible and stopped. They hadn't been in school together, but March said he remembered seeing her around. She remembered him, too, and offered him a cold drink and the chance to wash up if he wanted to drive to the house. He said he went. She said he was a liar. She swore she was home all day doing laundry. Her husband phoned several times during the day and came home after lunch to pick up some papers he needed. Suzie Tustman swore she didn't have any idea why March tried to use her as an alibi.

The D.A. introduced into evidence an issue of the *Pine Lake Courier*. A picture of Suzie Tustman riding in her red convertible in the Halloween parade was on the front page. The story gave her name and enough details, according to the D.A., for a con man like March to concoct an alibi. A copy of the paper was found on the back seat of March's car. The D.A. also pointed out that March's attempts to describe the Tustman house were generically vague.

Jack Tustman corroborated that he had called and gone home the way his wife said. He pinpointed his trip to the house during the time March claimed to be with her. The public prosecutor handling March's case couldn't punch any holes in their stories or even show they had reason to lie. Suzie hadn't lived in Pine Lake when March was there as a teenager. Jack Tustman vaguely remembered the trouble March had gotten in as a kid but had never known him. Liz Husby's identification of March as the man who ran out of her husband's office just before the body was discovered, along with the evidence of the bloody tire iron, brought the jury back with a guilty verdict in less than an hour.

Vince wondered if the Tustmans knew March was out of prison. Grabbing the phone book, he checked the area code for Pine Lake and dialed information, then Tustman's number. The phone was picked up quickly, and a deep-voiced man said, "Yeah?"

"Mr. Tustman?"

"He can't come to the phone right now. Who is this?"

Something in the man's tone set off a warning bell. "Vince Norris from L.A," he said without mentioning the paper.

The man covered the phone, but Vince heard his muffled call. "Sheriff?"

Vince hung up. Well, well. Cops. Could be a hundred reasons, but he wasn't going to waste time trying to sort them out. Cramming the clipping folder into his briefcase, he headed for the garage.

It was almost dark when he pulled into a gas station just outside of Pine Lake. When he asked the kid filling the tank where the Tustman house was, the kid's eyes bugged.

"You a cop?"

"No, a reporter."

"No kidding. Where?"

"*L.A. Times.*"

"Hey. How'd you hear about the murder so fast?"

The kid was impressed all to hell with a big time reporter. Vince gave him a knowing look. "Confidential sources. I hear everything soon as it happens." Before the kid could come up with another question, Vince said, "Do you know where the Tustman place is?"

"Sure." The kid pointed down the highway. "You go through town. 'Bout three miles out you come to County Road 17. The Tustman place is 'bout a mile in on the left. You can't see it from the road, but you can't miss the mailbox. It's the first one on that side." He leaned down to the window. "You gonna write a story 'bout the murder?"

"You bet." Vince pulled a pad and pencil from his briefcase. "Let me make sure I get your name right."

The kid's head bobbed as if it were on a spring. "Gary— G-A-R-Y—Kellog—K-E-L-L-O-G."

Vince printed it out in letters big enough for the kid to read. Then he said, "Now tell me about today. Did you see the victim anytime in the last twenty-four hours?"

"Naw. She don't come in here if she can help it. She gets Jack to fill up the car if it needs gas."

She. Suzie Tustman? He said, "Jack? That'd be her husband, right?"

"Yeah. I hear he had a heart attack finding her that way." Gary Kellog whistled softly through his teeth. "Come home expecting dinner and find your old lady butchered 'stead of the chicken. Shock like that could kill you."

"Is he in the hospital?"

Gary shook his head. "No hospital here in Pine Lake, and I'd of seen the ambulance go by if they took him down to Bakersfield. More'n likely Doc Philbin'll take him over to the nursing home if he wants to keep an eye on him."

Vince asked where the nursing home was. Gary said it was on the other side of town. Vince put out his hand, and Gary wiped his on his pants before they shook.

"You need anything else, you get in touch with me, y'hear?"

"Sure thing. Thanks, kid."

"I'll get Mr. Owens at the drug store to save me tomorrow's *Times*," Gary shouted as Vince drove off.

Vince whistled softly, barely able to contain himself. Suzie Tustman murdered. Rick March hadn't wasted any time. Vince had trouble staying down to the fifteen mile an hour speed limit through town. When the sidewalk ended, the town did too. Vince checked the odometer and hit the gas. He slowed when nearly three miles had clicked off, but he didn't spot the road. If there was a sign, he'd missed that, too. He went another quarter of a mile, then turned around and drove back slowly. This time he saw the narrow blacktop road that angled off among the pines. He turned onto it and drove almost a mile before he saw a cluster of cars at the foot of a driveway. A man in a tan uniform and a Smokey the Bear hat stood in the middle of the drive slightly apart from the others. Vince knew he'd found Tustman's place, even though he couldn't see the mailbox.

He parked fifty yards down the road and walked back. The middle-aged sheriff's deputy motioned with his outstretched arms for the others to step back.

"Go on home now, folks. There's nothing to see, and you know the sheriff's not going to let you near the house."

He jutted his chin in Vince's direction. "Something I can do for you, Mister?"

Vince pulled out his ID as the curious onlookers made a path for him. The deputy read the card and tugged at the end of his nose, not sure what to do. Finally, he handed the card back to Vince.

"Ask for Sheriff Mayville up at the house." He stepped aside.

The sun had long since disappeared. Darkness shrouded the pine trees bordering the drive. Even at this elevation, the hot dusty smell of the drought hung in the air.

Yard lights blazed everywhere, and the house was lit as if a party were in progress. The sheriff's car and two state Highway Patrol vehicles were parked close to the house. A black hearse and a white van were parked on the grass. A man with a deputy sheriff's badge pinned to his plaid sport shirt stopped Vince on the porch. Vince showed his card again. The man told him to wait while he checked with the sheriff. He closed the door behind him before Vince got more than a glimpse of a wide hall.

The sheriff who came back with the deputy was a small, pale-faced, balding man with features as sharp as a predatory bird. He motioned Vince inside and closed the door when the deputy went out. The hall was fifteen degrees cooler than outside. The sweat on Vince's back began to evaporate.

"I'm Sheriff Mayville. You drive up all the way from L.A., Mr. Norris? How'd you hear about the murder?"

Vince decided his growing reputation for speed was worth nurturing. "I was up this way on another story when I got a call from one of my contacts."

Mayville snorted. "Didn't your contact tell you the county D.A.'s investigators have been called in? Not much I can do to help you. Case may be out of my jurisdiction."

That wasn't any surprise after the mess Mayville made of the Husby murder investigation. But underlying the sheriff's words was an unmistakable touch of anger that might come in handy. Vince nodded sympathetically.

"How was she killed?"

Mayville said, "Knifed." Even though Mayville didn't shift position, he gave the impression of a man looking over his shoulder.

Butchered, according to Gary Kellog. "Any ideas who did it?"

"Maybe."

"Rick March got out of prison today."

"That he did." The sheriff's expression didn't flicker. His eyes were a peculiar shade of gray, like stones at the bottom of a clear stream.

"Anyone see him in town or hanging around?"

"Not that they told me about."

"Who found the body?"

"The husband."

"That'd be Jack Tustman, right? He was Gil Husby's business partner in the construction company, wasn't he?"

The sheriff's expression became wary. "Yep."

"You think there's any connection between the two murders?"

Definitely cautious now, Mayville said, "Now, I don't think we should be speculating 'bout that until we get some evidence, do you, Mr. Norris?"

Vince let it go. "Has the coroner been here?"

"Doc Philbin's here. We're waiting for the county crime unit and coroner now."

"Any idea how long she's been dead?"

The sheriff's shoulder hunched almost imperceptibly.

"Jack found her three hours ago when he came home, but Doc estimates more likely she's been dead six-seven hours anyhow. Hard to tell with the air conditioning." Behind him, a man in gray slacks and a white shirt appeared in the living room doorway.

"They want you upstairs, Sheriff."

Mayville put his hand out, and Vince shook it. "Sorry I can't be more help, Mr. Norris. Maybe if you call me at my office tomorrow?"

Jackpot! Vince gave a quick nod. The man in the white shirt stared a moment before he followed Mayville upstairs. Vince edged closer to the doorway and saw a knot of people in the upper hall. They separated to let the sheriff go by, then followed him into a room where the door was open. He stopped, they stopped, like cattle waiting to be let into the barn, and stood with their backs to the hall.

Vince crossed the living room in four strides and went up the stairs, sweeping his gaze like a camera lens, registering what he glimpsed in bits and pieces through the group of men in the doorway. The bedroom was neat, no sign of a struggle. The body was on the bed, on top of a white spread, as if the woman had stretched out for a nap. She was wearing pink shorts. Vince couldn't see the upper half of her body, but there was no missing the blood. It covered whatever she was wearing above the shorts and had soaked into the bedspread in dark, ugly blotches. A trail of it made a long exclamation point down the pink dust ruffle. A few feet away, a man sat in a pink-and-green flowered chair with his face hidden in his hands.

A rangy man in a pale gray suit turned and saw Vince. "Hey, who the hell are you? Who let you in?"

Vince held up his ID. "*L.A. Times.*"

"Well get the hell out of here. This is a crime scene." He

moved toward the hall, and Vince backed down the stairs. The guy stood with his arms folded until Vince reached the living room.

In the entry, Vince looked back. The guy had gone back into the bedroom. Vince switched direction and made a quick tour of the lower floor. Living room, dining room, kitchen. Nothing seemed out of place, but he couldn't be sure. There were no signs of a meal having been eaten or being prepared. Was she killed before lunch, or was she dieting or a meal skipper like a million other slender women? From what he'd seen of the body, Suzie had probably looked pretty damned good in those shorts.

He went out the front way so the man posted there would see him leave. The sheriff was playing it safe, but Vince had the feeling he was ready to cooperate. Those were county investigators up there, sure as hell, and they were ready to ace him out of the case. Mayville had a personal stake in finding March now. Like Vince, he knew it was too much of a coincidence to think anyone else could have killed Suzie Tustman. And if he'd taken her out, Liz Husby would be next.

What the sheriff didn't know was that Vince had already found Liz Husby, alias Beth Davies. He nodded to the deputy at the foot of the drive and loped toward his car.

CHAPTER FIVE

The alarm bolted Beth from a dark dream where menacing figures in hooded black masks crept around her in tightening circles. As a rule, she woke on her own before the alarm went off and showered leisurely before getting Jenny up, but now Jenny was already awake. Beth heard her murmuring softly to Sasha. Beth shut off the alarm and hurried to shower and dress.

She had talked to the therapist often enough the past year to know that her unsettling dreams grew out of the fear generated by how easily Vince Norris had found her. Rick March had been a specter lurking in her mind ever since the trial, but with so many immediate concerns to concentrate on all the time, she'd been able to keep it at bay. Now he was horribly real. He was out of prison and might be tracking her down right now.

Orange juice splashed onto the counter as she poured. She wiped it up nervously. Could he find her as easily as Vince Norris had? Her phone number wasn't listed, but that hadn't stopped Norris. She wondered if he had really gotten information from the power company. As a reporter, he probably knew tricks or had inside contacts to get what he wanted. Surely a utility company wouldn't give out information to just anyone who called, would they? The pitcher hit the refrigerator shelf as she let go of it too soon.

She leaned against the counter and hugged herself as though a winter wind had sprung up suddenly. She should have asked Norris more questions. She glanced at the phone. Should she call him at the *Times*? She'd been too frightened last night to think straight. But if she called him now, he'd assume she was willing to cooperate on the story he wanted.

My God—a story? This was her life! Didn't he realize she and Jenny deserved this hard-earned chance? No, she wouldn't call Vince Norris. She wanted absolutely nothing to do with him. She could find out how much information Pacific Power would give out by calling them herself. That would tell her whether or not Norris was lying. But there were probably other ways of finding people. Rick March wouldn't give up easily.

While she was looking for miracles, she might as well hope that Rick March had gotten over the rage that drove him to threats of revenge. She might as well wish for a lot of things.

The practical thing she could do was talk to Madelaine. The therapist always helped her see things more clearly. When they first came to L.A., Beth and Jenny had seen her every week. Gradually they'd been able to cut back on sessions. Jenny saw Madelaine every other week. Beth only called for an appointment when she needed to explore some fear that broke through the safety net of her emotions. More often than not the talks were about Jenny.

Was Jenny's appointment this week? Beth checked the calendar on the refrigerator. Yes, tomorrow. It made Beth feel a little better. Maybe Madelaine would be able to fit her in, too. She'd call when she got to work.

Jenny came in as Beth set out the cereal and milk. Beth forced a smile and patted down a blonde strand poking up from Jenny's bangs.

"The weatherman says it's going to be hot and dry all summer. I wish you'd think about going to that camp I told you about." She poured herself a cup of coffee and sat across from Jenny, who began shaking her head before Beth finished talking. "Just think about it, okay? Camp is fun. There are lots of kids to play with and things to do. You can go swimming every day. It would be a nice break from school and the sitter. I tell you what, we can drive up next weekend and have a look at it. Would you like that?"

"I don't want to go."

"Not even to look at? You've never been to camp. You might like it a lot."

Jenny looked at the cereal floating in milk. "I wouldn't like it."

"How do you know if you don't try it? There are horses. You still love horses, don't you?"

Jenny nodded but looked close to tears.

Beth backed off. "Well, I want you to at least think about it. You'll do that for me, won't you?"

Jenny nodded again, still staring at her cereal. Beth poured out the coffee that tasted sour all of a sudden and rinsed the cup. While Jenny finished eating, she put out fresh cat food for Sasha and refilled the water dispenser.

Jenny was waiting at the front door with her knapsack and petting Sasha while Beth checked the windows and gathered her things.

"Go eat your breakfast," Jenny told the cat, sliding her hand along its back and tail in a final good-bye. The cat meowed and strode toward the kitchen. Outside, Beth picked up the morning paper and shoved it out of sight in her briefcase as they went down the walk.

When Kim went to lunch at noon, Beth put up the chain and the lunch sign so she wouldn't be disturbed. More from the need to do something constructive than the conviction it would do any good, she looked up the number of the power company and dialed. She got a flat refusal when she requested information on a customer. No amount of pleading got her anywhere, nor did asking for the supervisor, who was even more adamant about not giving out such information. The woman suggested Beth call the phone company who might contact the party for her if it were an emergency. For what it was worth, Beth was sure when she hung up that Rick March couldn't get her address that way.

Los Angeles was a huge, sprawling city where hundreds of people lost themselves every year. Rick March had a lot more street smarts than she did. There were probably other ways for him to find her. The idea made her tense, and she picked up the phone again and dialed Madelaine's number before she made a nervous wreck of herself. She caught the therapist between appointments, and Madelaine said she had an opening at four. Beth said she'd be there. She'd let Kim close up, and she'd still be able to get to the sitter's to pick up Jenny at the regular time.

When she hung up, she heard someone hurrying up the stairs. She tried to pigeonhole her thoughts about Rick March so she could concentrate on work again, but when the man came into view, her heart sank. It was Vince Norris.

"Look, I know you don't want me coming around, but I saw the other girl leave. I waited for you to come out, but you didn't. I need to talk to you." His gaze searched the tiny empty studio behind the glass partition as he leaned on the counter. "Did you read the paper this morning?"

Beth was too angry to do more than shake her head. She hadn't thought about the paper since she shoved it in her bag.

Norris rubbed his fingers as if he'd forgotten how to

snap them. "Suzie Tustman was murdered yesterday."

Beth's heart rode a fast elevator to a sudden stop. She grabbed the counter as a wave of dizziness washed over her. Norris darted around the end of the counter and helped her to a chair.

"You okay? Look, I'm sorry I sprang it on you like that. You want some water or something?"

Beth shook her head and found her voice. "Was it Rick March?"

"They don't know. No one saw him, but you can bet they're looking for him for questioning."

"Pine Lake is only a few hours from here," she said in a thready voice.

"Look, maybe you should go somewhere for awhile, someplace he won't think of looking for you. If he is looking, that is."

Oh, don't think I haven't thought of it. But where? How do I live? What do I use for money? What do I tell Jenny?

"Don't you have some relatives? In another state maybe?"

"No."

"Friends?"

She didn't answer. Her mind was tripping and sprawling over thoughts. Rick March had killed Suzie. Yesterday. Where was he now? She had to run . . . get Jenny and disappear. *Talk to Madelaine first,* she told herself. Clear thinking, level headed Madelaine—

"Beth, are you sure you're all right?" Norris was leaning over her with a concerned expression.

"Oh, yes, I'm fine except for being scared out of my wits. But thanks for telling me. It's a lot better than reading it in the paper." *Or being taken by surprise the way Suzie must have been.* She got to her feet unsteadily.

"Let me help you."

"I'm okay." When she saw his expression, she realized he wasn't talking about the arm he'd taken. "I need time to think, Mr. Norris. Please."

"I'm going. I'll call you later to make sure you're okay."

She nodded distractedly. Norris glanced back as he went down the stairs.

"I understand your concern," Madelaine said with a compassionate look, "but worrying never solves anything. If you think March is anywhere in the vicinity or even headed this way, you must go to the police."

Beth swallowed the sour taste in her mouth. "I can't, not without telling them who I am. Don't you see, I've spent this past year building a new life for myself and Jenny. I can't toss that away."

Madelaine raised an eyebrow. "It's better than tossing your life away, isn't it? The man is a killer."

Beth's stomach churned. "I don't intend to let him find me. I'm going to leave town, hide somewhere."

Madelaine's face was expressionless, but her eyes mirrored her concern. "You can't hide forever."

"Just until the police catch him. I won't feel safe until he's locked up again."

"Where will you go?"

Beth let out a long breath. "I don't know. I'll think of something. But Madelaine, you have to talk Jenny into going to camp. Please! I want to get her out of the city right away."

"School isn't out until the week after next."

"I know, but I'm sure I can arrange something with the camp. If not, we'll go somewhere, the two of us, for a few days until it opens. I'll take her to Disneyland, or maybe to Mexico. She's never been there. Please, Madelaine, convince her, won't you?"

Madelaine's expression was guarded. "Does she know about March?"

"No. I hid the papers. There isn't much chance anyone at school will talk about it."

Madelaine was thoughtful a moment, then said, "I'll talk to her, if that's what you want, but I think it would be a mistake to push her too hard. She's come a long way the past couple of months. I wouldn't like to see her lose ground."

"What do you mean? How can going to camp hurt her?"

Madelaine met Beth's puzzled look. "I think it's time for you to start being more honest with her, Beth."

"About March? I can't! You don't know what it's been like all these months seeing her so withdrawn, hiding from life and her own childhood. I want my happy little girl back. I won't let her be frightened again!"

"Do you know what she's afraid of?" Madelaine asked gently.

"Everything! Death, violence, losing me the way she lost her father—"

"Are you sure that's all?"

Beth stared at the therapist. Of course she was sure. Wasn't that what Madelaine had been working on with Jenny this past year?

"What do you mean?" she asked finally, almost afraid to hear the answer.

"We're all afraid of death and violence and losing loved ones, but sometimes children view the loss of a loved one from their own internal viewpoint. Their need to make sense of the dreadful things that happen in life makes them look for reasons. Place blame, if you will. You and I have talked about your marriage. By your own admission, it wasn't the happiest, most carefree union in the world. Gil cheated on you. He demeaned your talent, your artwork. He teased Jenny about things she didn't do well and constantly broke his promises to both of you. You were thinking about divorcing him if he hadn't died when he did."

Beth listened numbly as Madelaine went on.

"Jenny loved her daddy, but she felt she couldn't please him. Nothing she did was ever quite good enough. How do you think that made her feel?"

Beth's voice came from a far memory. "Inadequate."

"There must have been times when she was very angry with him, even hated him."

Beth's mouth opened to protest, but nothing came out.

"In a child's mind, being angry or hating someone often translates into wanting him gone."

Beth shook her head in slow denial. "Did she tell you this?" Her voice was barely a whisper. She should have known, should have been able to read her child's turmoil. Guilt swamped her.

"She doesn't have to," Madelaine said. "It's a perfectly normal response in children. At times she must have been angry enough at Gil to want him out of her life. Then one day when she's hurt and not sure if she loves or hates him, she walks into her daddy's office and he's dead. 'Gone.' Her wish has come true. Is it any wonder she feels responsible?

"When she's ready to talk about that, it will be the major breakthrough we've been waiting for. But right now, she's afraid of getting angry with you. She doesn't want to wish you 'gone' like her father because it might happen. She blames herself for his death. Now she believes she can't let herself be angry at you. Camp is a threat. She's afraid she'll be angry if you force her to go."

"But I'm not forcing her! She needs to get away. It's only for a couple of weeks!"

"Her father was only supposed to be gone for the day. He was going to take her to the pony farm that afternoon, wasn't he? That was going to be fun too."

Beth sagged and tears stung her eyes. "What should I do?"

"I can't decide for you, Beth. I'll support your decision, whatever it is, but it may be easier for Jenny in the long run not to be coaxed into going away right now."

A light blinked on the phone, which Beth knew was a signal that the hour was up and another patient was waiting. She collected her purse.

"Thanks, Madelaine. I guess I need time to mull this over. I thought—" She sighed. "I don't know what I would do without you to talk to. You have a away of putting things in perspective, even if I don't like it."

Madelaine came around the desk with a smile. "If you didn't have me, you'd find someone else to confide it. It's human nature. The most important thing is you're learning to take charge of your own life. Now about Rick March, if you won't go to the police, I agree you should go away. Let me know what you decide. In the meantime, I'll keep Jenny's appointment in my book for tomorrow unless I hear from you."

All the way to the sitter's and home after picking up Jenny, Beth caught herself watching the rearview mirror to be sure no one was following them. Jenny glanced at her curiously several times but didn't say anything. When Beth asked about her school day, Jenny shrugged and said it was okay.

Jenny went to her room after supper. Beth didn't protest.

She hadn't come to grips fully yet with what Madelaine said. She was being forced to choose the lesser of two evils: keep Jenny with her and worry about Rick March finding them, or send her to camp and risk further trauma for the poor child.

When Jenny fell asleep with Sasha curled at her feet, Beth took the morning paper from her briefcase and read the story about Suzie Tustman's murder. Vince Norris had the byline. Amazed, she realized he'd been in Pine Lake. He had talked to Gary Kellog and Sheriff Mayville. His description of the Tustman house was as accurate as a photograph. She read the details of the murder quickly, shuddering when she came to the part about Suzie being stabbed repeatedly. The police had no clues, no witnesses. The article didn't mention Rick March, but anyone who'd read yesterday's story about his release from prison would remember the Tustman name and make the connection.

When the phone rang, it startled Beth so badly she almost knocked it from the table in her haste to answer. "Yes?"

"It's Vince Norris, Beth." She'd forgotten about his saying he'd call. She realized, too, it was the second time he'd called her Beth, as if they were friends.

"Have you heard anything?" She couldn't bring herself to say Rick March's name. They both knew what she meant.

"Not much. March took a bus from the prison to Sacramento. No one seems to have noticed him after that. There are a lot of towns between there and Pine Lake, so it's going to be pretty hard to pick up his trail. Have you thought about what you're going to do?"

She hadn't thought about anything else. "I don't know," she said.

"I have a suggestion," Norris offered.

"Oh?"

"One of the columnists here at the paper has a problem. His house-sitter backed out on their deal to stay at his place while he and his wife are on vacation. They're leaving tomorrow night, so he's got to find someone in a hurry. I told him I might know someone."

House-sitting. Lots of people didn't like to leave their houses empty when they went away. She felt a flutter of hope in spite of his presumptuousness. Dare she trust Norris? Was he being helpful or was he still after a story?

"They'll be gone two weeks," Vince said. "By that time the Tustman thing will be solved."

Her thoughts whirled. "Where is the house?"

"Up in the Hollywood Hills. It's a great place. I've been there a couple of times to parties. Terrific view, privacy, all the comforts of home and more. You're not allergic to dogs, are you? That's part of the deal. You get to walk the Doberman twice a day."

A dog. They wouldn't be able to take Sasha. Jenny would have to understand.

"I don't mean to push you, but I have to give him an answer right away," Vince said. "He hasn't got much time."

She took a deep breath. "Yes. All right, I'll do it. We'll do it."

"Good girl. I'll take you up there in the morning to meet the Fischers. Can you go in to work a little late? They have to leave for the airport at four, so they'll want you to start tomorrow evening."

"Yes." Kim could handle things for an hour or so.

"Okay, I'll see you, what, eight-thirty?"

"Make it quarter to nine. I drop Jenny at school on my way to work."

"I'll be waiting at the shop."

Beth hesitated. "What did you tell them about me?"

"I just said you were a friend."

"Thanks, Mr. Norris."

"Sure. Good night, Beth. I'll see you in the morning."

She hung up, praying she was doing the right thing.

CHAPTER SIX

The sun beat across his shoulders and dried the heavy sheen of sweat covering his bare chest and back. His skin felt tight as he raised the pick and brought it down with a smooth, strong swing. A splintered crack radiated like a bullet hole in the macadam. He rocked the pick to break apart hunks of paving, then pulled the pick free and raised it again.

Each blow gave him an almost sensual pleasure. For a year he'd been suppressing energy, resisting letting it out in prison yard fights or explosions of anger. During his first few stints in corrections facilities, he'd done hard time, fighting the system, other inmates and himself. It took a while, but he finally realized he was the big loser in those rounds. He couldn't beat the system. If he whipped another inmate, there was always someone else ready to challenge his reputation. Most of all, he couldn't beat himself. Fighting was a waste of time. It finally sank in that it was better to use muscle on whatever job he was assigned and work out, but save his real energy for important things. Like getting out.

This time he'd done it. In only a year. He felt a swell of satisfaction as he raised the pick axe again.

He had spotted the orange markers of the construction zone in the Chevy's headlights last night a few minutes before the engine began to sputter on its last drops of gas. He hadn't noticed how long the gas gauge needle had been on a quarter of a tank and cursed when he realized the damned thing was broken. He managed to get the heap off the road before it died. It was a good six or seven miles back to the last town he'd come through. A hell of a walk in the dark, and not much when he got there. He'd seen only one gas station, and it was already closed for the night.

Where the hell was he? He had cut off the main highway ten miles back when he spotted the flashing lights of cop cars ahead of him on the highway. It was probably an accident, but he didn't want to get close enough to find out. The last thing he needed was some jerk patrolman shining a light in his face and asking for identification. So he wound up in the middle of nowhere without any idea how far it was to the next town. The hell with it. He'd wait for morning.

By the Chevy's dome light, he had wiped his fingerprints from everything he'd touched in the car. Then salvaging the credit card, clothes, a bag of burgers and a six-pack he'd bought at a Quik Stop back on the highway, he took the Chevy out of gear and rolled it over the edge of a gully that ran along the side of the road. The car bumped down into the dry brush at the bottom of the wash. He could still see the top of it from the road, but it was hidden well enough unless you were looking for it.

He made his way back to the construction site. The moon gave the blacktop a silvery sheen as he checked out the work being done. A grader and a steam roller were parked off on the shoulder. Tire tracks showed where trucks had come and gone. The road was being resurfaced, not patched. That meant they'd be back in the morning. He found a place a few yards off the road and curled up under a tree with his rolled-up jacket for a pillow.

The morning sun and the sound of trucks woke him. Watching from his vantage point, he ate a cold burger and drank a can of warm beer as the road crew began breaking pavement. When the foreman yelled for the men to speed it up, Rick pulled off his shirt and wrapped it around the left-over food. He stashed the bundle behind the tree, then walked to the back of a truck and grabbed a pick. Nobody argued when he joined the crew. An extra pair of hands meant less work for the rest of them.

The men called the foreman Johnson. He glanced at Rick curiously several times but didn't say anything. When they broke for lunch, Rick sat by himself so he wouldn't be expected to join in any conversation. Johnson intercepted him as the men started back to work.

"I don't remember seeing you before."

Rick nodded. "I'm new."

"Yeah? When did you hire on?"

"Yesterday. Talked to the guy at the office." He gambled. "The big guy."

"Mulvaney?"

"Yeah."

"He's supposed to let me know any changes."

Rick shrugged. The foreman motioned. "Okay, go on back to work. I'll settle it with Mulvaney at the end of the week. You live in Harper?"

"No. I was on my way through when I decided I could use a few days' pay before I moved on."

"On your way through? Nobody goes through Harper except by mistake."

Rick smiled crookedly. "I was thumbing. Guy let me off in the middle of nowhere."

"That's Harper, all right. He sure as hell didn't do you no favor. Okay, get back to work. We're a day and a half behind schedule, and it ain't getting any cooler."

Rick lifted the pick. "Any chance I can ride back to town

with the truck when we finish?"

"Sure."

Harper was a two-bit town even smaller than Pine Lake. The construction truck pulled up behind a Quonset hut where two dump trucks, a backhoe and a small steamroller were parked. The sign on the Quonset said, "ACE CONSTRUCTION AND HEAVY EQUIPMENT."

Rick waited until the crew foreman drove off in a two-year-old Impala before he went into the office. A plain woman in her thirties with tired-looking eyes and graying brown hair was bent over a ledger at a desk. She looked up when the door banged.

"Can I help you?"

"I'm Joe Dominick." He smiled enough to look friendly but not pushy. "Johnson hired me on today. Just temporary till the job gets back on schedule. He said I should give you my hours so I can get paid."

She frowned. "Mr. Mulvaney won't like it."

Rick gave her a troubled look. "Do you have tell him?"

"Of course." Her eyes said she wasn't crazy about the idea or Mulvaney.

"My car died over in Bakersfield," he said. "I've been hitchhiking, trying to get to Phoenix. I got a job promised me there. If Mulvaney finds out I'm temporary and Johnson took me on without asking him, he may tell me to walk. Johnson said you were a good egg. Too good to be working here." He looked at his scuffed, dusty shoes as if he'd suddenly decided he was saying too much. Her fingers tapped the ledger rhythmically as she thought over his indirect suggestion. When he finally looked up, she gave him a hesitant smile.

"Okay, Joe. I'll fix it. The truck leaves at six-thirty if you need a ride out." He grinned. This time her smile was warm and friendly.

"There's a cafe down the street and a place that rents rooms at the other end of town. It's not much, but it's cheap." He looked at his shoes again.

"No money?" she asked quietly.

He took some coins from his pocket and spread his palm to show her. She sighed as if it were worse than she expected.

"How many hours did you work today?"

He told her. She opened a drawer and took out a cash box, counted out some bills and gave them to him. She filled out a receipt and gave him a pen to sign it. She slipped the receipt into the back of the book.

"If you need a place to sleep, no one locks the equipment. Out back. And if you don't mind cold chicken and potato salad from the grocery store, you can eat dinner at my place."

"Won't your husband mind?"

She looked at the receipt book. "I'm not married."

"A nice person like you should be." When she smiled, he was glad he hadn't said 'pretty girl'. She wouldn't have swallowed that one. "Okay, I accept, but only if there's something I can do for you. Maybe fix a screen door or chop some firewood?"

She laughed. "It's ninety-seven degrees outside. What would I do with firewood?"

He grinned. "Save it for a cold winter night."

She put the receipt book in the drawer and closed the ledger. "I have a back step that's loose. Will that do?"

"Yeah."

She took her purse from the bottom drawer and got up, glancing around the office as she turned off the fluorescent overhead lights and followed him out.

CHAPTER SEVEN

In the morning, Vince Norris was waiting at the front door of Creative Color Graphics when Beth got there. She put her briefcase in the studio and told Zane she had a personal errand and would be gone about an hour and Kim would handle things until she got back. He looked a little surprised but didn't ask questions.

As they drove up the hill above Hollywood and Vine, Vince filled her in on the background of the people she was going to meet. Ted Fischer had been writing a financial column, *Fischer On Finances*, for the *Times* for eighteen years. He and his wife spent two weeks traveling abroad every summer. This year they were going to the Greek Islands. They had no children and had built the house when they were married in the forties. Although it had been renovated and redecorated a number of times, it was still a testimony to art deco style of Hollywood's heyday.

Vince took so many twists and turns on the way up, Beth wondered if she'd ever be able to find the way on her own. Vince laughed and told her Ted sent maps with party invitations for guests who were finding their way to the house for the first time.

The house crowned a small plateau on the crest of a hill above Hollywood Boulevard. The final stretch of road to it was a narrow blacktop not wide enough for two cars to pass without one pulling onto the shoulder. It was bordered on one side by the face of the hill and the other by the steep drop of a canyon. Several houses perched on the lip of the canyon, but there was none directly across from the Fischer house that Vince pointed out as he drove past. At the top of the hill, he turned the car around in an unpaved clearing where the peak fell away to a dramatic view of the city below. Vince told her the space was used for guest parking by the hilltop residents. He drove back down to the Fischer house and let Beth out before he parked on the concrete apron in front of the garage.

When he shut off the engine, the hilltop was suddenly quiet. The noise of the city vanished except for a faint hum of traffic from the freeway far below. It was like being in the country ten minutes from Hollywood and Vine.

The Fischers' garage was entrenched like a bunker in the hillside under the house. The room above it had a curved solarium window of bronzed glass running its full length. Two flights of steps angled up to the front door. Except for the pebbled glass panes on either side of the door, the wall facing the road on this side of the house had no windows. Flowering hibiscus bushes and an array of succulents in pots and planters surrounded the entry to complete the feeling of total privacy. When Vince rang the bell, a dog's deep bark responded and there was a scrabble of claws on a hard surface. The big dog's shape appeared behind the pebbled glass. Beth wondered nervously if Jenny would be frightened of him.

A man silenced the dog with a soft command, and the door opened. Ted Fischer was tall, straight, and gray-haired with a small neat mustache. Dressed in pale gray slacks and a slightly darker La Costa shirt, he put out his hand to Vince.

"And you must be Beth," he said, smiling at her and extending his hand again. "Come in, come in. Don't be afraid of Baron. He's an overgrown pussycat." The dog watched them, tail wagging, tongue lolling.

The entry was an open foyer with a flagstone floor and tall, lush, green plants in recessed planters on either side. The dog whined softly but didn't move from where it had been told to stay. It looked so friendly, some of Beth's concern began to evaporate.

A smiling, gray-haired woman who barely came up to her husband's shoulder joined them and immediately suggested that her husband give Beth a tour of the house while Vince keep her company in the kitchen where she was making coffee.

Beth followed Ted into the living room. The walls facing away from the entry were glass and gave a one-hundred-eighty-degree view of the city. Ted pointed out downtown in the distance to the southeast and a glint of the ocean in the far southwest. He drew her attention to the Capitol Records building phonograph-needle spire almost directly below them.

A fieldstone fireplace flanked by planters and a recessed cupboard for firewood covered one end of the living room. The wall she'd thought windowless from outside defined a narrow atrium of lush plants behind another wall of glass, which was undetectable from outside, and which helped flood the room with light. The furniture was of simple lines in muted colors.

Another planter was recessed into the floor at the opposite end of the room where a dining room table, also built-in, curved from the back of a kitchen counter around the planter and its greenery. Eating there would give the feeling of being on a secluded tropical terrace, Beth thought. She felt herself falling in love with the house.

They bypassed the kitchen for the moment and walked through the rest of the house, which contained surprise after surprise. A glass-walled master bedroom shared the magnificent view and had a thirty-six-inch television set concealed behind a wall panel operated by remote control, as were the drapes and lighting. The master bath had an atrium behind its glass wall and glassed-in shower. On the street side of the house, the huge den with the smoked glass bubble wall faced a view of the valley and neighboring ridge of hills. In the distance in the hazy morning light, Beth saw the famous HOLLYWOOD sign. Ted Fischer showed her how the room could be left open to the hall or shut off behind sliding *shoji* screens. Off it, the guest bath had a sunken tub and a sky-lighted roof. Beth ran out of superlatives.

When Nancy called from the kitchen that coffee was ready, they sat at a small table in a glassed alcove overlooking the terraced hill.

"The house is wonderful," Beth said.

"We like it," Nancy said simply. "Vince tells me you have a daughter. How old is she?"

"Eight." Beth saw the small flash of relief in the other woman's eyes. Eight was old enough to be beyond the destructive stage. The house had been built for the comfort and pleasure of the owners, but was hardly child proof. "She's more of a reader than she is a runner," Beth said reassuringly.

Nancy nodded and passed a plate of freshly baked bran muffins. She didn't look offended when Beth refused. "I'd worry about a small child with the terraces outside," Nancy said. Vince took a muffin with a wolfish grin.

"I don't mean to rush you," Ted said, "but as Vince told you, we're on a tight deadline. Our plane leaves at seven tonight. We have to start for the airport by four." He glanced at his wife and a wordless signal passed between them.

"We'd like you and your little girl to stay here tonight."

Beth sipped the hot coffee. Jenny would love the house. It would mean she could finish the school term.

"We can be here by six," she said. It wouldn't take long to stop at the apartment and pack. She could pick up something for dinner, too. They could eat right here looking out at the city.

"Good," Ted and Nancy said in unison. Ted got to his feet. "Bring your coffee and I'll show you the patio." He slid open the door and screen, and she followed him out. Vince and Nancy and Baron trailed behind them. Outside the sudden chatter of a mockingbird broke the hum of traffic on the Hollywood Freeway below.

Beyond the bedroom end of the house, part of the patio was under a trellis of flowering bougainvillea. A metal table and chairs were set up in the dappled shade. The rest of the terrace had concrete planters of orange and lemon trees and ripening strawberries. Along the high cinder block wall that sealed off the road and the neighboring house, beds of daisies and early roses were splashes of color.

The steep drop off on the city side of the hill had been terraced into two-foot-wide beds that ended in a high chain link fence fifteen feet down the slope. Ted pointed out where he'd planted lettuce, carrots and radishes, and he encouraged her to pick as much as she and Jenny wanted.

"There's a sprinkler system for everything including the greenhouse and atriums. I'll leave you a printout of the watering schedule for the house plants," Nancy said.

"It's all so—breathtaking," Beth said as Ted led her to the opposite end of the house where a small, narrow greenhouse was lush with bedding plants and delicately flowering orchids. Beyond it, the rest of the yard continuing uphill to the fence was terraced and planted in rows of sweet corn just beginning to ear. There were stone steps leading up to a gate. Beyond it, there was only one house above them. It was a square cinder block structure surrounded by low-maintenance ivy.

"Amos Westerland's place," Ted said. "His house was the only one up here when we came. He does special effects for Paramount. Right now he's in Utah working on a film, but even if he was home you wouldn't see much of him. He stays to himself pretty much." Ted grinned. "You could call him the perfect neighbor. Nice guy."

Inside again, Nancy showed Beth some of the kitchen gadgetry, then gave her the plant watering instructions and a set of house keys. She showed Beth where Baron's dog food was and explained his feeding schedule, cautioning her not to feed him table scraps or raw meat because they upset his digestion. Ted gave her a hand-drawn map showing the turns and landmarks for coming up the hill. He also gave her another map on which he'd drawn the routes for walking Baron. At the front door, he explained how the security system worked. Once set, anything that broke the circuit set off a silent alarm that would bring an armed guard response unless she canceled the call within thirty seconds. To do this, she had to talk into a hidden microphone behind the tall bamboo that filled a planter against the dining room wall.

As they drove back down the hill, Vince gave her a friendly grin. "Not a bad hideout, huh?"

Hideout . . . A sober reminder of the serious reason behind the pleasant half hour she'd just spent. "It's a remarkable place. I didn't expect anything like that right in the city."

"Yeah, it's something," he said.

"I was surprised the Fischers didn't ask how come I

want to get away. Are you sure you didn't tell them anything about me?"

"Hey, I said I didn't. They're so happy to have you, they don't care if you've been living out of the back seat of your car. I vouched for you. That's enough for them."

She didn't argue, but she was still uneasy.

"Is there any problem about coming right after work tonight?" Vince asked.

She looked at him sharply. "Have you heard something about March?"

"No, nothing like that, but if he's on the move, every minute could bring him that much closer. I think it's a good idea for you to get out of that apartment as soon as possible."

Her euphoria vanished as she came back to grim reality. He was right. She couldn't afford to forget Rick March for a minute. She'd tell Jenny where they were going when she picked her up after school. They'd make a game of packing. Sasha would be a problem. Jenny wouldn't want to leave her. She wondered if Mrs. Hackett would take care of the cat while they were gone? The building manager would ask a million questions about such a sudden trip. Beth would have to think of something to tell her. What about mail and the phone? She asked Vince.

"You can put a temporary forward on your mail. I'll pick up a card and drop it by the office for you to sign. Do you get a lot of calls you don't want to miss?"

"Yes." Most of her freelance people contacted her by phone. And if anything happened to her mother, the nursing home had instructions to call.

"I'll get call forwarding for you. I know someone at Pacific Bell who can expedite the order. The Fischers have an answering machine, so you can screen calls."

She felt another wave of relief. "Why are you doing this for me, Mr. Norris?"

He glanced at her briefly, then looked back to the road. "I don't know . . . I guess I don't like to see anyone terrorized. Or maybe I'm still looking for that story."

CHAPTER EIGHT

Rick woke with the first dull flush of morning. Momentarily disoriented, he scowled at the unfamiliar blue chenille bedspread folded neatly over the iron foot rail of the bed. Memory edged back, and he glanced at the sleeping woman beside him. Vera's bed was a lot more comfortable than the ground or the cab of the truck would have been if he hadn't accepted her shy invitation to stay.

He picked up his clothes and dressed in the tiny bathroom at the end of the hall. In the kitchen, he helped himself to a couple of sweet rolls he found in a bag in the bread box, then ate the leftover chicken and potato salad right from the bowl. His six-pack was gone. She didn't have any beer around, but he found a couple of cans of diet pop in a cupboard and took those. On the way out, he took forty bucks from the purse she left on the spindly-legged hall table. If she got to the office before the truck pulled out, she'd know he was gone, but she was the kind of woman who'd expect that. She wouldn't say anything to anyone. She'd live on the memories of last night until the next guy came along. If one did.

His stride lengthened when he saw an eighteen-wheeler pulled off the road not far from ACE HEAVY EQUIPMENT AND CONSTRUCTION. The hood was up, and a man was lying on the fender leaning into the engine. Rick waited until he finished and slid to the ground, wiping his hands on a rag.

"How about a ride?" Rick said.

The driver pointed to a sign on the windshield that said, "No Riders."

"Just as far as 99? Not many cars passing at this hour."

The driver hesitated, then shrugged. "What the hell, I can understand wanting to get out of this burg." He put out his hand. "My name's Bud."

"Joe." They shook.

"My fuel pump began acting up last night. Thought I could find a garage here." Bud glanced down the deserted main street.

"God forsaken place. The whole damned town was dark at 2 a.m. so I figured I might as well catch a few hours sleep. Fixed the damned thing myself as soon as it got light. Hop in. I gotta make up for lost time. I'm headed for Los Angeles. You can ride that far if you want."

"Couldn't ask for anything more," Rick said as he climbed into the cab. He let Bud set the pace on conversation, and there wasn't much of it. It gave Rick plenty of time to think.

Suzie Tustman said Liz Husby moved to L.A. after the trial. Taken back her maiden name, according to her in-laws who wanted to keep their grandkid in Pine Lake. With a little encouragement, Suzie had even managed to dig up an address she had copied from her husband's Rolodex.

Rick leaned back against the warm leather of the truck cab. Things were beginning to fall in place. They'd be in Los Angeles by mid-morning.

Stepping into the shaded entry to the apartment court, he squinted at the names next to the bells. *E. Davies—1-C.* "E" would probably be for Elizabeth. Maybe she liked to be called Elizabeth now.

Shifting the small tool kit he'd bought at a K-Mart, he

scanned the bell cards again and found the one marked *Hackett, Mgr.—1-H.* He glanced through the gate. The numbering system began at his left. Four apartments to each side. 1-C would be the one by the leggy oleander bushes. If the numbers followed in order, the manager would be up front on the right, closest to the gate. In a direct line of sight with the door of 1-C.

He pushed the manager's bell and waited. Nothing. With a glance back at the hot, hushed street, he hit the bell again. This time when there was no answer, he took a piece of heavy wire from his pocket. Bending it, he worked it down through the metal grillwork surrounding the lock plate. When it caught the latch, he pulled up slowly. The lock clicked, and the gate swung open.

He walked to 1-C as if he belonged and knocked on the door. The hairs at the back of his neck prickled, but he resisted the urge to glance around the two-story court. He was in plain sight if anyone looked out or came in from the carport out back, but it was a risk he had to take. He raised his hand and knocked again, barely brushing his knuckles on the wood, all the while listening. Somewhere a kid was crying and a radio or television was playing, but that was it.

Standing with his back to the courtyard, he propped the screen door open with his hip. He got out the set of lock picks he'd bought from a guy in Echo Park who had fenced a few things for him in the past. He had the door open in no time.

The apartment was hot and stuffy. He was in the living room. The kitchen opened off to the right, and on the left a short hall led to the bedrooms and bath. All the drapes were closed. He checked the bedrooms first. The first one was the kid's. Half a dozen stuffed animals stood like a police line-up on the pink-flowered bedspread. The room didn't look lived in. There were no clothes or toys thrown around, nothing stuck up on the walls except a neatly framed picture of some pink and blue flowers. He lifted the cover of a book on the desk. "Property of Vista Elementary School Library" was stamped on the inside.

The other bedroom was hers. He sniffed the faint scent of perfume and wondered what it was called. The room was neat, but not like the kid's. There was an open book face down on the night table and an assortment of makeup in front of a mirror with light bulbs around it on top of the dresser. Next to them was a silver frame with a picture of a little girl in it. He studied it for several moments. She'd grown since he last saw her, but there was no mistaking the wide eyes and blonde hair. She must be about eight now.

There were several framed pictures on the walls. He moved closer for a better look. Liz was always drawing in high school. She did this one. Her initials were written in tiny script on a bottom corner: EDH. The picture was a lake scene, blue water against a background of towering, dark pines with a cabin tucked under them. Damned if it wasn't the cabin on Sullivan Lake. He remembered seeing her sketching it once. Maybe this wasn't the same, but it was the same cabin. He wondered how many of them she'd done.

The closet door was ajar. He opened it and ran his hand along her clothes. Most of them were blues, greens and rosy pinks that went with her fair coloring. He pushed the door almost shut the way it had been. He pulled open dresser drawers one by one, but there was nothing interesting in them.

As he stepped back into the hall, something flashed by at floor level. He almost jumped out of his skin. A damned cat. He caught a glimpse of it as it disappeared into the kid's room.

In the living room, he went to the card table set up near the window. A chipped coffee mug held an assortment of pencils and pens. There weren't any papers except for some bills stuck between the wires of an oversized paper clip. He went through them without finding anything interesting. From a shelf of the bookcase behind the table, he picked up a stack of papers held together by a rubber band. He grunted when he came to a paycheck stub with the name and address of a printing company on Sunset Boulevard. He memorized it and put the bundle back where he found it. He started for the kitchen but stopped when he saw the phone with her number written on the little card under the buttons. He memorized that, too.

Like the rest of the place, the kitchen was clean and neat. There were no dishes in the sink. The towels were folded and hung over a metal rod attached to a cupboard. A green bowl and an inverted plastic jug stood on a newspaper near the sink. A few pellets of dry cat food had fallen around the bowl. Using the edge of his finger, he opened cupboards and drawers, careful to close them the way he found them, even the one that wasn't quite shut.

Back in the living room, he tried to get a feeling for the way she lived. Pretty damned simply, from the looks of it. The place wasn't fancy by a long shot. The carpet was cheap gold shag. The furniture was okay, but it wasn't expensive. Maybe she rented the apartment furnished. The stuff didn't look like anything she'd buy.

There was no central air conditioning, only a window unit behind the drapes. He eased them open and checked outside. The ground fell away abruptly to the lot next door. There was a ten-foot drop from the window he was looking out. A cinder block retaining wall between the yards came about halfway up. The next building was only twenty feet away, but the window levels were offset, so he couldn't see in anywhere. The ground level of the building was a garage. Almost empty now.

Sweat trickled at his armpits. He unfastened the latch on the window before he let the drape fall back in place and looked around one last time. He eased the front door open and checked the courtyard. He muttered a curse as the damned cat streaked past him and made a beeline for the thick shrubbery. Cursing again, he pulled the door shut and reset the dead bolt with the lock pick.

CHAPTER NINE

Beth honked as Jenny emerged from the medical building where Madelaine's office was. Jenny walked toward the car slowly. Her solemn face made Beth wince.

My poor baby, she thought. *So serious all the time.*

"Hi, sweetie. How was it today?"

"Okay." Jenny slid in and pulled the door shut. She buckled her seat belt, then sat with her hands folded on top of her knapsack.

No excitement, no enthusiasm. Beth took a deep breath to lift her own spirits.

"I have a surprise," she said as she pulled out of the parking space. Jenny turned to look at her, her expression frightened. *Dear God, she thinks I'm talking about camp.* Beth went on quickly. "We're going to baby-sit a house. The two of us. Just for a couple of weeks while the owners are away."

Jenny's brow puckered as if she were trying to understand a complicated problem. Beth went on in a rush of words.

"Wait until you see it! It's way up on top of the hill there." She pointed to the hazy hills ahead of them. "It has plants growing inside and glass walls so you can see the whole city. There's an orange tree and a lemon tree and strawberries in the garden."

"Whose house is it?" Jenny asked curiously.

"Some very nice people named Fischer. They're going away for two weeks and they can't leave the house and dog alone."

Jenny frowned again. "Sasha's afraid of dogs."

Beth took a deep breath. "I'm sorry, honey, Sasha can't come. I know you'll miss her, but she might run away if we take her to a strange place. Cats do that sometimes, and we wouldn't want to lose Sasha."

"Who'll take care of her?"

"I thought we could ask Mrs. Hackett."

"Sasha doesn't like her."

"It's only for two weeks. As long as someone feeds her and makes sure she has water, she'll be all right."

Jenny turned to stare out the window. *I'm handling this badly,* Beth thought. She tried again. "She was okay last summer when we went to Disneyland for the weekend."

"She wouldn't sit on my lap when we came home."

"Cats are like that," Beth said reasonably, "but they get over it. Sasha may be a little unhappy, but she'll forgive us and love us all the more when we come home."

Jenny kept staring out the window, and Beth reached over to pat her knee. "You'll see. It will work out just fine. I promise."

Jenny looked resigned. "Can I come home to see her sometimes?"

Beth hesitated. If Rick March was caught quickly, they could stop by the apartment every day. If he wasn't . . . She wouldn't consider that possibility. "We'll see."

When they got out in the carport, Jenny was silent while Beth unlocked the back gate and the apartment door. Then she hurried inside calling the cat.

"Sasha. Sasha?"

There was no answering meow, and the cat didn't stroll out to meet them the way it usually did. Jenny went into her room still calling. She came back to the living room and opened the drapes to see if the cat was on the windowsill, then went through the entire apartment looking in all the cat's favorite hiding places.

"She's gone," she said in an anguished voice.

"She can't be, honey," Beth assured her. "There's no way for her to get out of the apartment."

"But she's not here. I looked everywhere." Jenny was close to tears.

Beth put her arm around her. "I'll bet she found a new hiding place. Under the bed. Or maybe she managed to lock herself in a closet. Let's look." She was down on her hands and knees peering under the bed when someone knocked on the door. She scrambled up and hurried to answer it. Mrs. Hackett was standing outside the screen holding a wary Sasha in her arms.

"Oh, we were just hunting for her," Beth said with relief. How in the world had the cat gotten out? Over her shoulder she called, "Jenny, here she is."

Jenny ran in as Beth opened the screen door. The cat gave the manager a malevolent look as it escaped into Jenny's arms. Jenny carried the cat to her room, crooning and hugging it.

"I found her under the bushes near the back gate," Mrs. Hackett said.

A slash of uneasiness cut through Beth's surprise. "Really? When was this? I don't know how in the world she got out."

"It was about three o'clock. I was coming back from the market. I wouldn't have seen her all crouched behind the jade plants that way if I hadn't dropped my keys. I decided I'd better take her into my place before she took a notion to slip out the gate and go exploring. What with the traffic on the avenue and all, who knows what might have happened."

"Well, thank you, Mrs. Hackett," Beth said sincerely.

"Jenny would be devastated if anything happened to her."

The manager clucked. "She really loves that cat, doesn't she?"

Beth nodded. "As a matter of fact, Mrs. Hackett, I was going to come over to talk to you. Jenny and I are going on a little vacation, and I wondered if you'd be willing to feed Sasha while we're gone?"

Mrs. Hackett's benevolent expression became strained.

Beth said, "I'd pay you for it."

The smile came back, showing the woman's prominent dentures. "Well, I suppose I can do it. How long are you going to be away?"

Rick March would surely be caught before the Fischers came back. "About two weeks."

"Don't you know for sure?" Mrs. Hackett asked, frankly curious now.

Beth improvised. "We're invited up to Tahoe to visit friends. We've never stayed with them before. They don't have children, but if Jenny is having a good time, we may stay a little longer."

Mrs. Hackett's head bobbed as she accepted the explanation. "When will you be leaving?"

"Right away. We just have to pack some things."

"So soon?"

"I'll put out fresh water and food for Sasha, but if you'd look in on her tomorrow?"

"I'm surprised you're taking Jenny out of school so close to the end of the year, but then she's such a bright little girl she won't have any trouble catching up. You two have a good time. Send me a postcard from Tahoe. When my Bill was alive, we used to go up there sometimes. I always loved the lake. Bill liked the casinos. He'd play Twenty-one all night if I let him. I always said we had to decide ahead how much we could afford to lose. When it was gone, he had to quit, that's all there was to it. I always made him promise or I wouldn't go." She paused for breath, and Beth broke in before she could go on.

"Thank you, Mrs. Hackett. I really appreciate your doing this. Now I have to pack. I'll leave out the cat food, and if you'll keep an eye on the water dispenser?"

"Of course, dear. You can trust me. You two just enjoy yourselves."

Beth was relieved to say good-bye and close the door. To her chagrin, Jenny, still holding Sasha, was behind her.

"You said we were going to a house up on the hill," she said with a puzzled look.

Beth tried to justify her lie. "We are, honey. I didn't want to tell Mrs. Hackett we were going to be that close or she might ask why we can't come home and feed Sasha ourselves."

"Why can't we?"

Beth remembered Madelaine's advice about honesty. One lie certainly led to another, but this wasn't the right time for total honesty. Maybe she should have taken Jenny and Sasha and run, hidden far away from here. "You just have to trust me for now, sweetie. Please? I can't answer your questions. Let's go pack, okay?"

Jenny retreated in silence to her bedroom as Beth got two suitcases down from the closet and opened one on Jenny's bed. She took the other to her own room and began putting clothes into it.

A half hour later, with tears in her eyes, Jenny hugged the cat and checked its food and water and clean litter box for the fifth time before she followed Beth out of the apartment.

CHAPTER TEN

He ditched the car in a crowded parking lot in front of a supermarket, then walked several blocks to a busy intersection where five streets came together like crossed wires. God, it was hot. It felt worse than it had out in the blazing desert. The buildings held the heat and sprayed it back into the streets like hot oil. He spotted a bar across two streets and headed for it.

Inside, the air conditioning was going full blast and felt icy for the first minute. He ordered a draft beer from the gray-haired bartender who reminded him of an actor in a TV sitcom.

Sitting here was better than hanging out near the apartment complex until she got home from work. The place had been deserted this morning, but people worked crazy hours in this town; some came home in the middle of the afternoon. Last thing he needed was for someone to spot him and wonder what the hell he was doing hanging around. Liz probably didn't get home until five or six. This was as good a place as any to kill time.

She'd changed her name back to Davies. Funny, he'd never thought of her as anything *but* Liz Davies. He had recognized her right off that afternoon nineteen months ago when he crashed into her at the foot of those damned stairs. The lousy year he spent in Pine Lake as a teenager flashed through his mind like a shot. Liz Husby sat next to him in home room. The rest of the jerk kids weren't worth remembering, but she was different. She was a quiet little mouse, but she was always nice to him, not like the rest of the kids who wouldn't waste spit talking to a welfare kid.

He'd been so surprised seeing her outside Husby's office that day, he did a double take. It was a big mistake. It slowed him down just enough to let her get a good look at him, good enough so she wound up being a prosecution witness against him. Her and that lying bitch, Suzie Tustman. He spent plenty of time thinking about her the past twelve months, two weeks and four days in a cell block.

For a minute he let himself savor the memory of Suzie's warm, silky skin. She actually tried to pretend she was glad to see him. What kind of a dummy did she think he was? Like he'd come back to see her when he could pick up a woman in any bar for the price of a few drinks. They were always a mistake, just like Suzie. He should have known better. Broads always spelled trouble.

He glanced at the bar mirror as someone slid onto a stool one down from him and ordered a Jack Daniels straight. The guy had his suit coat off, and he dropped it onto the empty seat between them. Rick went back to his beer and unfolded the newspaper he'd bought from the box outside. He glanced at headlines without much interest until he spotted a headline near the bottom of the page. *PINE LAKE WOMAN MURDERED.*

He read quickly, squinting in the dim light. Suzie Tustman had been stabbed to death. He cursed silently and read on. No one had been arrested. The Kings County district attorney's office was investigating the case. Jesus, how the hell did they get into it so fast? It looked like they weren't going to give that hick sheriff a chance to botch things again. Rick finished the article and stared at his reflection in the mirror.

The article didn't mention his name. Maybe the D.A.'s

office was playing it smart, but as sure as he was sitting there, they were looking for him. All that wild stuff he'd said in the courtroom when the jury brought in the verdict . . . He wiped sweat from his upper lip. The county D.A. had a lot more connections than that stupid sheriff. That meant the cops here in L.A. might be on the lookout for him already.

He glanced at the bartender who was talking to the guy in shirt sleeves and decided it was time to move on. No sense giving anyone enough time to think about him. He left enough change on the bar so he wouldn't be remembered as a cheapskate or a big spender. Outside, he crossed one intersection and went down a side street to look for a car.

An hour later he drove past the place where Liz Husby worked. It was a small shop in the middle of a strip mall set back from the street. The parking lot in front was full. He drove through it slowly, hoping to get a glimpse of Liz inside the shop, but the afternoon sun glared off the windows in a bright sheet. He couldn't see a damned thing. It would be dumb to walk in there when he didn't know if she worked behind the counter or in back somewhere. If she spotted him first, she could call the cops before he even knew she'd seen him. Besides, there were too many people around. Right now the fewer people who saw him the better. He'd cruise around a while, then go back to her apartment and wait. She and the kid would come home eventually.

He straightened when he saw a car turn in at the alley. The dashboard clock showed five-thirty. He got out of the Toyota as the other car disappeared behind an oleander hedge. He got to the mouth of the alley in time to see a woman and kid get out of the blue Honda. As they walked to the rear gate of the complex, the woman's back was to him, but he had a good look at the kid. The kid in the picture on the dresser. She was taller and skinnier than she was that day when she walked into Husby's office, but he recognized her all right.

The woman opened the gate and they went in. He ran down the alley in time to see them go into Apartment 1-C. No mistake about it, even though he hadn't see Liz up close. He pulled out the wire and started to fish for the latch, but stepped back quickly when the door of the apartment next to Liz's opened and a woman carrying a laundry basket headed right for him. He drew back into the shadowy carport and listened to the slap of her sandals on the paved walk. When she didn't come past the gate, he took another look. The laundry room must be on his right. He should have checked the damned layout when he was in there. He looked at the rest of the complex when he realized he could hear voices, but he didn't see anyone. Open doors and windows maybe. No telling how many people were home. He'd better go back to his original plan and wait until dark. He checked out the license number on the blue Honda Civic before he left the carport.

He drove back to Sunset Boulevard. The knapsack the kid was carrying was probably full of schoolbooks. It was the middle of the week, so she'd be going to school again tomorrow. That probably meant Momma wouldn't go out partying tonight. She'd stay home and make sure the kid got to bed on time. It made him feel better about coming back later. He'd have a couple more beers and be invisible for awhile. In L.A. he didn't have to worry about sticking out like a canary at a cat show the way he did in those little burgs up north. Not that he planned on staying here any longer than he had to.

The Toyota's engine missed a few times before it caught and settled to a rough idle. The car was a heap of junk. He decided to ditch it and pick up something more reliable. He made a U-turn and headed back toward Echo Park where he abandoned the car a few blocks from where he'd picked it up. If the owner missed it and reported it stolen, the cops would find it easily enough and chalk it up to joy riding kids.

He found a different bar, sleazier than the other one, where there was a mixed crowd of Hispanics and Anglos and plenty of loud music. He nursed a couple of beers he paid for with the last of the tens from Vera's forty bucks. When the sun began to set, he found a Mexican restaurant with strings of lights shaped like jalapeno peppers along the bar mirror. He ordered two tacos and two burritos and washed them down with another beer. It was dark when he came out.

He went up and down several hilly blocks near the park in search of another set of wheels. The neighborhood was full of beat-up jalopies that would be easy to start, but tonight he wanted something in good shape that would blend into Davies' middle-class neighborhood. There was no way he could tell about the engine until he had it going, but anything would be better than the crappy Toyota he'd ditched.

On the fourth block he tried, he spotted a five-year-old Chrysler Imperial with the window rolled down far enough for him to get his hand through to unlock the door. He sat a moment behind the wheel. It felt right. He popped the ignition and started the engine. It purred, and he grinned as he maneuvered the car out of the parking spot. He drove down the hill before he turned on the headlights.

He parked on the side street across from Liz's alley. He

slipped the set of lock picks, knife and cord into his pocket and got out. Crossing to the alley, he checked hedges and fences and listened for dogs. If anything went wrong, he didn't want any surprises.

He swore softly when he saw the Honda was gone. Bitch. Peering through the gate, he couldn't tell if there was a light behind the drapes of her apartment. Where the hell had she gone? Was the kid with her or was there a sitter in there? He heard voices but couldn't tell if they were coming from an apartment or the patio that was screened from his view by a row of tall bushes.

He went back to the street and around to the front of the complex. A steady stream of cars was going by on the avenue, but the sidewalks were empty. L.A. wasn't a walking town. People drove to the corner liquor store. He glanced through the front gate, and sure enough, four people were sitting on the damned patio. He decided to have a look at the narrow strip of yard and cinder block wall he'd spotted from her window.

Light spilled from windows along the sides of both buildings, but most of the shades were drawn. He walked along the narrow strip of grass until he came to the windows of her apartment. The one next to the air conditioning unit was ten feet above him. He wasn't sure if there was a light behind the closed drapes. He stood on tiptoe to feel if the air conditioner was on, but his reach was short so he couldn't be sure. He considered climbing the wall to check the window he'd unlocked, but that might be pushing his luck. Someone could look out a window behind him, or the sitter, if there was one, might grab the phone before he could get to her.

Damn! Everything was going wrong all of a sudden. He didn't like it, but he'd have to wait for Liz or Elizabeth

Davies, or whoever the hell she called herself now, to come home.

He made his way back to the car and settled down. He'd come this far. There was too much at stake for him not to be patient a little longer.

CHAPTER ELEVEN

As they drove up the hill, Jenny was silent and withdrawn. Beth knew she was unhappy about leaving Sasha and uncertain about the great adventure Beth was trying to convince her lay ahead. But in spite of herself, from time to time Jenny's eyes lingered with childish curiosity on the dramatic hillside houses and landscaped yards. Beth decided to leave her to her thoughts for the time being. The Fischers' house would captivate her, and maybe Baron would win her over completely.

When they turned into the last road, Beth used the automatic door opener Ted Fischer had given her and drove into the garage to park beside the Fischers' beautifully restored 1958 Thunderbird. As Beth lifted out the suitcases and led the way up the front steps, Jenny's growing excitement was obvious. The house and neighborhood were much nicer than anything they'd ever lived in, and Beth knew Jenny was impressed.

Baron barked as they came up the steps. Jenny backed away from the door nervously. Beth punched in the security code and unlocked the door far enough to poke her head inside.

"Sit, Baron," she commanded. The dog plopped to its haunches, whimpering softly and wagging its stubby tail. "Good dog!"

She opened the door and carried in the suitcases. Jenny followed cautiously, her gaze on the dog. Sitting, the animal was almost as tall as she was. Baron whimpered, and Jenny put out a hesitant hand to pet its massive head. Baron licked the hand happily, and Jenny laughed. Encouraged, Baron licked her face. Still laughing, Jenny hugged the dog. Beth breathed a sigh of relief. Mission accomplished.

"Come on, I'll show you the house," Beth said, leaving the suitcases where they were for the moment. Baron bounded across the room and came back with a soft bean bag which he dropped at Jenny's feet. Jenny picked it up and threw it carefully across the living room. The dog brought it back, tail wagging, ready to play again. Jenny threw it, then followed Beth along the hall to the kitchen and bedrooms. Baron followed at their heels with the bean bag clutched in his jaws.

The house delighted Jenny as much as it had Beth, and she ooh-ed and ahh-ed over the spectacular view. After they carried the suitcases to the bedroom, Beth suggested Jenny take Baron out on the patio to play while she got dinner ready. She had decided to leave cooking in an unfamiliar kitchen for another day and bought Chinese take-out on the way up. She set the small table in the kitchen alcove where they could enjoy the view. While they ate, Baron stretched out in the shade outside the screen door, tongue lolling, eyes closed.

"I like Baron," Jenny declared. "But I miss Sasha," she added loyally. "Do you think Mrs. Hackett will remember to feed her?"

"I'm sure she will."

"Can we go see tomorrow before we come here?"

"Not tomorrow," Beth said. "Maybe in a few days." *Not until I know where Rick March is . . .*

When they finished eating and Beth had rinsed the dishes and put them in the dishwasher, she said it was time to walk the dog. When she took his leash from the hook in the closet, Baron woofed and galloped to the front door.

"He knows," Jenny said.

"Mr. Fischer always walks him about this time," Beth explained. She made sure the sliding doors were locked, then found the keys and the "dog-walking map" Ted Fischer had given her. Baron sat without being told as she fastened the leash. When Jenny wanted to hold it, Beth said first they'd make sure the dog was well behaved outside. Jenny would be no match for the powerful animal if it bolted; she wondered if she would be. Baron sat on command while she locked the door and punched in the security code.

Ted Fischer had told Beth the dog had to be leashed outdoors except in two areas of undeveloped hillside where he could run free. While Baron sniffed shrubbery at the foot of the steps, Beth consulted the map and decided to take the longer walk that ended in one of the free zones where the dog could run. She gave Jenny the map and assigned her to navigate as they set out.

They followed the curving streets, from the peak where the house stood to a winding road that dipped into a valley then rose again toward another ridge. The air was unnaturally still, and only thin patches of shade under the trees broke the grip of the scorching heat. When they came to the end of the climb, Jenny pointed to the trail marked on the map.

"This is where Baron can play," she said. The dog was already whining and looking up expectantly. "Can I take his leash off?"

"Sure," Beth said.

Jenny snapped open the clasp. The moment the leash fell away from the collar, the dog gave one short woof and raced up the hill. When he disappeared around a curve in the path, Jenny ran after him. Beth hurried to catch up. Baron had already come back with a stick in his mouth.

"He wants me to throw it," Jenny said, giggling. The dog dropped the stick. Jenny picked it up and threw it. Baron thundered after it. Jenny's laughter rang out as the dog bounded back for another play.

They made slow but pleasant progress along the path between patches of dry brush and weeds. Beth reveled in the sound of Jenny's laughter as she tossed the stick and went through mock wrestling matches to get it away from the dog each time he brought it back. Such a simple thing, yet it brought Jenny to life more than anything had this past year and a half. Madelaine would be pleased. As soon as they had a house of their own, Beth vowed to get Jenny a dog. They'd had one in Pine Lake when Jenny was small. Sighing, Beth thought how perfect the picture would be if the specter of Rick March wasn't hovering in the background. But she was doing the right thing coming up here. No matter where Rick March was, she was safe for the moment.

When she realized the sun was sinking behind the western ridge, Beth told Jenny they had to go back. On the way, Jenny held Baron's leash as the tired dog was content to walk at a slow pace.

When Jenny asked to watch the sunset before she got ready for bed, Beth fixed glasses of lemonade and carried them to the table on the patio. Baron lay close to Jenny's chair and she rubbed his back idly with her bare foot while they watched the sun brush the city with fiery color as it sank slowly into the distant ocean. Finally Beth collected the glasses.

"It's past your bedtime," she said.

Baron jumped up at the sound of her voice, but when

Jenny reached to pet him, the dog walked away, straining into the growing gloom. Without warning he sprinted down the length of the house and up the stone steps beyond the greenhouse, deep growls issuing from his throat.

"Baron!" Jenny sounded frightened.

Trying to recover from her own alarm at the dog's sudden change of behavior, Beth said, "He probably hears a rabbit or a raccoon. Mrs. Fischer said there are lots of them around."

Jenny clutched her hands into each other, and her face was suddenly pale. Beth put an arm around her shoulders and led her inside.

"Will Baron be all right out there?" Jenny asked.

"Of course he will. He's just being a good watchdog. He'll come in soon. Now go take a shower, then I'll show you where the Fischers hide their TV. Maybe we can find something fun to watch for a little while before you go to sleep."

"Can I sleep with you, Mommy? It's so quiet. I'm scared alone."

"Sure. Come on. After your shower I'll show you how the magic drapes and lights work in the bedroom."

When Jenny had the water running in the shower, Beth went out on the patio and called softly to Baron. To her surprise, he was still sitting by the upper gate. He turned to look at her, and when she called again, trotted down slowly.

"What is it, boy?"

He rubbed his head against her leg and pushed a wet nose into her palm. She went into the kitchen and held the screen open for him, but the dog stayed where he was, looking from her to the gate.

"Leave the rabbits alone," she said in a coaxing tone, but he didn't accept the offer of the open door. Instead he lay

101

just outside it, head on paws, gazing into the darkness beyond the greenhouse. Nervous, Beth turned off the lights and sat at the table where she could see the end of the house and the path leading up to Amos Westerland's place.

His house was dark. She hadn't seen any sign of his return, but she supposed he could be back. Would Baron react to Westerland's presence this way? It didn't seem likely when they'd been neighbors so many years. Maybe someone was keeping an eye on the place while Westerland was gone, picking up the mail and checking doors and windows. It might even be a security patrol the Fischers forgot to mention.

Don't go imagining things, she told herself. Most likely Baron heard some wild creature exploring the bank of ivy, just as she had told Jenny.

The phone rang. It startled Beth and she picked it up without thinking.

"Hello?"

"Beth? It's Vince Norris. I just wanted you to know your call forwarding is connected."

"Oh, thank you." She had completely forgotten his promise to see to it.

"Are you settled in okay? Need anything?"

"We're fine. Thanks for helping us get this place. Jenny loves it." She knew her voice was strangely stilted, but she still wasn't at ease with him. He had helped, but he also had told thousands of readers that she lived in L.A.

"I figured she would," Norris said. "Ted's a gadget nut who believes in making life easy and fun."

She smiled, thinking of all the buttons and levers and switches Nancy and Ted had explained to her.

Jenny called from the bedroom. Beth said quickly, "Well, thanks again, Mr. Norris. The house is wonderful. I have to go now. Jenny's getting ready for bed."

"Sure. If you think of anything you need, just call. You have my card."

"Yes. All right. Thanks." She hung up and went to Jenny.

Lying on the king-size bed together, Beth explained the row of buttons hidden in the headboard that controlled the electrically operated gadgetry. Giggling, Jenny closed the drapes and activated the spring that swung back a large, framed oil painting on the wall opposite the bed to reveal the enormous television set. Beth let her play with the remote control to change stations and volume, even split the screen so two stations could be viewed at the same time. When a news program came on, Beth shut off the set.

"Past your bedtime," she said. She let Jenny swing the picture back in place and dim the lights, then kissed her good night, saying she'd be to bed soon.

Half an hour later when she was sure Jenny was asleep, Beth turned on the small television set in the kitchen and listened to the news. The story came on after two others about a local gang war and a fire in West Hollywood.

"In the town of Pine Lake, a hundred fifty miles northeast of Los Angeles, authorities still have no clues in the murder of Suzie Tustman, who was found brutally stabbed to death in her home yesterday. Mrs. Tustman was one of the key witnesses in the trial last year of Rick March, who was convicted of bludgeoning her husband's business partner to death. March was sentenced to twenty years to life, but several days ago, the conviction was overturned after the appeal he filed through the ACLU's appellate program showed a significant break in the chain of custody of the alleged murder weapon. March's appeal was based on the trial transcript which showed the Pine Lake sheriff had left the alleged murder weapon in his vehicle at the scene of the crime for two hours while March was being questioned.

"March was released from Folsum Prison earlier this week and is currently being sought for questioning because of threats he made against Mrs. Tustman and several other people he deemed responsible for his conviction. Security measures have been reinforced at the Bakersfield courthouse where Judge Willard Hastings, who presided at March's trial, still presides in the Criminal Courts Division. Los Angeles police are trying to contact Elizabeth Husby, wife of the murder victim, whom March also threatened."

Beth's mouth was dry when she tried to swallow. She stared at the screen. The terror she'd been holding at bay rushed over her like a tidal wave. *No picture of me, please—* She let out her breath when the anchorman went on to another story. Shaking, she turned off the set. Should she call the police and admit her identity? The idea frightened her. Would they give her police protection or simply warn her? She looked at the phone, but couldn't bring herself to make the call.

Baron woofed softly, and she jumped, her heart thudding against her ribs. She'd forgotten about the dog. She hurried to the door. He came in, tail wagging, his vigil apparently over. When she locked the screen and the inside door, she found the box of canine treats Nancy had left with the dog food and gave one to him before she turned out the lights. In the bedroom, she undressed quickly and climbed into bed, resisting the urge to hold Jenny in her arms to make sure she was safe.

CHAPTER TWELVE

Vince had been trying for two days to reach Sheriff Mayville, but the woman who answered the phone kept saying he was out and she didn't know when to expect him. Vince left his number each time, but now at 10:00 p.m., Mayville still hadn't called. Vince rang an information number and asked for Mayville's home number. To his surprise, he got it.

He got a cold Corona from the refrigerator in the closet-sized kitchen of his apartment, then sat in front of the air conditioner with the phone in his lap. He'd call all night if he had to. The phone rang a long time before it was finally picked up.

"Sheriff Mayville here."

"Vince Norris, Sheriff."

"I heard you've been calling."

"You asked me to, remember?" Vince worked to keep his tone unchallenging. "You seem pretty busy. Anything new?"

"Not a damned thing I know for sure. The D.A.'s investigators are talking to people in town and poking around the Tustman place. If they turned up anything, they ain't telling me about it." Resentment was heavy in his voice. He was probably taking a lot of heat about March getting out because he fouled up on procedure.

"Someone must have seen March around town." People would recognize the biggest newsmaker the town ever had.

"I'd know if they did. Folks here are pretty upset about there being another murder. They don't like to think something like this can happen twice. The only killings we usually get are hunting or car accidents. There was that fight over in Mac's Bar a couple of years back when one drunk landed a lucky punch and the other one cracked his head on the bar rail as he went down. Died the next day."

No wonder Mayville was out of his depth with the Husby murder case. "What about unfamiliar cars? March made damned good time getting from Folsum to Pine Lake. He must have had wheels."

The sheriff sighed. "Mr. Norris, maybe you didn't notice, but a state highway goes right through town. A couple of hundred cars pass through here every day. We don't have any traffic lights or cops on corners. The Tustman place is three miles out of town. Who's to say which direction March came or went? Not many houses on that road and damned little traffic. Neighbors claim they didn't see anyone around except those who belong there. Hell, March could have driven back and forth ten times or pulled right up to the Tustman place with no one the wiser."

Vince made a note to check the neighbors. "Did Mrs. Tustman have any other enemies who might want her dead?"

The sheriff was quiet a moment, as if the idea had never occurred to him. Finally he said, "Everybody has enemies, Mr. Norris. I don't suppose Suzie was any different. She was a beautiful woman."

Was he hinting at something? Vince probed carefully. "Were she and Jack happily married?"

"Seems so. Usual squabbles, I suppose, but all couples have them. I haven't heard any stories the past year or so."

The past year or so? Gil Husby died eighteen months ago. "What about before that?" he asked.

"You know how it is in a small town."

Vince's instincts tingled. When people were evasive, there was something to hide. "Did any of those stories link her to Gil Husby?"

The sheriff was quiet for such a long time, Vince thought he wasn't going to answer. When he did, he was evasive again.

"Don't seem right bad mouthing the dead."

That sure as hell meant 'yes.' None of the clippings Vince read said anything about Suzie having a reputation for running around, but the Sheriff sure was hinting at it. Vince thought about asking Beth, but she wasn't likely to admit it if her husband had been involved. He made another note to check for rumors. He tried a different tack with Mayville.

"Sheriff, how do you figure March found the Tustman house without asking for directions?" He would never have gotten there unless Gary Kellog had given him directions. If the gas station attendant and the gawking crowd on the Tustman driveway were typical citizens of Pine Lake, folks would be knocking on the sheriff's door to let him know someone had asked for directions the night of the murder. "Maybe you should find out if March called Tustman's office. He could have pretended to have a delivery."

"Wanda says no calls like that came in to the office."

Mayville wasn't as dumb as he seemed. Vince jotted down the secretary's name. "How long has Wanda worked for Tustman?"

"Five years, give or take."

She'd been there when Husby was killed, so she would have recognized March but not recognized his voice. But if no one called, that blew holes in the theory.

"I don't know how he found the house, Mr. Norris," Mayville said, "and I don't much care. Point is, he did. The county district attorney's investigators are running around bumping into each other. They have a bulletin out that March is wanted for questioning. Ondavin means to wrap this up fast and have March behind bars again. Ask me, March is probably halfway across Arizona or down in Mexico by now." Mayville made a noise that might have been a chuckle. Vince figured he'd be a happy man if the county investigators fell on their butts.

Vince needed something to keep him ahead of the pack. "Sheriff, do you know where Liz Husby went when she left Pine Lake?"

Mayville hesitated. "Some say L.A. She doesn't stay in touch with folks here, far as I know."

"Has she ever come back?"

There was another pause, as if Mayville wasn't sure how much to say. "I think the girl should be left in peace, Norris. She had a hard time last year and for awhile before that. She deserves a chance."

Mayville was protecting Beth. Interesting. Vince decided he needed to know more about Liz Husby's life in Pine Lake, but he knew the sheriff had said as much as he was going to for the moment. Was it common knowledge that she'd changed her name and moved to Los Angeles? If Suzie Tustman knew, March could have gotten the information from her before he killed her.

"I guess she does," Vince said. "Thanks, Sheriff. I appreciate your talking to me. I'll call again in a day or two, if that's okay. Maybe one of us will come up with something useful. Should I call the office number?"

"No matter. Calls get switched here after hours."

So Mayville had been screening his calls and ignoring Vince. Vince gave Mayville his office and home numbers and asked the sheriff to call if he heard anything. The sheriff hung up so fast, Vince doubted he'd written the numbers down.

Vince pulled at the Corona. Pine Lake was far enough out of L.A. that his editor wouldn't consider the story worth following very long unless March could be tied to the killing. Or if he found Beth Davies and killed again.

L.A. was a hell of a big city. Even if March had learned Beth's address, she was gone now. There was nothing to tie her and the kid to the Fischers' place. Stashing her up there was a stroke of pure genius. March would never find her. Neither would any other reporters. For the time being, she was all his. And when the media began linking March's name to Suzie Tustman's murder, Beth would be scared enough to trust Vince completely.

In the meantime, he'd stick close to Mayville and do some checking on his own.

CHAPTER THIRTEEN

March struck a match and looked at the dashboard clock. *Midnight.* Where the hell was she? He got out of the car and walked down the dark alley to make sure she hadn't slipped past him somehow. There was no blue Honda. He could still hear a murmur of voices from the patio, but all he could see was a pale blur beyond the tangle of vines. Didn't people ever go to bed around here?

He walked back along the alley and stood in the darkness considering his next move. If there was a sitter in there with the kid, it would screw things up. Better make sure first. He walked toward the avenue. Across the street in front of a closed mom and pop market was a phone kiosk. He fished in his pocket for coins and dialed the number he had memorized from her phone earlier. It rang twice and was picked up.

"Hello?"

He scowled. It was Liz. He recognized the soft inflection she always gave whatever she said.

"Hello?" she said again a little breathlessly. "Who is it?"

He cradled the phone gently. She was in the apartment all the time. Where the hell was her car?

He hung up, crossed the street and walked up to the front gate of the complex. Standing in the shadows beyond the faint pool of light thrown by a light above the mailboxes and bells, he peered into the courtyard. From here he could see two people sitting in lawn chairs. They had drinks, and one held a glowing cigarette. He went back to the sidewalk and went around the side of the building where he'd checked the windows earlier. The windows in the next building were dark. So were the ones along Husby's building. The only light was a dim glow from the alley.

He vaulted onto the block wall, adrenaline flowing. His running shoes were quiet on the hard surface as he made his way to the window he'd unlocked earlier. Looking up, there wasn't any way to tell if it was still unlocked. Maybe he should wait a while to be sure she went back to sleep, but he was too psyched up to sit around anymore. He took a breath to steady himself, then let his weight fall toward the wall below the window, palms flat to take the impact. Stretched like a buttress, he balanced on one hand and reached up to push at the window. His gut strained as the window moved upward. He got it open about six inches before he ran out of leverage and had to reposition himself and stretch on tiptoe.

When the window was up far enough to climb through, he stood back and checked to make sure he hadn't attracted any attention. He flexed his knees and jumped, feet aimed, grabbing the window ledge and pulling himself upward. In spite of the good shape he was in, his arms strained as he slid through the opening head first, not bothering to look first to see what he was getting into. He slithered to a heap on the carpet next to the card table.

A lamp on a table near the sofa was on like a night light. It left the room half in shadow. He got to his feet and glanced into the dark kitchen before he made his way to the hall. He stopped when he saw the cat that had run past him before sitting outside the kid's door. When he took a step toward it, it slid into the shadows. Damned thing moved so fast. Holding his breath, he looked into the room. The bed was empty except for the row of stuffed animals. What the hell—

He stepped across the hall to the mother's room. It was empty too. Damn! Where the hell was she? She had answered the phone a few minutes ago. He picked up the phone on the nightstand and listened. For a moment he was puzzled by the dial tone, then realized she must have call forwarding. *The bitch.* He'd waited all this time, and she and the kid were gone. Angry now, he turned on a lamp and opened her closet, trying to remember what clothes had been there this afternoon. They all looked the same, but there were some empty spaces among the hangers. There was also an empty space on the shelf where a suitcase could have been.

He went into the kid's room and turned on another light. The schoolbook was gone, and there was no sign of the purple knapsack she had when she came home. He swore softly. Liz had probably read the story in the *Times* about Suzie Tustman and run like a rabbit. She always was scared of her own shadow. He could still see her on the witness stand answering questions in that little voice of hers. The district attorney kept asking her to speak up. She'd managed to do that all right, and she had pointed right at him as the man she'd seen run out of her husband's office.

Where would she go now? The kid had her schoolbooks. Did that mean they were still in town? Had she gone to a hotel or some friend's place to hide out? That was the kind of dumb thing that would make sense to her. She was a mouse, and mice didn't plan ahead. When they smelled a cat, they ran blindly.

The more he thought about it, the more sure he was that Liz hadn't gone far. She was waiting for the cops to pick him up. Maybe they figured he would head for L.A. and suggested she hide out. Did they have a line on him or were they guessing? Maybe it would be a good idea to head south and cool it for awhile. But that would be wasting time, and time was something he didn't have. He had to do it now, before the cops found him. The sooner the better. He knew where she worked and the name of the kid's school. One or the other would lead him to her.

He opened the drawer of the nightstand and took out her address and phone book. He glanced through the almost empty pages, then crammed the book into his pocket. There was a leather jewelry box on the dresser, but the stuff in it was junk no fence or pawnbroker would look at twice. As he picked up a necklace, the strand caught on something and broke. Beads scattered all over the place. The cat streaked out from under the bed and pawed one of them across the carpet. Rick grabbed for the animal, but it scooted under the bed. The hell with it. He wondered who was going to feed it with Liz and the kid gone. Maybe she figured on stopping home each day so the stupid thing wouldn't starve.

He lifted the silver-framed picture from the dresser and studied it in the light. The kid looked like her old man. Same big blue eyes and thin face, only the kid's were solemn. Husby's had the shifty look of a guy who was figuring out his next move. Rick remembered Husby as a swaggering, bragging jock as a senior back in high school. He had the look then. He still had it ten years later when he stopped and offered Rick the tire iron so he could fix the flat.

He pried off the back of the frame and pulled out the picture. When he put the frame back on the dresser, it skidded on some of the beads and fell to the floor before he could grab it. When he picked it up, the glass was cracked in three directions. He put it back on the dresser, then folded the picture and shoved it into his pocket. On second thought, he picked up the frame and polished his prints from it before he put it back and turned off the light.

The kitchen looked the same as it had earlier. Either they didn't eat here or she was a hell of a housekeeper. He opened the refrigerator and saw a meager supply of food. No milk or vegetables that would spoil fast, only a package of cheese wrapped in plastic and half a bag of carrots. He looked in all the cupboards for a supply of booze, but there wasn't any.

Using a towel from the rack, he went through the apartment, wiping down everything he'd touched. Except for the broken beads and the picture frame, everything was the way he found it. He shut off the lights except for the lamp she'd left on and pulled aside the drape for a look at the patio. It was finally empty. He left through the front door.

He woke at six-thirty. He never needed a clock. Since he was a kid, he'd been able to wake up at whatever time he decided. He first used the talent to sneak out of foster homes before anyone was stirring for the day. Sometimes he just wanted to get out of the house so he didn't have to help get younger kids ready for school or change a baby's stinking diapers. Sometimes he needed to get away from the whole scene, to be alone for awhile so he wouldn't go crazy with so many people yelling at him all the time.

When he was a little kid, he used to believe each new place was going to be better than the old one. It never was. No matter where they put him, he was somebody's ticket to a few bucks every month from the welfare department. He was a nobody, a nothing. Some of the foster mothers never even bothered to get his name straight. Called him "Kid" or

"You." It made him feel like a drained beer bottle
deposit on it. When it got real bad, he'd run away to
for a while. They always found him and sent him
sometimes to a worse place than the one he'd run from
it didn't stop him from trying.

Once when he was about seven, he got as far as
Bay. It was the first time he'd seen the ocean. He re
bered sitting on the beach fascinated by the waves cu
and slamming against the sand and rocks. He felt as
was part of it, or it was part of him. Strong. Powerful. I
structible. No matter what happened, it came back ha
than before. He fell asleep on the sand and stayed ther
night. He woke up with cold rain soaking him and the w
whipping at his wet clothes. The sea had become a rag
demon, spewing froth and towering waves that devoui
everything in their path. It was awesome. He shivered as
clawed furrows in the sand then washed them away in a
other burst of energy. He'd been so hypnotized by it, l
never heard the cop car pull up on the road behind him
They took him back, but he never stayed anywhere ver
long after that.

He used the toilet, then dropped to the floor and began
his push-ups. He counted aloud softly as sweat began to
coat his body, concentrating totally on the rise of power in
his muscles. When he reached one hundred, he sprang to
his feet and grinned at the thought of a shower. He could
shower whenever he wanted now. Doing what he wanted
when he wanted was one of the best parts of being out.
That and being in control.

Naked, he experimented with the temperature of the
water until it was hot enough to feel good, then stood under
the spray for a long time as he soaped and rinsed. When he
finally toweled himself dry, he studied his torso in the wavy

mirror above the sink, flexing his biceps and pecs and running his palm over the crude prison tattoo of a knife on his left arm.

Sipping his second cup of coffee, he watched the parking lot behind the print shop from a restaurant across the street. His senses sharpened when he saw a blue car turn in. He couldn't make out the driver, but a couple of minutes later, Liz Davies came around the corner of the building and went into the shop. He picked up his check and paid the cashier.

"Have a nice day," she chirped as she handed him his change.

"I plan to," he said, smiling at her.

He dropped two quarters into the box near the front of the restaurant and pulled out a *Times*. Now that he knew she was where she belonged, he had time to read. But not here. The restaurant was the only place he could wait around and not look out of place, but if he sat there all day, he was sure to attract attention. Best thing would be to re-park the car where he could watch the Honda. She wouldn't go far without it.

He started around the corner of the block where he'd parked the car and stopped. A cop car was double parked next to the Imperial. Without breaking stride, he turned around and quickened his pace to put distance between himself and the Imperial. Damned thing must already be on the hot sheet. He shoved the *Times* under his arm and tried to look as if he were headed home or to work. Trouble was the street was deserted. No one walked in this damned city. He went two blocks then cut down a side street and onto one that paralleled Sunset.

He should have picked up a different car this morning,

but the damned Imperial was right where he'd left it two blocks from the motel. He'd given in to the temptation of easy pickings. He wouldn't make that mistake again. Still, there was nothing to connect him to the car. The owner would be happy to get it back in one piece, and the cops wouldn't bust their balls trying to find out who'd taken it.

Then he remembered the flight bag he left on the seat. Damn! He should have taken it into the restaurant with him. Another mistake. He had to watch it; he was getting careless. He reviewed what was in the bag: a couple of cheap razors, the shirts and socks he took from the jerk who didn't fix the gas gauge on the Chevy, two pair of shorts he bought in a discount store on Western. Nothing that would help the cops make him. Nothing he couldn't replace easily. Still, it ticked him off that he'd slipped up on a detail. He had to be more careful from here on out.

He walked a long time, cutting back to Sunset Boulevard at Western Avenue where the action picked up and he wouldn't be the only one on the sidewalks. He needed another car, but it wouldn't be smart to sit around in it all day. He'd play it safe and get off the street until the Husby kid got out of school.

A couple of blocks past Vermont Avenue, he bought a ticket at a porno movie joint and sat in the empty back row. He slouched to watch the flickering screen. From time to time he got bored and went to the men's room where there was enough light to read the paper. The story about Suzie Tustman was recapped, but there was nothing new. His name wasn't mentioned again, but that might be a trick to lure him into the open.

He walked out onto the oven-like street at one o'clock. By two, he was in a silver Ford Escort parked outside Vista School. He had the windows open, but it was like sitting in a sweat box. Beads of perspiration trickled along his jaw as he studied the kid's picture. When he heard the muffled sound of a bell, he focused his attention on the doors of the school. They opened and kids began to spill out. He studied them, wishing the Davies kid had red hair. He'd never seen so many little blondes in his life.

She came out in the second wave. He spotted the purple knapsack and took another look at the photograph to make sure. Her hair was pulled up in a ponytail, but it was her all right. And she was walking alone.

She turned down the street away from him. He started the car. When she got to the corner, he pulled out and followed slowly. He had to stop for a crossing guard at the corner, but he had no trouble keeping the purple knapsack in sight. She walked slowly, as if she weren't keen about where she was going. Two kids her age were only a few feet ahead of her, but she didn't try to catch up. She was probably a mouse like her mother.

She turned again at the next corner. He got there in time to see her open the gate of a house in the middle of the block. She was already out of sight by the time he drove past the small, frame bungalow with a fenced yard. In back, a kid about five hung from the bar of a jungle gym, and a toddler with dark ringlets played in a sand box.

He drove around the block and found a shady place to park and wait.

CHAPTER FOURTEEN

The air was like hot sand as Vince drove through Pine Lake to Jack Tustman's office. The weathered-siding building loomed in the center of town like a brown bunker. The sign above the door said Tustman Construction in red letters. Apparently Tustman got a new sign but no new partner. The word Livery was faintly visible on the weathered wood over the hay doors, which had been converted to a picture window. On one side of the building there was an outside stairway to the upper floor. According to what he'd read, Gil Husby's office had been up there.

Inside, cool air washed over Vince like a waterfall. The office was bright, with louvered awnings on the large windows to keep out the direct sun. The color scheme was pale green desk, chairs, and carpeting, accented by dark green lush plants flanking the windows. Not what he expected in a small town construction company. Jack Tustman did okay for himself.

Vince smiled at the gray-haired woman sitting behind the desk separated from the entry by a wood-railed partition.

"Can I help you?" she asked.

"Good morning, Wanda. Is Jack in today?"

She looked a little surprised. "No, he isn't, Mr.—?"

Vince leaned across the partition, his hand out. She shook it tentatively, her eyes questioning. "Norris. Vince Norris. I was out at the house Monday night. He looked pretty bad. He's okay, isn't he?"

Her face sagged. "He's been through so much. Doc Philbin has him under observation. There isn't anything here I can't handle for the rest of the week, and what with the funeral and everything, he has more than enough to worry about." She straightened her shoulders as if marshaling her strength.

"Has a time been set for the funeral?"

"Friday afternoon. Jack's sister and her husband are coming in from Illinois. Doc doesn't want Jack to go home until there's someone there with him. Poor Jack . . ."

"What about Suzie's family?" he asked with what he hoped was the right note of concern.

Her face hardened, and she gave an inaudible sniff. "I imagine they'll come over from Bushville in force for the funeral."

Did Wanda hold Suzie in the same disdain as the rest of the family? Vince made a mental note to get Suzie's maiden name and check out the clan. "Have the police come up with anything on the murder?"

There was no mistaking Wanda's feelings on that subject. She pursed her mouth and almost clucked. "They're not trying too hard, if you ask me. Why they ever let a man like that out of prison is a mystery. Sheriff Mayville's taking a lot of heat, what with the election coming up this fall. And him doing his job is all. The law bends over backwards to make sure criminals' rights aren't violated, but what about poor innocent citizens? What about Jack's rights—and Suzie's?" She reached for a tissue and dabbed at her nose.

"Yeah, it's a hell of a mess." Vince waited while she blew her nose and dropped the tissue into a pale green wicker wastebasket. "Well, I guess I should let you get on with your work."

"I'll tell Jack you came by."

"No need. I'll drop in on him and say hello. See if he needs anything." Remembering Gary Kellog's remark about no hospital in town, Vince said, "He over at the nursing home?"

She nodded and smiled wanly. Vince said good-bye and left. When he looked back through the plate glass window as he climbed into the car, Wanda was drying her eyes and blowing her nose again. He wondered if any of the tears were for Suzie or if they were all for Jack.

He studied the town as he drove through. No one was out in the scorching midday heat, but a few cars were angled at the curb in front of the market and along the block where the bank and the town's only restaurant were. Through the window of Stella's Cafe, he saw the tables and stools were filled. He considered going in to see what he could pick up in the way of gossip, but in a town this size he'd be an obvious outsider who'd be stonewalled by silence. He'd better have a shot at Jack Tustman before his relatives set up a buffer.

Small towns were all the same. The nursing home was on the edge of town, on a quiet street with lots of trees. The health care business always put the aging population out to pasture in tranquil surroundings, as if getting back to nature somehow made dying easier. Given a choice, most old people would probably rather be smack-dab in the middle of town where the action was.

The nursing home went under the pleasant euphemism of Pine Lake Residence. It was a low sprawling building with concrete ramps instead of steps and well-tended lawns and gardens with paths and benches here and there. Vince parked in a visitors' lot screened by a border of pines.

The reception desk in the entry was empty. Along the corridors, he could hear the clinking of lunch trays being distributed. Steeling himself against the smells of old age and fresh antiseptics, he glanced down the two halls branching off the reception area. In the interest of peace and quiet, the doc would keep Tustman as far away from the other patients as possible. The end of a wing, but which one? He shrugged and turned right, reading the nameplates beside the doors as he passed.

Gray scarecrows of both sexes were propped in wheelchairs with tray tables holding their meals. One shrunken specter with no teeth, his face caved in by the weight of age, yelled and flopped an arm like a netted fish. Vince turned away. A nurse's aide came out of a room and smiled at him as if noonday visitors were commonplace, probably welcome if they helped out with feeding. She reached for another tray from the cart in the center of the hall and carried it into a room.

Vince reached the end of the hall without seeing Tustman's name or anyone the size and shape of the huddled figure he'd seen in the dead woman's bedroom Monday night. At the end of the hall, double glass doors opened to a bright dining room where tables for four or six were arranged in seating groups. Several patients in wheelchairs sat snug against tables. Others, able to get around under their own power, stood on line at a food counter where women in white uniforms and hair nets portioned out food from containers the size of dish pans.

Vince retraced his steps and went down the other wing. This one seemed to be the express route to the grave. No one was sitting up in chairs. A few beds were elevated and the occupants were attempting to feed themselves, but most lay unmoving despite the trays beside them. Two aides were working their way down the hall feeding the helpless.

Vince got to the end of the corridor without finding

Tustman. The last room on his right didn't have a name-plate; the single bed was empty and made. Had Tustman been released? About to turn back, Vince did a double take on the name card posted outside the door across the hall: Ethel Davies. As in Beth Davies? A mother in a nursing home would account for her coming back the way Mayville had hinted. Vince ventured into the room.

The woman in the bed was so shriveled and thin, she looked like a wispy-haired corpse except for her eyes, which swung to him like a motion detector. As he approached the bed, the woman's gaze followed him, but despite the speed with which she had sensed his presence, there was no awareness in her expression.

"Hello, Mrs. Davies," he said quietly.

No light snapped on behind the clouded eyes. Vince wondered if she was blind. He tried again.

"Beth sends her love," he said. The name didn't bring any response. Uncomfortable, he stepped back as an over-weight nurse with blonde hair came in. She smiled as she put the tray on the table.

"I didn't know Ethel had a visitor," she said with the determined cheerfulness nurses always exuded. She began to crank up the bed.

"I'm a friend of her daughter's," Vince said.

The woman's smile froze somewhere between friendly and disdainful. "How is Liz?"

Liz. That was it. He should have remembered she'd always been Liz in this town.

"She's fine. I was up this way and thought I'd stop by to say hello to Ethel. I didn't realize she was—"

"Has been for five years," the nurse said, glancing at him with frank curiosity. "Where do you know Liz from?"

On guard now, Vince lied easily, recalling the biographical material that said Elizabeth Davies had gone to art school for two years in Los Angeles. "We were in art school together. We keep in touch."

"I see. You'll have to excuse me," she said, glancing at her watch. "I have to feed Ethel. Unless you want to do it? We encourage visitors to—"

"Sorry, I have to go." He stepped aside to let her move the table close to the woman in the bed, who had already slipped sideways like a rag doll.

"Has Liz been here lately?" he asked as the nurse stuffed pillows around Ethel to keep her upright.

The woman's plump cheeks fell to jowls when she scowled. "Not since Christmas. You'd think—" She clamped off whatever she started to say and turned to her patient. "Here we go now, Ethel. It's lunchtime. My, doesn't this look good today."

Vince walked out as she chattered on in a loud voice, as if to conquer the old woman's physical and mental infirmities by sound waves. Back at the reception desk, a young woman with bangs and shoulder-length hair was on the telephone. When she hung up, Vince said, "I'm looking for Jack Tustman. I was told he was here."

"Oh, you missed him. He left about an hour ago."

"Is he coming back?"

"I don't think so. The doctor released him this morning."

Vince gave her a 'that's life' smile. "Okay. Thanks. Guess I'll have to catch him at the house."

The girl smiled back. Jack's tragedy hadn't incapacitated him for long, Vince thought as he walked out into the shimmering heat of the parking lot. He hadn't found Jack Tustman, but he knew now that Beth Davies had come back to Pine Lake at least once since she left.

He sat in the car with the engine running and the air conditioner on high, wondering if he should try to find Tustman. He might be home, or he could have gone to pick up the relatives Wanda mentioned. Vince decided to put him on hold for the moment.

The sheriff's outer office was empty, but his door was open. Vince walked in. Mayville cocked an eyebrow. "Didn't expect to see you back in these parts so soon," he said.

"Mind if I sit down?"

"Suit yourself."

Mayville leaned back in the oversized leather swivel chair that made him look like a kid playing the role of sheriff in a school play. Vince sat on the straight-backed wooden chair that was the only other one in the room.

"Anything on March?"

"I already told you, Mr. Norris, the county D.A. isn't taking me into his confidence. Technically, I'm still in charge of the case, but I don't have the manpower or the jurisdiction to go outside the township limits. I guarantee you one thing, March isn't here in town."

Vince remembered the election Wanda mentioned. "You wouldn't think unkindly of the idea of solving the Tustman murder on your own, would you, Sheriff?"

Mayville's eyes narrowed, and Vince knew he'd struck a nerve.

"Rick March is a thorn in your tush," Vince said. "The D.A. has more equipment and manpower than you do, but March is just another case to him. Now you, you've got a personal stake in finding March."

The only change in Mayville's expression was a glint of cold steel in his eyes.

"I want to work with you, Sheriff. You know this town. I

know March. I've studied his file. I want to find him before he finds Liz Husby."

The silence drew out for a long time. Finally Mayville said, "What's in this for you, Norris?"

"The story. The hunt, the chase, the capture from both viewpoints, the hunter and the hunted."

Mayville smiled wryly. "You going to write a book about March's life?"

"Not only his life story. March's *mind* story. How he thinks, how he plans, how he feels."

"That's a mighty ambitious project, Mr. Norris, but it sounds pretty cold."

"Not cold, realistic. March is clever, and he's on his guard now. We have to anticipate what he's going to do next."

The sheriff swiveled the chair slightly and considered Vince with a mixture of skepticism and interest. He didn't want to commit himself, but he was hooked. Vince knew the prospect of beating out the district attorney was a red cape waving in front of Mayville.

"And just how do you think you're going to find March before the county boys do?"

Vince aimed a finger in Mayville's direction, then at his own chest. "We're going to figure out how he got here and where he went. Something you said the other night started me thinking. March went right to the Tustman place without asking directions. How could he know where it was—*unless he'd been there before?*"

The sheriff's face was impassive.

"That's what you've been thinking all along, isn't it?" Vince said. "He didn't have to ask directions because he already knew the way. He was there the day of Gil Husby's murder, just like he said he was."

The sheriff held up a palm. "No way I'm going to believe he didn't kill Husby, if that's what you're saying."

"Sure he killed Husby, but if he was at the Tustman place that day, it puts a different light on the murder."

"How so?"

"Why did Mrs. Tustman lie about his being there?"

Mayville's chair came forward. "You're jumping to conclusions, son. Maybe he was there to burgle the house."

"Mrs. Tustman said she was home alone all afternoon."

"He could have seen her and decided it wasn't the easy job he figured."

Vince challenged him with a hard look. "Suppose they were there together? Suppose she invited him like March claimed?"

Mayville folded his arms on the desk. "The woman is dead, Norris. Killed by a maniac who got out of prison on a fluke. He said he would kill her and he did."

Vince held up a hand. "I'm thinking like March. Hear me out. Antisocial personalities believe everything they tell themselves. He had a lot of time to think about Suzie Tustman's testimony. He headed straight for her when he got out. In less than twelve hours, she was dead. Why was he so obsessed?"

"Revenge. She testified against him."

"Possibly. Or maybe because she put him up to the murder, then double-crossed him by not backing his story."

Mayville's chair rolled into the desk as he straightened with surprise. "That's crazy," he said.

"But not impossible," Vince pointed out. "Maybe she made passes at Husby and was rejected. Maybe they had an affair, but Husby got tired of her and broke it off. Maybe she only wanted March to scare Husby, and things got out of hand.

"If she invited March back to the house the way he said she did, there are any number of scenarios she could have fed him to convince him to do murder for her. No point in admitting the whole thing in court because no matter how he sliced it, he was still confessing to murder. So he came up with a story he expected her to go along with, but she double-crossed him."

The sheriff shook his head. "That's pretty far-fetched."

"Okay, put that aside for a minute," Vince said. "March needed a car to get to Pine Lake and out again as fast as he did on Monday. I say we start by checking stolen vehicles between here and Sacramento. If we can get a line of the kind of car he was using, someone's memory may be jogged.

"March could have taken Suzie's car, but he didn't. And you didn't have any cars reported stolen in town that day, did you? That means March used the same car to get from here to his next stop." Vince leaned forward. "I've been reading March's file. He's stolen enough cars in his lifetime to start his own used car lot. His pattern's always the same: dump a car and pick up another one first chance he gets. That way he's in and out before the cops get a line on the vehicle. So how far can he get if he was lucky enough to grab a car that was all gassed up? Then he either has to get another set of wheels or buy gas. He's not loaded with dough, so my bet is he finds himself a new car. We check towns between here and Sacramento for cars stolen Monday morning. South of here, we check for abandoned cars. When we come up with a match, we know where he's headed. We also check for petty thefts in case he decides he needs money. He's not going to risk anything big. He'd hit something easy, like a grocery store till when the clerk's back is turned, or a woman's purse left on a counter for a minute, maybe a flea market cash box. Something like that."

Mayville looked surprised. "You *have* thought this out, haven't you?"

"Are you arguing with my theories?"

"Can't say that I am, leastwise not about the car. But I don't buy that bullshit about Suzie getting him to kill Husby for her."

Vince settled for half the pie. "Do we have a deal then?"

Mayville thought it over. "I guess there's no harm in giving it a whirl. But tell me, what are you going to be doing while I'm tracking all this down?"

"Trying to figure out how March would go about finding Liz Husby next. Sure as fate he's after her. Is the old lady in Pine Lake Residence her only relative?"

The sheriff looked surprised again. "Emmett Davies died ten years ago."

"How long has Ethel been over there?"

"Five years."

"Why didn't you tell me Liz comes back to see her? How many times has she been back since she left?"

Mayville's eyes narrowed, and he hesitated before he said, "Twice. There's not much point in coming very often. Ethel doesn't recognize her."

"What's wrong with her?"

"Early senility, maybe Alzheimer's. She had a hard life. Liz was born when she was past forty. Emmett Davies was a drinker who made life miserable for his family. You would have thought Ethel would throw a party when his temper sent his blood pressure skyrocketing once too often and he dropped dead of a stroke, but she was a lost soul. Guess she was so used to him telling her what to do she didn't know how to run her own life anymore. Liz came home from art school to give her a hand. Even after she married Husby, she went to her ma's every day to see she was okay. Then Ethel began having little strokes that did funny things to her mind. Couldn't be left alone, so Liz took her in. Husby wasn't crazy about the idea, but there wasn't anyplace else for her to go. Wasn't long until Ethel fell and broke a hip. Then she had another stroke. She hasn't walked or talked since. Nothing to do but put her in the home. Not likely she'll ever get out, and she's taking a long time dying."

The Pine Lake Residence was too fancy to exist on Social Security checks. Vince asked who paid for her stay.

"Husby did until he was killed, I'll say that for him, but his old man was the one with money. He isn't one to hand it around much, even to kin. Gil didn't leave Liz anything to amount to a row of corn. The business went to Jack as sole survivor of the partnership. Jack figured helping Liz was the right thing to do. He paid Ethel's bills until Medicaid took over."

Conscience money for screwing Beth out of her husband's share of the business, Vince wondered? "What about the stories about Gil Husby and Suzie?"

"I never said that."

"C'mon, Sheriff, now that we're working together, I need to know all of it."

Mayville hitched uncomfortably in his chair. "There were stories about Gil and just about every woman in town. He was a hellion as a kid, and being away four years at college didn't tame him. Smart as they come except about women. Couldn't keep his mind or hands off them. Suzie's name cropped up more than once those last few months, but that didn't make it so. She was too much of a looker for Pine Lake. That kind of pretty always spells trouble in a town this size. Women figure she's after their men, and men think that's mighty green grass on Tustman's side of the fence."

"Did Liz know about them?"

Mayville shrugged. "May have. Hard to say. She kept to herself mostly."

"You said there haven't been any rumors about Suzie the past year or so. How come?"

"Tustman and Husby were friends as well as partners. The murder shook him up. Both he and Suzie have stayed pretty close to home since."

Eighteen months was a long time to mourn, Vince thought, but he let the matter drop. Something else was clicking in the back of his brain. He wanted to read the trial transcript before he dug anymore. He asked the sheriff if he could get him a copy.

"Probably."

"Today?"

"In a damned big hurry, aren't you?"

"So's March," Vince reminded him.

"Okay, I'll see what I can do. A couple of people over at the county clerk's office owe me a favor."

"How soon will you have the stolen car report?"

"The Highway Patrol can FAX it. Shouldn't take long, but I'll need more time to get in touch with the local sheriffs who may be able to help on the abandoned vehicle angle."

"Just try not to tip anyone to what we're doing." Vince got to his feet.

"Where you headed?"

"To see if I can find Jack Tustman. Then I want to talk to Suzie's and Gil's families."

"Forget Tustman. He's on his way to Bakersfield to pick up his sister and brother-in-law. They're flying in today from Illinois."

"Okay, I'll put him on hold. Where will I find Suzie's folks?"

"Over in Bushville, twenty miles north of here. Name's Abbott. Don't expect much from them."

"Why not? Don't they care their daughter was murdered?"

The sheriff snorted. "Ain't for me to say."

"Okay. I'll stop back about four and see what you've come up with."

CHAPTER FIFTEEN

As they left the sitter's and drove to the supermarket on Sunset Boulevard, Beth wondered if it was her imagination that Jenny looked happier than she had in a long time. She wasn't bubbly, but some of the tension that usually pinched her pretty face had eased. Even her movements seemed more relaxed. She walked jauntily beside the cart as they went through the crowded store aisles choosing supplies for dinner and staples for several days. Jenny spotted a display of pet toys and asked Beth if she could buy one for Baron. She chose a squeaky, bright colored, rubber bone and then asked to carry it separately when the groceries were bagged. When they were finally driving up the hill, with Jenny navigating by the map of turns and landmarks, Jenny chattered happily about playing with Baron again.

Vince Norris hadn't called or come to the shop, and Beth wondered if she'd been too suspicious in questioning his intentions. His offer to help seemed genuine if he wasn't going to pester her. She was relieved, though she had to admit she'd had trouble sleeping last night after the dog acted so peculiarly, and even more at midnight when the phone woke her and the caller hung up without saying anything. It had taken her a long time to convince herself it was a wrong number or someone who was expecting the Fischers to answer. In the bright light of morning, she made up her mind not to torture herself about coming here. If Rick March tracked her to Los Angeles, he'd never find her.

The real bonus was that Jenny was happy. She hadn't

asked to stop and see Sasha. And staying at the Fischers' meant she could finish the school term.

Baron danced when they came in, then dashed for his beanbag. Jenny showed him the new bone. When she squeaked and jiggled it, the dog cocked its head quizzically. Jenny threw the bone and Baron dropped the beanbag and raced after it, not the least disturbed by the substitution. Laughing, Beth sent them to play on the patio while she fixed dinner. Using a cookbook from Nancy Fischer's collection, she experimented with the microwave oven to do the chicken and vegetables and was pleased with the results. Jenny ate quickly, impatient for the evening dog walk.

Because of their limited time this morning, they had walked Baron along one of the shorter routes on the map. Tonight they followed another long one where Baron could run free and chase sticks again. Beth let Jenny and the dog wear themselves out playing before they set a leisurely pace for home.

Beth set up her artwork on the desk under the bubble window. Jenny stretched out on the floor of the den to watch television, her arm flung over the dog curled at her side. Beth couldn't get over the difference the dog made in her daughter's mood. Jenny loved Sasha, but the cat was a sedentary companion, not a romping playmate like Baron. In Pine Lake, they'd had both a dog and cat, but dogs had to be leashed and walked in the city, and Beth simply didn't have time on top of everything else, nor was there room in the apartment.

She gazed through the bronze-tinted glass at the Hollywood sign on the distant ridge. From a screen of shrubbery, there was a sudden flash of light as the sun glinted off something. A bird watcher with binoculars? If they lived up here, they could go bird watching. They could have a dog.

Wishful thinking . . . This kind of neighborhood was too far out of her financial zone. Scrimping and saving, she'd be lucky to be able to afford a tiny bungalow down on the flats. She'd been lucky to sell the house in Pine Lake, but her profit after the mortgage wasn't much. Her savings were a far cry from the down payment on a quarter or half-million-dollar house like one of these.

Sighing softly, she began to work on the ideas for the electronics chain account ad.

He relaxed but didn't take his eyes from the house where the kid had gone in. At quarter after five, his guts did a slow roller coaster ride when he got his first good look at Liz as she climbed out of the Honda. She hadn't changed much. She didn't look as tense as she'd been up on the witness stand. She'd done something different with her hair. It was shorter and softer, the color of dark honey when the sun splashed it. It made her look young, the way she did in school. Funny, he didn't remember her being so pretty.

She went into the house and came out a few minutes later with the kid. When they got in the Honda and drove off, he stayed a block behind until she put on her blinker for Sunset Boulevard. Then he closed the gap so he wouldn't lose her in the rush hour traffic. She turned into a supermarket parking lot a few blocks down. He followed, but there weren't any empty spaces near where she parked the Honda, so he pulled into the yellow zone in front of the store where he could watch the front door. No sense following her inside. It would be too easy to be spotted. A horn honked behind him, but he ignored it. When the driver swung out to pass and shouted an obscenity, March cocked his finger and aimed. The guy turned eyes front and drove off, bouncing over the speed bump in his rush.

She was in there half an hour. A tall, gangly kid in a red apron followed her out with a cart full of sacks. When she pulled out of the lot, he let one car get between them. She went north to Franklin Avenue, then west, the opposite direction from her apartment. She'd bought enough groceries for a week, and the kid had her knapsack. From the looks of it, they were headed for the Hollywood Freeway. Maybe a nice isolated spot in the suburbs? She was making this easy. A few minutes later he cursed when the Honda made an unexpected swing onto a street right behind the freeway entrance. He cut the wheel sharply and almost stalled the Escort on the steep incline. He jammed the gear shift into second as he saw the Honda turn again and vanish behind a hedge. He pressed the gas pedal to the floor. The car spurted ahead.

She was making a sharp right at another corner a block ahead. Damned road twisted all over the place. He gave the Ford all it had, but when he got to the turn, the Honda was gone. He gunned the engine, then slammed on the brake when the street dead-ended in a T. Which way? He pulled out into the intersection so he could look both directions, but the Honda was nowhere in sight. Cursing, he turned left, shifting quickly when the car strained on another steep climb. He had to hit the brakes again at another right angle turn almost hidden behind a stone wall. He could only see a few yards before the street curved again.

It was a damned maze. Rage spread through him like hot pain. His knuckles were white on the steering wheel, and a muscle in his jaw pulsed. He turned onto the next steep street, hoping this was the way she went, then laughing out loud when he saw the tail of the blue Honda go around a curve two blocks ahead of him. He closed the gap between them so he wouldn't lose her again but didn't get close

enough to worry her. She was probably too intent on nego-
tiating the turns and curves to spot him in her rearview
mirror, but if she did, he wanted to be sure she didn't recognize him.

He lost sight of the Honda twice more but found it again
as they neared the summit of the hill. When she turned onto
a narrow blacktop road with a sign, DEAD END, he
stopped. It would be crazy to follow her up a dead-end
street. He shut off the Escort's engine and listened for the
sound of the Honda. It stopped in about twenty seconds.
Enough time to go only a house or two, he figured. The
dead-end road couldn't go far before it ran out of mountain. He'd wait. When it got dark, he could walk up there
and find her without any trouble.

He memorized the name on the street sign before he
started the car and made a U-turn. He tried to retrace his
route back down to Franklin, but after a few corners, he realized the houses he was passing weren't the same ones he'd
seen on the way up. What the hell, it didn't matter. There
were probably a dozen ways to get off the friggin' hill. He
kept heading down and eventually came out on Franklin
Avenue. Relieved, he pulled in at the first drugstore he
came to and bought a six-pack of cold beer and a city street
map. He popped a beer and studied the streets on the map
that crisscrossed the hill he'd just come down. He recognized a few names and found the one he wanted. Leaving
the map open on the seat beside him, he set out again.

At the summit, he turned the opposite way from the
dead-end street. He made a few dips and turns, checking
the map, and finally came to a road that ended at a high
wire mesh fence. A red Corvette was parked on a small plateau where there was room for three or four cars to park. A
woman about thirty, dressed in bright red shorts and a loose

T-shirt, was doing leg stretches against the rear bumper. Rick flipped down the sun visor and parked as far from the Corvette as possible. The woman glanced up but kept stretching until she reached her count. Then with another glance in his direction, she went through an opening at the side of the gate and set off at a slow jog.

A sign on the gate said *Hollywood Reservoir   No Dogs Allowed   Area Closes at Dark*.

He considered following the woman, but the distraction didn't interest him now. He wouldn't mind getting rid of the Escort, but he didn't want a high profile car like the Corvette. Besides, the fox probably had a good enough look at him to describe him to the cops.

He got out. The Corvette was locked. An expensive looking pair of binoculars lay on the passenger seat. He glanced toward the gate where the woman had gone. There was no sign of her. He went back to the Ford for the Slim Jim he'd bought this morning from a locksmith supply shop downtown where the owner wasn't too fussy about credentials. They'd done business a number of times in past years. The guy wasn't the type who could afford to talk to the cops.

He slid the bar down along the Corvette's window and caught the lock. He opened the door and grabbed the binoculars. Raising them, he studied the ridge across the valley where the dead-end street was. Adjusting the focus until he could pick out individual houses, he counted three along the top of the ridge.

The first one had a driveway that curved around some trees so he couldn't see the end of it. The middle one had a garage carved into the hillside. There was no driveway to the top house unless it was on the other side.

The other side of the road fell away sharply to the valley.

Five houses were built around the curve to the top. He could see the carports of the last two. One was empty. There was a car in the other, but he couldn't tell the color or make.

At most, he had eight houses to check out. It wouldn't take long.

He turned the glasses to the valley. Streets curved like jumbled wires on the slopes, sometimes doubling back with only the depth of one or two lots separating them. Most of the houses had fences—stone, wood or growing stuff. Except for the occasional hum of a car winding uphill and the steady drone of cicadas, it was quiet. He moved the glasses back to the ridge, from one house to another, wondering which of them Liz Husby was in.

He considered keeping the binoculars, but the woman in the red shorts would probably miss them right off. He wiped his prints from them and put them back where he found them, then locked the car door and slammed it. Back in the Ford, he started down the hill.

CHAPTER SIXTEEN

Bushville was two miles off the main highway and fifty years behind the calendar. It reminded Vince of archival photos of the Great Depression. The town was a block long, with houses scattered like dead bugs on a windshield. Most of the buildings were unpainted or dusty enough to look it. There was a tiny grocery, a bar, a hardware and feed store and a steepled community center that looked as if it had once been a church.

For a small town, Bushville had more than its share of cars. There were two or three in every yard, mostly old wrecks that probably hadn't run for years, more parked along both sides of the main drag and in front of the community center where a sign on the door said: BINGO FRIDAY NITE.

He parked and walked back to the bar with *Charley's* printed on the glass. The afternoon clientele numbered half a dozen men in overalls or T-shirts and jeans. They all turned when the door opened then transferred their scrutiny of Vince to the mirror behind the bar as he took an empty stool and ordered a beer. The bellied bartender put a bottle and glass in front of him.

"Passin' through?" the barman asked as he slid Vince's change toward him.

"I came over from Pine Lake." All eyes were still on him. "Hell of a thing, that murder."

The bartender nodded, and there was a low exchange between two men a few stools down.

Vince said, "She came from here, didn't she?"

The bartender nodded again. The man beside Vince said, "You know her?"

"No. I hear she was a beauty, though."

Down the bar, someone barked a short laugh. Vince glanced at the mirror and saw a young, dark-haired guy in his thirties with a day's growth of whiskers on his chin and a pack of cigarettes rolled in his shirt sleeve.

"A beautiful tramp," the man said.

Beside Vince, a man in overalls and a white line on his upper arm where his tan ended said, "That's not what you were calling her before she sent you packing, Johnny."

Everyone laughed. The kid with the stubble leaned forward to look down the bar.

"Elwood, you wouldn't know a good piece if it bit you. How long's it been since you got it up?"

The bartender grinned as if the exchange was nothing new.

"Where can I find the Abbotts?" Vince asked.

The expressions on faces in the mirror blanked. Vince was the outsider again. The bartender said, "Who's looking for them?"

Vince pulled out his press card. "Vince Norris, *L.A. Times*. I'm doing a story on the murder."

A bleary-eyed drunk at a table in the back said, "Suzie finally made the big time. Had to get herself killed to do it." He coughed and picked up his glass with an unsteady hand. In the mirror, Vince saw the men along the bar grin.

"I'm not going to force them to talk to me if they don't want to," Vince said, staring down the bartender.

"For crissake tell 'im, Charley. What the hell—" someone said.

The bartender pointed to the drunk at the table in back.

"That's Pete Abbott, her old man."

Vince's head swiveled. The drunk was slumped in the chair, his eyes barely focusing. The glass in front of him was empty.

"Give me another beer and a drink for him," Vince said, sliding off the stool. At the table, Pete Abbott raised his head as Vince sat down and said, "I'd like to talk to you about Suzie."

"If you're looking for someone to say something good 'bout her, you'll have to talk to her ma. She was a tramp, Mr. Reporter, a no-good tramp from the time she was twelve. Nothing or nobody here was good enough for her." He looked surprised as Charley set a drink in front of him. Abbott lifted it quickly as if afraid it might be taken back. He drank and put down the glass without taking his hand from it.

"How long ago did she marry Jack Tustman?"

When Pete seemed to ponder an answer, someone at the bar said, "Three years."

So much for privacy. Vince considered taking Pete Abbott somewhere, maybe the car, but from the looks of him, he'd have to be carried.

"Where's your wife, Pete?"

Abbott took another swallow of the drink and lowered the glass shakily. "Over to the funeral home. She's got the crazy notion Jack'll let her pick out Suzie's dress for the funeral."

Vince studied Abbott who, despite the glazed look, seemed able to think. At closer range, Pete Abbott wasn't as old as Vince first thought. Maybe fifty, but too much sun had aged his face to cracked leather, and too much booze had given him the gaunt look of a chronic drunk. He got the glass to his mouth again and finished the whiskey.

Still holding the glass, he asked, "Why you interested in Suzie?"

"I want to help catch her killer."

Abbott snorted, and his head flopped forward. With effort he looked up again. "What good's putting killers behind bars if the damned state lets them out again?" The slurred words seemed to exhaust him. His chin sank to his chest and bobbed a few times as he worked to lift it. He squinted at Vince.

"Were Suzie and Jack having problems?" Vince asked.

Someone at the bar said something in a low voice, but Vince didn't catch it. Someone else laughed. Abbott leaned forward to rest his arms on the table.

"Jack's a bastard," he said. "Always was. He can afford to be, with his money. What made him take a shine to Suzie, don't ask me, but Suzie knows a good thing when it comes along, and money's a good thing t' her. Always wantin' what she couldn't have. Always dreamin' big dreams. She was goin' to L.A. and be in the movies. Sure, rich and famous. Big dreams. Suzie was full of 'em, but when Jack started droolin' over her ass, she got hip to the altar faster'n you can blink. The hell with famous if she had rich."

"Is Tustman's construction business that good?"

"He ain't hurtin'. His old man left him enough money to get a partner and start up the business. Fix up that old house, too." Abbott shrugged and the motion made his body sway dangerously before he dropped his weight back to his arms on the table.

"Any problems between Tustman and Husby?" Vince asked.

Abbott scowled as if an answer required heavy thought. "Always problems when it comes to money."

Interested, Vince probed. "What kind of problems were they having?"

Abbott concentrated again, then said, "Dunno." His eyelids drooped heavily and his mouth went slack. His head nodded to his chest and he let it stay there as if he had to keep an eye on the empty glass still in his hand. He didn't move when Vince got to his feet and went to the bar to pay his tab.

"Give him another drink when he wakes up."

The bartender nodded and made change. As he put it in front of Vince, he said, "Jack's not as bad as Pete makes out. Just that he got sick of handing out drinking money, but you can hardly blame him for that. He was good to Suzie in spite of everything. And he did right by the widow too, more'n most partners would do."

"You mean Mrs. Husby?"

Charley nodded. "Bailed her out on the house so's she and the kid could move. Paid for her mama over in the nursin' home."

"What about the Husbys?"

"They'd pay anything to keep Liz and the kid in town, or I should say the kid. Only grandchild. They ain't happy the mother took off with her."

"They keep in touch?"

Charley shrugged.

"Anything to what Pete said about trouble between Tustman and Husby?"

"Naw, leastwise not that I heard. Even with the slow-down in construction, they were busy all the time."

"I hear Husby had an eye for the ladies. Anything between him and Suzie?"

"Gil?" Charley looked surprised. "I never heard it. He did his share of looking and more, but frankly, if he wanted something on the side, he could do a lot better than taking up with his partner's wife. Besides, he'd never play that close to home, his folks being pillars of the community and all."

"What do the Husbys do?"

"Family owned most of the property the town sits on. Glen Husby ran the town council 'til he retired a few years back. Some say he still does. Some say he still owns the town, too."

Vince was beginning to understand why Liz Husby wanted to get away. "How can I find the Husby place?" he said.

Charley detailed a route back through Pine Lake and a few miles past the county road turnoff to Tustman's. Leaving a couple of bills on the bar, Vince thanked him and left.

The Husby house was a sprawling ranch type that wouldn't look out of place in Beverly Hills. The drive curved around a grove of birch that didn't show any effects of the heat or drought. Vince pulled up in front of a covered portico leading to the pillared entrance.

A big-boned woman with a lined face and a mouth that turned down answered his ring so quickly he wondered if a buried cable rang a warning bell when a car approached. She was wearing a flower-print dress with a white apron over it.

"Mrs. Husby?"

"Who should I say it is?" She folded her arms as if she were used to dealing with magazine salesmen.

"My name is Vince Norris. Is Mrs. Husby home? Or Mr. Husby? I'd like to talk to them."

"What about?"

A dragon at the gate. "About their son and his family."

The man appeared behind her so silently and swiftly, he must have been standing out of sight behind the door. The woman moved aside as if he'd pushed her.

"My son is dead," he said. He started to close the door, but Vince put his hand to it. Husby was curious enough to let the door stay where it was.

"I know that, Mr. Husby. And I know that his killer got out of prison and that Suzie Tustman was murdered that same day."

"Who are you?"

"Vince Norris, *L.A. Times.* I'm covering the story of the murder. Do you realize he may be after your daughter-in-law next?"

Husby swung the door open. "Do you know where my granddaughter is?" he demanded. He was thin and tall enough to hold a pitchfork in a Grant Wood painting. "If anything happens to her, it'll be Liz's fault. March is crazy. He'll use the child to get to her."

For a split second Vince was tempted to tell him Beth and Jenny were safe, but the undercurrent of anger in Husby's tone bordered on hatred. Vince figured he hadn't been crazy about the idea of his son marrying Liz Davies.

"I'm trying to get a lead on March," he said. "I know Liz moved out of town. I was hoping you could tell me where she is. Has anyone been asking about her lately?"

Husby ignored the question. "If March shows his face around here, I'll shoot before I stop to call the sheriff. Mayville won't have the chance to botch things again." He fixed a steely gaze on Vince. "You didn't answer my question. Do you know where my granddaughter is? Is she in Los Angeles? Is that why you're here? Have you seen her?"

You didn't answer mine either, Buster, Vince thought.

"No. I've been asking around. No one seems to know where she is."

"I know where she ought to be. She ought to be right here with people who love Jenny and can take care of her properly. Any kind of a decent mother would have brought the child here right off." Husby closed the door in Vince's face.

Vince turned and walked back to the car. Husby was a miserable bastard. No wonder Beth wanted to get away from him. As he fastened his seat belt and started the engine, the front door of the house opened and a woman in a fashionable blue silk dress and matching pumps hurried toward him. He rolled down the window. The woman leaned to it.

"If you find Liz, Mr. Norris, tell her to let me know Jenny's all right. Tell her I'm not angry. I miss Jenny too much." Tears filled her eyes and she didn't brush them away. "If anyone knows where Liz and Jenny are, it would be Jack Tustman. Glen's tried everything to get him to say where she went, but Jack won't tell. Please, Mr. Norris, tell Liz I'll come anywhere she says, and I won't tell Glen. If I can just see Jenny for a little while—" The tears spilled as she straightened and turned to walk back to the house. When she saw her husband standing in the open doorway, her shoulders squared.

Vince rolled up the window and drove down the curved driveway and back to the highway.

CHAPTER SEVENTEEN

March weighed the risk of going back to the dead-end street while it was still light. He was wasting time, but there was no telling who might come along. On the other hand, how long did he have before the cops started looking for him in earnest? *Wanted for questioning.* That was a laugh. Wanted for murder was more like it. They'd dump him back in the slammer so fast he wouldn't have time to breathe.

With the load of groceries Liz lugged home, they were probably in for the night. Still, he had made that mistake last night. He could camp at the foot of the dead-end street to make sure she didn't slip past, but that would be asking for trouble. All these places had private security stickers or signs, and there was a Neighborhood Watch sign on a pole at the head of the street. A guy sitting in a car would attract attention.

The smart thing would be to check out the route down the other side of the hill, but that would mean risking the possibility of Liz taking off without his seeing her. No way he was going to do that again. Instead, he found a place to park half a block from the reservoir road where he could wait for the Corvette to leave. While he waited, he studied the map and traced the long, looping, curved road he'd seen through the binoculars down to Cahuenga Avenue. There were a couple of turns, but not as many as on the other side of the hill. He'd be in a hurry when he left this time and couldn't afford to box himself in some damned dead-end street. Half the roads up here went nowhere or around in circles. He studied the new route again, memorizing the turns. He'd go that way. He was ready. He had everything he needed except her.

Ten minutes later the Corvette with the blonde behind the wheel came out of the reservoir road and turned the opposite direction. When the car was out of sight, Rick drove back to the fence and parked.

The temperature dropped a few degrees when the sun sank behind the ridge where he'd last seen Liz Davies' Honda. He'd been watching the stretch of street he could see from here. Two cars had gone up and none came down. He'd seen some people walking dogs, but they were too far away to identify. With the No Dogs sign, he didn't worry about them coming up to where he was. Two couples jogged around the reservoir, but they came from somewhere else, not the gate he was at.

The sky began to darken and lights came on in a couple of the houses on the ridge. It was time for him to move closer. He started the car and drove without turning on the headlights. At the foot of her street, he parked beside a high brick wall covered with vines, far enough away from the nearest streetlight to be all but invisible in the shadows. He sat listening and looking around. It wasn't perfect, but it wasn't as risky as driving to the top of the ridge where another car coming up the road could block him in.

He got out and closed the door. The sound seemed to crash against the chirp of crickets and the drone of traffic on the freeway. The beginning stretch of the road up the ridge was dark. The first house with the driveway was dark. The next one had a room over the garage with a curved glass solarium wall. Light spilled down across the road from it, and Rick stopped to look for someone inside but didn't see anyone. The garage door was shut. He wondered if the Honda was behind it.

The houses on the other side of the street clung to the drop-off like bats in a cave. The first one had a carport with two cars in it. He went close enough for a look. A Porche and a BMW. The next one had a Jag convertible.

He stopped to look back at the smoky glass bubble of the house with the garage. He had a good view into the room from higher ground, but he still didn't see anyone. He continued up the hill. The last three houses on the outer curve were dark and the carports empty.

The third house on top of the ridge stood against the skyline like a guard tower without lights. There was a paved pad beside the house where a car could park, but it was empty. There was a car parked on a wide flat clearing where the road ended. It wasn't the Honda, but there was no telling which house it went with. He squatted behind it and studied the block house. The shades were drawn and the rooms behind them dark. If anyone was in there, they were asleep or dead.

He crossed to the parking pad and squatted again to look down at the first two houses on the ridge. The farther one was only a dark blur among the shrubbery and trees. He couldn't even tell if there was a carport or garage. He focused his attention on the middle house. There was a light in the kitchen that jutted out past a long room with floor-to-roof glass. He made out a table and two chairs fitted into a glassed-in corner across from the counter and cupboards. He couldn't see the rest of the house or the lighted room under the bubble.

A bank of ivy spilled downhill in front of him, and a path ran from the edge of the car pad to a gate in a chain link fence between the two yards. He started down what turned out to be broad steps, but he hadn't gotten five feet when a huge dog came out of nowhere and rushed the gate. Its deep-throated growl froze him for an instant before he was able to leap back into the shadows. The dog stayed at the gate, barking wildly, sensing his presence.

Rick breathed in shallow bursts. Damned mutt. The noise would bring out half the neighborhood. There was no way he could make a run for it. He kept his gaze glued to the lighted window. A couple of seconds passed, then a woman came into sight. She opened the door.

"Baron!" The dog paused, then barked sharply again. "Baron! Here boy, come here!"

The dog woofed softly but stood his ground. After a moment, the woman said, "Okay, but you be quiet now, you hear?" The dog whined.

Rick let out his breath. It was Liz Davies. But he hadn't counted on the dog. He watched it for several minutes, trying to decide what to do. He'd have to put it out of the way before he could make his move. Damn. It meant another trip down the friggin' hill.

The dog growled as he moved back to the road. No lights had come on in the dark houses. Maybe the Doberman barked often enough that no one paid attention. He hoped so. As he came around the curve, he spotted Liz Davies behind the solarium window. She seemed to be talking to somebody, but he didn't see anyone else. The kid? The owner of the house? He had no way of telling, at least not now.

But he'd found her. That was the important thing.

151

CHAPTER EIGHTEEN

"If March was in Sacramento at eight-thirty and here by one o'clock, I figure he didn't have time to go over the Sierra or the Diablo," Sheriff Mayville said as he handed Vince a FAX copy. "He might've come down Interstate 5, but Highway 99 is a straight shot for anyone who knows this area. This covers the whole San Joaquin Valley."

Vince scanned the stolen car list. "How about abandoned vehicles and thefts?"

"Nothing yet. I put the word out, but it may take a while."

"I'll get started on these and check back with you later."

Vince drove to the motel on the edge of town across from the station where he'd talked to Gary Kellog. It was a long way from fancy and had the hot, dry smell of a closed attic, but it had a phone and a place to spread out a map.

He turned the air-conditioner to high and opened the drapes, then pulled the table close to the window and jockeyed the only chair around to it. With a felt-tip pen, he went down the list, marking the spread-out map with locations where cars had been stolen. He skipped trucks for the first go-around. March had always been into cars.

He began with the towns south of the Sacramento city limits. According to reports, March got off the Folsum bus about eight. The M.E. put the time of death at between one-thirty and two o'clock. March made good time, which meant he either picked up a car fast or started south to look for one.

March was comfortable in big cities, but he was smart enough to know city cops got on things like stolen cars faster than rural sheriffs. Vince's guess was March got out of Sacramento before he went car hunting. Hitchhiked, or took a bus maybe.

There was one theft along the thirty-mile stretch between Sacramento and Stockton. Vince started with it. A half hour later he was on his ninth call.

"Duane Cass? My name is Vince Norris. I'm calling about the Chevrolet you reported stolen."

"It's about time. I don't get why you guys need three days to find one lousy car!"

"I'm not with the police, Mr. Cass."

"I don't care who the hell you're with if you've found my Chevy. Where is it? When do I get it back?"

"It hasn't been found yet." Cass swore. Vince went on before he could go off on another tirade. "What time was the car stolen, do you know?"

"I sure as hell do. Between nine-thirty and quarter to eleven. I've told Valerie a million times to close the damned garage door when she goes out, but I can't get it through her thick head. She was only going to the market, she says. She called me at the shop at quarter to eleven."

"Was the car gassed up?"

"Damned near a full tank. I gassed it up last week. Haven't been driving it much because the plugs and carburetor need work. I was gonna get at it next weekend."

"How many miles does it get to the gallon?"

"What the hell has that got to do with anything?" Cass said.

"I'm trying to get an idea of how far the thief could have gotten before he had to gas up."

Mollified, Cass said, "Fifteen, sixteen. Once I get it

tuned up, it'll get eighteen, easy."

Vince felt a stir of excitement. This could be it. He was anxious to get off the line.

"You gonna let me know soon's it's found?" Cass demanded.

"Someone will. Thanks, Mr. Cass."

"Yeah, sure, thanks for nothing. Any damage, someone's going to pay for it, you hear?"

"Right." Vince hung up and leaned over the map.

La Puerta was three miles off Highway 99, thirty miles south of Stockton. If March grabbed a bus out of Sacramento, he could have been there by nine o'clock. Using his thumb as a ruler, Vince estimated the distance to Pine Lake. Under two hundred miles. An easy drive in four hours. If the Chevy had, say, fifteen gallons in the tank, that was enough to get March to Pine Lake and beyond. Not much farther, though. Say twenty-five to fifty miles, tops.

He drew a circle with a fifty-mile radius from Pine Lake. South it went almost to Bakersfield. What then? March would want to stay out of sight as much as possible. Chances were he'd pick up another car as soon as possible. Half a dozen thefts had been reported in the Bakersfield area.

Vince finished calling the rest of the list and came up with two more possibles, but Duane Cass' car fit the bill best. La Puerta was a cheap bus ride from Sacramento, and the car disappeared in the time frame when March could easily have been there.

Vince stretched and went out to the Coke machine for a cold drink before he drove back to the sheriff's office. In response to Vince's question, Mayville read from scribbled notes on a pad.

"Couple of wrecks and one abandoned car down near

Harper. Some teenagers have been using it for a bar and bedroom the past couple of nights. The license number's on our hot sheet."

Vince glanced at the paper the sheriff turned toward him. The Chevy from La Puerta. Pay dirt.

"Where the hell is Harper?" he asked. He didn't remember seeing it on the map.

"Down near Tulare."

Tulare was dead south, almost to Bakersfield. "That's on the way to L.A.," Vince said. "He could be there by now."

"Even us country boys are smart enough to figure out that's where he'd head if he's after Liz Husby," the sheriff commented dryly. "Mind telling me how you think he's going to find her in a city that size?" He peered at Vince. "You holding out on me, boy? You know where Liz is?"

"I have a couple of leads, but she's covered her tracks pretty well. March will have his work cut out for him."

"But you think he can find her, is that what you're saying?"

"It'll take a lot of luck and looking." He wondered if Beth had the sense to skip work and school for the kid. Maybe he should call her.

Mayville looked skeptical. "Word is the D.A. has March's description spread statewide, unofficial like, of course, but you can do that when you have clout." Mayville studied Vince. "You better follow up those leads and get to Liz first, boy."

"Where did you hear she was in L.A.?" Vince asked.

The sheriff dismissed the question with his hand.

"C'mon, Mayville, it's important. If you heard, others did, too. How about Suzie Tustman? Any chance she knew?"

The sheriff's brow wrinkled. "The nursing home has a number for Liz in case her mother takes a turn for the worse."

Vince gritted his teeth for being ten kinds of idiot for not thinking of that. Still, the aide he'd talked to didn't seem to know or care where Ethel's daughter was.

"Who's in charge over there?"

"Dermott and Fannie Haskell own the place."

"They the ones who'd call Liz?"

The sheriff scratched the faint stubble on his chin. "They'd leave it to Dolly Raisch. She's head nurse, but believe me, she's not one to give out information, especially to someone she doesn't know."

"Did she know Suzie Tustman?"

"Not enough to gossip. Thirty years difference in their age."

"What about Jack? You said he paid the bills for a while."

The sheriff was thoughtful a moment. "Jack doesn't go to see Ethel. Don't see Dolly would have the chance or reason to tell him. It would be more likely Liz would tell him herself. Jack was about the only friend she had around here."

"Let's hope March is searching blind. The longer it takes him to get a line on Liz, the more time we have to find him. I'm going back to L.A. I'll call you as soon as I have anything."

"You do that, Norris," Mayville said, leaning on the desk. "And you find both of them before anyone else does, y'hear? There isn't much chance I'm going to be able to arrest him personally, so you make damned sure my interests are protected."

Vince reassured him and left. In the car, he turned back toward Highway 99. No point in nosing around Tulare or Harper. By this time, Rick March was in L.A. sure as hell.

CHAPTER NINETEEN

March bypassed the parking spot he'd used earlier. It would be tempting fate to take it just because it was convenient. That would be a mistake, just like the Imperial the cops spotted. Things went wrong when he took the easy way. It was some kind of fucking law. Not Murphy's. March's.

This time he'd stay in control and not go off half-cocked. He'd made a mistake not coming prepared for a dog, but it hadn't cost him anything but a little time. Now he was ready. He'd gone over his whole plan and knew it would work. He was thinking smart now, and he was still three jumps ahead of the law.

That newspaper story said they wanted him for questioning. It didn't mention any evidence to tie him to Suzie Tustman's murder. They'd take him in and move him around so a lawyer, if they let him call one, wouldn't be able to find him. It was one of their favorite tricks. Stupid bastards. They were good at tricks. His picture was probably in every police station and patrol car in L.A. by now. Liz's apartment would be staked out, too. Maybe she'd done him a favor coming up here.

He'd seen a couple of private security cars making rounds on his way up. They probably hit each street a couple of times a night, but they didn't go by often enough to be a problem as long as he didn't stay in one place too long. He hadn't spotted any cop cars or unmarked cruisers, no fuzz hiding behind newspapers in parked cars, no vans with peepholes or directional scopes aimed toward the house where Husby was holed up. The chances of a trap were pretty slim.

So why was he jumpy?

No matter where he looked, he seemed to be alone. Maybe that was it. It wasn't normal. Not in a city. Not when he knew damned well there were people behind those hedges and walls and fences. How could he be sure one of them wasn't looking out right now? One busybody who noticed he went up and down these streets a couple of times could spell trouble.

He was glad he'd checked out another way down the hill. When you had options, you used them. He closed his eyes for a minute and concentrated on remembering the names of the streets that would take him down to Cahuenga. Satisfied he could do it without a trial run, he turned the car the opposite direction from Liz's street. Half a block down where the road began to curve downhill, cars were parked along both sides of the street. Voices and laughter and the sound of water splashing came from behind a high, grapestake fence. He parked in front of the first car and angled the wheels to the curb. Carrying the plastic grocery bag, he got out and walked back to the dead-end street.

The room with the humpbacked glass was still lit up. It was past ten. The kid should be asleep. He didn't see Liz Davies, but he sensed her presence the way he felt the heavy air move against his hot skin. He skirted the patch of light under the windows, half expecting the dog to set up a racket. When it didn't, he worried that she'd taken it in for the night.

Back at his vantage point on the car pad of the cinder block house, he crouched to study the lighted kitchen where he'd seen Liz earlier. The rest of the house was dark. There'd be a bedroom in the back at the other end. Was that where the kid was? Where was the dog? He peered at the gate, but nothing moved. There wasn't enough moon to do much good. He couldn't tell if the mutt was lying in the dark down there or if she'd taken it in.

The plastic bag rustled as he reached for the ground beef laced with rat poison and Seconal. Staying low, he moved toward the gate, trying to be as quiet as possible. He was almost there when the dog tore out of the darkness at the other end of the patio, barking furiously. Rick tossed the meat over the fence and scrambled back, then threw himself onto the bank of ivy as the Doberman leaped at the gate. Rick pressed flat, trying to keep his eye on the dog and the lighted kitchen at the same time.

The dog's barking cut off as it began to sniff around. Seconds later, Rick heard it gulping down the meat. He grinned. Stupid mutts were all the same.

Liz Davies came through the kitchen and opened the back door. "Baron, come here, boy! Come on inside now."

The dog finished the meat and sniffed around to be sure it hadn't missed any. It looked through the fence, whining. Rick held his breath until the animal finally trotted down to the woman when she called again.

"Good boy," she said, patting its head. She stepped back so the dog could go in, but it stood its ground and looked toward the gate. It started back, but Liz snapped her fingers.

"No, Baron. Here. Come here." She clapped her hands. The dog stopped and looked at her. Finally it turned and went inside. She shut the sliding glass door. The dog sank to its haunches in front of it. Husby said something, and the dog looked up, its stub of a tail wiggling its whole rear as she walked out of sight.

March stayed where he was and watched the dog shift its

bulk a few times and settle down. It wouldn't be long. The Seconal would dope it up fast and the poison would put it out of the way for good. The dog lay its head on its paws, then lifted it and tried to get up. Its paws skidded on the tile, and it flopped like a drunken clown. It tried again and finally managed to stand. Wobbling, it staggered out of sight.

March sprang to his feet and bounded to open the gate. He left the gate open in case he needed to get out in a hurry, then made his way past the greenhouse and the wall of glass where the drapes were pulled. He peered into the kitchen. No sign of the mutt or Davies. They were probably in that front room.

He moved to the other end of the patio where he could make out a couple of white tables and chairs. The patio angled around the end of the house. The front part was full of planters with trees and vines faintly outlined against the dark sky. Behind them, an eight-foot cinder block wall sealed off the street and the neighbor's driveway. There was a gate in the middle of it. He went close enough to see that it was fastened with a padlocked chain. If he had to, he could get a leg up on one of the corner decorations and go over the top.

The south side of the lot was what people paid for up here. A steep bank dropped away into darkness. Occasional lights glinted among the treetops. Way down, the city was spread out like a blanket of lights. He hadn't seen anything like it since he was seven years old sitting on that beach at Moro Bay, trying to count the stars reflected in the ocean, telling himself if he counted a thousand, tomorrow would be better.

He brought his attention back to the bank. There was a chain link fence about fifteen feet down. Nothing else to keep you from falling a hell of a long way. In the dark, he could break a leg, or worse, so it was one of the gates or nothing.

He took out the knife as he made his way back to the kitchen door.

CHAPTER TWENTY

Beth looked up from her sketches when Baron whimpered. The dog came into the den unsteadily, falling against the stereo cabinet and whimpering again.

"What's the matter, boy?" Baron's front legs buckled, and he fell. Beth rushed to him. "What is it, Baron?" Even as she asked the unanswerable question, the dog gagged and vomited onto the rug.

Oh, God . . . Beth struggled with nausea as the dog retched again. Too late to do much good, she ran to the guest bath and grabbed a towel to spread under the dog's head. The sight of the slimy vomit made her gag horribly.

What in the world had he eaten? Certainly more than the mixture of canned and dry dog food she'd given him several hours ago. Something outside? Something dead? She grimaced and tried to erase the picture from her mind as she stroked the dog's neck.

"There, boy, feel better?" She spoke as she would to Jenny, soothing, comforting. The dog's eyes tried to focus then rolled back. Alarmed, Beth lifted the massive head.

"Baron? Hey, boy, come on now—"

The dog tried feebly to respond, but its eyes rolled as it fell back. Beth's panic mounted. The Fischers had left a list of emergency phone numbers. She jumped up and ran to the desk, turning on the lamp and sliding her finger down the list of names and phone numbers tacked on the bulletin board. *Veterinarian: Dr. Albert Martin 555-1432.*

She dialed quickly and got an answering service. The girl

promised to have the doctor call as soon as possible. Truly frightened as she looked at Baron who lay almost comatose, Beth stressed that it was an emergency. She hung up and hurried back to the dog. Its eyes were slits showing only a sliver of white. She put her hand on Baron's chest to be sure he was breathing and choked up with relief when she felt the rhythmic fall and rise of his massive rib cage. Steeling herself, she began to clean up the mess, telling herself it wasn't any worse than what she'd done when Jenny was a baby. The phone rang as she was rinsing out the towel. She raced for it.

"Dr. Martin?"

"It's Vince Norris, Beth. Who's Dr. Martin? Jenny's not sick, is she?"

"No. He's the vet. For Baron. I don't know what happened. He ate something, I think. He—he isn't moving." In spite of herself, she started to cry.

"I'll be there in a couple of minutes. You hear me, Beth? I'm calling from my cell phone. I'm on my way."

CHAPTER TWENTY-ONE

He worked the blade of the knife between the door and the frame. The scrape of metal against metal sounded loud, but he knew the noise wouldn't carry to the other end of the house. The dog sure as hell wasn't going to hear it.

Inside, the phone rang suddenly. He jerked back out of the light, holding his breath until he heard the murmur of Liz's voice in the other room. He went back to work on the door and soon felt the latch lever move. He slid the door open and closed it behind him as Liz stopped talking and hung up the phone.

He looked around to get his bearings. The big room on his left was a dining and living room. There were plants everywhere. They seemed to be growing out of the damned floor. He walked softly past the curved table, avoiding a plant the size of a small tree. He crossed to a sofa that was in line with the hall and squatted behind the arm.

The dog was sprawled in the doorway of the lighted room, its hind end half in the hall. It wasn't moving. It should be dead by now or close to it.

Liz came out of the room, and he dropped like a stone, then peered again cautiously. She crossed the hall, but no other light came on. She came back a couple of seconds later and knelt by the dog, stroking its flank.

Maybe it wasn't dead yet, but it was far enough gone that he didn't have to worry about it anymore. He started to get up, but Liz sprang to her feet suddenly and ran toward him.

Startled, he ducked back out of sight, sweating as he held the knife ready. But she didn't come into the living room. She opened the front door.

What the hell—

He was on his feet before he realized a car had stopped out front. Swearing, he crouched again. The car door slammed and someone ran up the outside steps. Rick pulled himself into a tight ball as he tried to figure out what the hell was going on.

If they didn't come into the living room and turn on the lights, he was okay. If they did, he'd go out fighting. He shifted the knife and breathed softly through his mouth.

CHAPTER TWENTY-TWO

Vince sprinted up the steps. "What happened?"

Beth made a gesture of helplessness. "I don't know. He came in from the yard and suddenly was sick. He vomited, and now I can't wake him. Oh, God, what if he—" She couldn't voice the fear that had been tormenting her since Baron collapsed.

Vince hurried down the hall and knelt beside the dog, pressing his palm to its chest and lifting one of its eyelids.

"I called the vet," Beth told him. "His service said they'd have him call back." She sank to her knees beside Vince. "Is he going to be all right?"

"He must have eaten something outside. Any ideas?"

She thought about the mess she had cleaned up. "It looked like raw meat."

"A dead animal, maybe?"

Beth shuddered, forcing herself to picture the slimy mess she'd flushed down the toilet. "I don't know. Not really. I don't think so. I mean, it could have been, but I'm not sure. Jenny and I didn't give him anything but his dog food. He didn't go out of the yard after we took him for a walk."

The phone rang, and she leaped up. It was Dr. Martin. In a rush of words, Beth told him what had happened. The vet said to bring the dog in. He'd meet them at his office. When she started to ask directions, Vince took the phone and told the doctor he'd be the one bringing the dog in. When he hung up, he asked Beth for a rug or blanket they could carry Baron on.

166

She grabbed the afghan from the chair near the TV and spread it beside the dog. Together, she and Vince lifted the heavy animal onto it, then carried it like a stretcher through the house and down to Vince's car.

"Will you let me know if—" She couldn't finish. Vince touched her hand where it rested at the open car window.

"I'll call. Better still, I'll come back, okay? Maybe with Baron. He could pull out of this in nothing flat. You can't tell."

She stepped back as he started the car, then retreated to the steps as he jockeyed the car around on the garage apron instead of driving up the hill. She went back inside when the taillights vanished. She leaned against the door, weak now that the matter was out of her hands. The poor dog. She felt terrible that something happened to him while he was in her care. Close to tears, she set the security code on the inside panel. A red light flashed, and she stared at it, trying to think what she'd done wrong. An incomplete circuit, that was it. The flashing light meant she'd left a door or window open somewhere.

Relieved at something to do, she started through the house to check.

Front door, living room doors . . . The sliding door in the kitchen was unlocked. She would have sworn she locked it after she let Baron in, but even so, it didn't account for the interrupted circuit. She snapped the lock as a growing uneasiness filled her. She had to be more careful from now on. Down the hall, she opened the bedroom door to check on Jenny. She was two steps into the room before she realized that the faint slash of light she was seeing came from the drapes that should have been closed tightly. The curtain was caught back on a chair. The sliding glass door was open.

"Jenny?" It was half whisper, half cry of mounting terror. Beth groped for the light switch and a bedside lamp came on.

"Jenny!"

The bed was empty.

"Jenny, where are you?" She jerked back the covers as if expecting the child to pop out laughing. She raced to the bathroom, snapped on the lights. Jenny wasn't there. Back in the bedroom, she stepped through the open door to the patio.

"Jenny!"

A faint hint of breeze sighed through the trellised bougainvillea, but the only answering sound was the distant hum of traffic on the freeway. Beth ran toward the ghostly white tables and chairs, looking in all directions, her heart thundering when she didn't see any sign of Jenny.

The other way. Turn on the outside lights! She reached through the doorway, groping until her fingers found the switch and snapped it. Light flooded the patio. She ran the length of the house, beyond the kitchen and the greenhouse to the steps.

"Jenny?" Her voice was a terrified whisper when she saw the open gate at the top of the path. She ran blindly. Where was Jenny? What had induced her to come out into the dark that had always frightened her so much?

"Jenny? Jenny! *Jenny!*"

Only the soft humming traffic broke the quiet. She stumbled up to the parking area where Vince Norris told her guests parked. It was empty. Amos Westerland's house was dark; so were the houses on the outer rim of the curve. She ventured cautiously to the edge of the clearing and looked down at the steep spill of darkness. She put her hand over her mouth.

Fear spawned nightmarish visions too horrible to contemplate. Stumbling, she raced back down the path. She yanked at the kitchen door before she remembered she had locked it. She ran to the open door of the bedroom. Inside, she grabbed the phone and dialed 911 with furious stabbing motions. It took several moments to realize she was listening to a dead line. She hit the plunger, trying to activate the dial tone. When nothing happened, her brain registered what had been on the edge of her vision. The phone cord dangled from the handset. The wire had been cut.

Beth threw aside the useless phone and ran for the one in the den. Tears rolled down her cheeks when she heard the dial tone and hit 911. A mewling cry escaped her lips when she got a busy signal. She depressed the plunger and hit the re-dial button. Again. Again. And again.

She took a deep breath and tried to think clearly. Should she call the Hollywood Police? She remembered reading somewhere that the police wouldn't take a missing person report unless a child had been gone several hours. Would 911 respond faster? Too upset to sit still, she went back into the bedroom and turned on all the lights. She pulled back the bedding and got down on her hands and knees to look under the bed. Jenny's slippers were there side by side. Beth sank back on her heels. Jenny would never walk around without her slippers. She was gone. *Kidnapped.*

The word jolted Beth so her heart slid through a beat too rapidly and made her gasp. She jumped up and ran back to the phone and began re-dialing. After what seemed an eternity, someone answered. The woman asked questions and finally said a police unit would respond as soon as possible.

In fear that she might have missed something, Beth went outside to search the patio again. She was peering through the locked gate at the neighbor's dark driveway when the phone rang.

She raced inside and grabbed it.

"Yes?"

"Beth? It's Vince. Are you all right? You sound out of breath."

"Oh, Vince. God. Jenny's gone! She's been kidnapped! You did this. You led him here!"

"Hey! Hey! Slow down. What are you talking about? What do you mean Jenny's gone?"

"She's gone. I came in after you drove away. The bedroom door to the patio was open and she was gone." A sob tore from her throat as she sank into the chair.

"Beth, listen. Are you saying you think March took her?"

It was the only possible answer. No one else would want to hurt Jenny.

When she didn't answer, Vince Norris said, "Are you sure she didn't just go off on her own?"

"Yes, damn it, I'm sure!"

"Sleepwalk? Has she ever done it?"

"No." She'd been a fool to trust Vince Norris. "The bedroom phone wire is cut. Does that sound like a sleep walker?" Fear came back in full measure and Beth's body trembled. She slammed down the phone.

Rick March had found her. She should have run while she had the chance. He had killed Suzie Tustman, and now he was torturing her through Jenny. A knife in the heart would be easier to bear.

CHAPTER TWENTY-THREE

March dumped the kid onto the passenger seat and slid behind the wheel. He had carried her down the hill wrapped like a mummy in the blanket he grabbed from the bed. He wanted to make sure she didn't yell, and he hadn't heard a peep out of her. He'd check on her as soon as they were out of here, but he loosened the blanket around her face so she could breathe. For a second, he thought she was dead. Her pale eyes stared at him from a dead-white face. Finally she scrunched her eyes shut as if she were trying to get rid of a bad dream. She was clutching a teddy bear, curled around it in a tight ball, her eyes still shut.

"I don't want to hear a sound out of you, understand, kid?" he said. She didn't move a muscle. She was scared to death. Good. It made things easier. When they were away from here, he'd give her a dose of Seconal just to make sure she stayed quiet.

He released the emergency brake and put in the clutch. The car rolled slowly, then began to pick up speed as it free-wheeled down the hill. Before he got to the hairpin turn, he put the car in second and popped the clutch. He turned on the headlights as he rounded the curve. Beside him, the kid made a choked, whimpering sound. He glanced at her. Only the pale blur of her face showed from the tangled blanket.

He kept the car at an even speed as he tried to watch for street signs and remember the turns he had to make. One wrong one would put him in a maze. Maybe he should have made a trial run, but it was too late to worry about that now. He wiped sweat from his lip when he finally spotted the last turn he had to make before Cahuenga.

There was an underpass and a stretch of road where there were no houses. He pulled over and took out the packet of reds he'd bought from a dealer in Echo Park. He had used most of them in the meat for the dog, but he picked up one of the ones that was left. Leaning over to the back seat, he grabbed a can of beer from the six-pack and popped the top. It foamed out over his hand, and he drank some before he put the can on the dash.

"Okay, kid, sit up," he said. When she didn't move, he poked her. "You deaf or something? I said, sit up!" He jerked her up, and her eyes popped open as she fell against the back of the seat. She didn't make a sound.

"Take this." When she didn't react, he grabbed her chin and forced her mouth open. He pushed the capsule onto the back of her tongue, then tilted the beer can to her lips and clamped her mouth shut to force her to swallow. She gagged, but he didn't let go until he was sure the pill had gone down. Beer trickled from the corners of her mouth, but her eyes were vacant. He wondered if she was retarded or something. Wherever she was, it wasn't here and now, but that was okay with him for the time being.

The headlights of a car coming down the hill behind him flashed in the rearview mirror. He let go of the kid, and she flopped like a rag doll to the seat. He threw the blanket over her. The pill couldn't have worked that fast, but he didn't have time to worry about her now. He shifted gears and got the hell out of there before the approaching headlights got close enough to outline the car.

At Cahuenga, he tuned the car radio to a soft rock station and headed for the freeway.

CHAPTER TWENTY-FOUR

Vince ran the yellow light, barely beating the oncoming traffic as it started across the intersection. He cut sharply onto Vine Street and started up the twisting route into the hills.

Beth Davies sounded frantic. If the kid was gone, he didn't blame her, but how the hell could anyone have kidnapped Jenny? Beth wasn't out of the house more than a few minutes, and they were right at the front door. They would have seen anyone go in that way, and they weren't gone long enough for someone to break in through the back. Unless Beth hadn't locked up. Given the state she was in, he would have bet money she'd double-bolt every door and window, but she could have been careless. Maybe she figured Baron would keep intruders out and alert her to any danger.

The vet's first impression was the dog was drugged. He'd know more after he took a blood sample and pumped the dog's stomach to examine the contents, but judging from the slowed heart rate and lack of reflexes, the vet ventured the opinion that Baron had probably swallowed a potentially life-threatening dose. The vomiting may have saved his life.

A dose that size couldn't be an accident. Someone deliberately wanted Baron out of the way. In order to get to Jenny? *Jesus!*

Vince pulled the wheel sharply and the tires screeched around a turn. Questions raced through his mind as he

173

spun around another turn, barely missing a parked car. It sure as hell was no chance snatch. This neighborhood was one of the least likely places to find kids in the whole city. It was a planned caper. An adrenaline rush hit him like a double martini on an empty stomach. Beth was right. It had to be Rick March. How the hell had March found Beth and the kid so fast?

He turned into the dead-end street and slammed to a stop in front of the Fischers' house. He was out and up the steps in seconds. A pale and terror-stricken Beth opened the door. When he came in, she turned away without saying anything. He followed her to the bedroom where she stared at the empty bed as if she could make the kid come back.

He had a million questions, but he gave her a couple of minutes. He walked around the room without touching anything. The telephone receiver, its cord dangling, lay on the bed. He leaned close enough for a good look. It was a clean cut.

Beth looked so shaken, he felt sorry for her.

"What about the phones in the den and the kitchen?" he asked, trying to draw her out so she wouldn't keel over.

"The one in the den works. I didn't check the kitchen." Her voice was oddly flat, devoid of energy and hope.

"Did you call the police?" She nodded as tears welled in her eyes. "Let's go sit down," he said, taking her arm.

She pulled away as if he'd jabbed her with a pin. She hugged herself and drew a quivering breath. "It's your fault. I never should have listened to you." She turned and went into the den where she sat on the edge of the straight-backed chair at the desk. When he followed, she didn't look at him.

"Beth—"

She gave him an agonized look. "You're the only one

who knows we're here. I don't know how, but you led him to us. Now he has Jenny, and I'll never forgive you. If anything happens to her—" She covered her face.

He tried to think of some way to comfort her but couldn't. After a while, he said, "What did the police say?"

She wiped away tears with her fist like a kid. "The woman said they'll send someone. Maybe I should call again. Maybe she didn't understand—"

"It takes a little time," Vince said. "I was right at the bottom of the hill when I phoned. They have a longer way to come." She looked away with an expression so full of pain he was afraid she was going to cry again.

"Why didn't he kill me and get it over with?" she asked in a shaky voice.

He couldn't answer that one. It didn't make sense for March to grab the kid when he could have waited a couple of minutes and grabbed Beth. March had gone for Suzie Tustman like a heat-seeking missile as soon as he got out of prison. She was dead within hours. Why start playing games now? He realized Beth was watching him.

"I don't know," he said honestly. "Look, why don't you tell me what happened? Everything, from the time you left work this afternoon. I know it hurts like hell, but you're going to have to tell the cops when they get here."

She clenched her jaw, then chewed at her lower lip. She began in a low voice, telling how she picked up Jenny at the sitter, did some grocery shopping, cooked dinner, walked the dog. He listened for a clue in the minutia. He hadn't caught anything by the time she reached the part he already knew.

"I was working here in the den. Jenny—" her voice broke. "Jenny watched TV a while. I let Baron out when she went to bed. Some time later, I don't know how long it was, he started barking. I went to call him."

"Which door?"

"The kitchen. He was up by the gate. He didn't want to come in. He stopped barking, so I let him stay out. Then a while later, he started barking again. He still didn't want to come in, but he finally did, and I locked up."

"Go on. What happened next?"

She chewed at her lip. "He lay down in the kitchen, and I came back to work. After a bit, he came in here. He was whining and had trouble standing up. Then all of a sudden he was sick. Everything happened so fast, I'm not sure what I did. I got a towel. He looked so awful, I was scared. When he fell over, I remembered the list of phone numbers the Fischers showed me. I called the vet and asked the service to have him call me as soon as possible." Her gaze brushed Vince's and slid away. "Then you called."

"And after I left with Baron, what did you do?"

She spread her hands as if she were tired of talking. She sounded exhausted. "I came in the house. When I tried to set the security system, the red light kept blinking, so I went to check the doors and windows. The kitchen door wasn't locked but—"

"You said you locked it."

"I thought so, but it wasn't latched. I knew that didn't account for the broken circuit, so I went to check the bedroom." She swallowed visibly. "The patio door was open. Jenny was gone." She covered her face, and her shoulders heaved.

Vince let her cry. He walked back to the bedroom and bent to look at the latch on the patio door. There were no scratch marks or chips in the finish. Even an expert with a complete set of burglary tools would have left some evidence. He went outside and walked to the kitchen. The police would have his ass if he touched anything, but they sure as hell wouldn't tell him anything once they took over.

Even with the patio and house lights on, pools of shadow made it hard to get a good look at anything. He took out the pencil flashlight on his key chain and examined the door and frame. There were scratch marks and nicks near the lock that looked pretty fresh. These latches were easy enough to force once you got a blade in there. He went back through the bedroom and walked around to the kitchen. The wall phone cord was intact. Three phones and only one disabled. If March came in this way, why would he walk right past this phone, then a few minutes later take time to cut the bedroom wire when he snatched the kid? It didn't make sense.

CHAPTER TWENTY-FIVE

Beth was relieved when Vince left her alone. She was sorry she had let him in, but her desperate terror for Jenny had blotted out reason. Why had she told him everything that happened when he asked? Was she really hoping he could explain why March had taken Jenny, not her? The question kept rushing through her brain in a dizzying spiral. With the front door open, March must have known she'd be right back, that she wouldn't leave Jenny alone for long.

The realization that he had poisoned Baron made her stomach roll dangerously. With a twinge of guilt, she realized she hadn't asked how the dog was. She glanced toward the door but couldn't bring herself to talk to Vince Norris again. Not when she was torn to pieces about Jenny being in the hands of a killer.

Dear God, keep her safe . . .

She turned away as Vince came down the hall. To her relief, he went out the front door. She heard a murmur of voices and only then realized another car had driven up. A few minutes later Vince led in a uniformed policeman. Beth got up as the officer nodded politely.

"Ma'am." The nameplate on his shirt said "Rastman."

"This way," she said crossing the hall to the bedroom without waiting to see if he followed. She pointed to the bed. "She was sleeping there. Jenny. Her name is Jenny. She's only eight. I checked on her just minutes before—" She glanced at Vince. "Before he came. We took the dog out. I wasn't gone five minutes!" Her voice broke.

"Have you checked around outside?" Rastman asked.

"Yes, of course I did." Beth found a tissue in her pocket and blew her nose. The policeman walked around the room then went out onto the patio where the lights were still on. He took a flashlight from his belt and disappeared toward the patio. A few minutes later he went by the other way.

"Beth—"

She gave a nervous start at the sound of Vince's voice. Without turning, she said, "Please leave me alone."

He stood a minute, then followed the cop outside. They came in a few minutes later followed by another uniformed policeman with a flashlight.

"The gate's open up there." Rastman pointed with his thumb.

"It was open when I went out to look for Jenny. It was closed earlier."

"Locked?"

When she shook her head, the policeman looked at Vince.

"The Fischers and the neighbor up there are friendly," he said. "He works for Paramount Studios. He's on location somewhere."

"Utah," Beth said mechanically. "I know the gate was closed because the dog was up there barking." Baron had been barking because someone was there. Why hadn't she realized it? If only she'd checked. Her eyes blurred with tears, and she reached to the box on the night stand for another tissue.

"The vet thinks the dog was given a pretty hefty dose of sedative along with the poison," Vince told the cop.

Beth looked at him. "You didn't tell me that." Her stomach lurched dangerously. Rick March had come prepared to get the dog out of the way. He must have been watching the house. She had accused Vince Norris of leading March to her and Jenny, but now she realized that was impossible. Vince Norris hadn't been here since the morning he brought her up to meet the Fischers, and tonight he hadn't gotten here until after Baron was sick. Rick March couldn't have followed Norris; he had followed *her*. She pressed her hand to her mouth, then realized Vince Norris was watching her.

"When will the vet know for sure?" the policeman asked.

"He's doing some tests," Norris said. "He said I could call in a couple of hours."

"Better give me his number." Rastman jotted it in a notebook. "We'll call in a report."

When the two cops went out, Vince followed them. Beth leaned against the front door and listened to the crackle of the police radio as Rastman made his report. Vince was talking to the other officer, but she couldn't hear what he was saying. She was so incredibly tired, her body ached. All she could think about was Jenny and how terrified she must be.

After a bit, Rastman came back to tell her detectives were on the way. She nodded, aware he was trying to be kind, but thinking of how much time they were wasting talking when they should be searching for March and Jenny. She was relieved when the policeman walked down the hall to the bedroom.

Beth rubbed the back of her neck where the muscles radiated pain. The same questions went round and round in her mind like a spinning disc: Why had March taken Jenny, and how had he found them? The story in the *Times* might have led him to Los Angeles, but how did he track her down once he got here? The nursing home had her phone number. Had he gotten it from them? The only other person who knew the number was Jack Tustman, and he wouldn't give it to March or anyone else. Beth realized with horror that Suzie might have known where Jack kept the number and been forced by March to tell him before he killed her. *Brutally stabbed* . . . Beth shuddered and rubbed her arms. The air-conditioning unit clicked, and she realized it was running with the doors wide open. She got up and turned it off.

She sank into a chair in the semi-dark living room and stared at the hill where the policeman's flashlight was playing over the steep drop-off. He was doing his job, but she knew Jenny hadn't wandered off or fallen. Rick March had followed them from the apartment. She remembered Mrs. Hackett coming to the door with Sasha in her arms. The cat had gotten out when *March* opened the door! Her bills and check stubs were on the shelf right above the card table. If he'd gone through them, they left a clear trail to Creative Color Graphics. All he had to do was follow it. And her. Coming here, she had been concentrating so hard on driving the unfamiliar streets, it never occurred to her to wonder if anyone was following her.

She looked up as the flashlight went past the kitchen. A minute later the policeman came through the living room as a car stopped out front. He returned with two men in plain clothes. One was tall and bulky, rumpled looking, as if he'd been in the same suit for several days. The other was an inch or two shorter, Hispanic, and looked as if he were sniffing something unsavory.

The big man held out his hand. "Ms. Davies. I'm Detective Atkins and this is Detective Montoya." The dour-faced man nodded without offering his hand. "Do you mind if we sit down?"

Beth switched on the lamp beside her as the two detectives sat on the sofa. Rastman stood near the bamboo plants as Vince Norris came in and shut the door. He stood in the entry like an uninvited guest.

Atkins took out a notebook and pen. "If you don't mind going over your story, we'd like to hear it in your own words. Take your time, and try not to leave anything out. Okay?" He smiled, and Beth nodded. "Start with how you happen to be here. I understand this isn't your house."

Beth took a deep breath. "My name is Elizabeth Davies. I changed it legally after—after my husband died."

Atkins said, "Vince Norris told us about the murder and the killer getting out of prison."

Beth's cheeks flushed. There was no hiding the past now. "I accepted Mr. Norris' offer, or rather Mr. and Mrs. Fischer's, to stay here for two weeks. I thought—I thought March wouldn't find me here." She felt naïve and stupid.

"Mr. Norris says no one knows you're up here. Is that right?" Atkins said.

"Yes. Only he and the people who own the house. They left for Greece last night."

"How long have you known Mr. Norris?" Montoya asked. His glance stabbed toward the entry.

"Three days."

"What about the Fischers?"

"I met them yesterday morning."

"Have you done this sort of thing before? House-sitting?" Atkins said.

"No, but I was frightened. I wanted to hide from March. I was afraid he'd come looking for me the way he did Suzie—" Her stomach cramped and she fought for control.

Atkins glanced at Montoya, who got to his feet and, motioning to Vince Norris, went down the hall to the den.

"Why did you think March would come after you?" Atkins asked.

"He said he'd get even. Then when he murdered Suzie—"

"Why didn't you call the police?"

"I—I thought I could hide. I know it's hard to understand, but I've spent the past year trying to erase all traces of Liz Husby. I wanted to start over and make a new life for me and Jenny. She's had such a bad time of it. Then when I saw how easily Vince Norris found me, I was terrified March might too. God, don't you see? I thought I was doing the right thing."

A thin film of sweat shone on Atkins' brow, but Beth shivered as though an icy wind had sprung up. Everything she'd done sounded stupid now.

"Why did he take Jenny?" she asked miserably. "I was here. I'm the one who testified against him. Why didn't he take me?"

"I can't answer that, Ms. Davies."

Montoya came back and said something to Atkins in a low voice. Atkins closed his notebook. Standing, he said, "The Kings County District Attorney's office is in charge of the Tustman case, Ms. Davies. They're sending someone to talk to you. Our crime scene unit is on the way. We'll need a picture of Jenny."

Beth went to the closet for her purse and took out her wallet. She extracted the school picture of Jenny taken last winter and handed it to Atkins.

"I have a bigger one at the apartment. I can get it."

Atkins slipped the picture into his notebook. "This will be fine." He turned toward the door. "An officer will be outside until the others get here. We'll be in touch."

"What about Jenny? Aren't you going to look for her?"

"We'll do everything we can. We've got floodlights on the way to check the hillside up there, just in case."

In case Jenny had fallen or been thrown down? Beth's heart plunged then staggered back.

Atkins took a card from his pocket and gave it to her. "Call if you think of anything."

Beth watched the two detectives descend the steps and drive away. She'd completely forgotten about Vince Norris until he spoke.

"Beth, why don't you go lie down? I'll call you when they get here. It may be hours."

"I can't."

"It's going to be a long night. You won't help Jenny by wearing yourself out."

She hugged her arms across her waist. "Do you have children, Mr. Norris?"

"No."

"Then don't tell me how I should feel or act. It's my little girl Rick March took!" Her irritation spilled. "Please go away, Mr. Norris. I can't take any more right now."

"I'll hang around until—"

"Go! I don't want you here!" She turned and walked down the hall. She needed to be alone, to think, to figure out what had made Rick March do this terrible thing. And more important, where he had taken Jenny.

She heard the front door close. A few minutes later, a car started. Beth let her breath out in a miserable sigh as she went back to the living room to turn the dead bolt and set the security system. Back in the den, she curled up on the sofa, physically ill from her churning stomach and mentally tortured by her churning thoughts. No matter how she asked herself the questions, she couldn't find answers. It was too far-fetched to think that anyone but Rick March had taken Jenny, yet there was no reason for him to have done it. For the millionth time in the past year and a half, she wished she had not stopped at Gil's office that day. If only—Shivering, she pulled a crocheted afghan around her and swallowed the sour taste in her throat. She closed her eyes as new tears overflowed. If he hurt Jenny, she would never forgive herself.

When the doorbell rang, she realized she'd dozed off. She jumped up, tripping over the afghan that fell around her feet. Her muscles ached and her head was fuzzy. She recognized one of the men outside immediately: the district attorney who had prosecuted March. A shiver touched the back of her neck as she remembered his cold, impersonal smile as he led her carefully through her testimony. She couldn't think of his name. She'd never seen the other one who stood a pace behind as if he'd been told to heel. Two uniformed state policeman were on the steps behind them.

"Hello, Mrs. Husby. Kings County District Attorney Peter Ondavin. May I come in?" He was tall and broad-shouldered, with thinning brown hair and eyes the color of faded denim. Eyes that still looked at her as though she were on the witness stand.

"Davies. Elizabeth Davies," she said automatically.

The two men sat on the sofa where the detectives had. Beth took the gold chair farthest from them as if to give herself breathing space. She folded her hands in her lap and tried to clear away the dull pain that throbbed behind her eyeballs.

Ondavin introduced the other man as a special investigator. He explained that he had no jurisdiction in Los Angeles County but had been granted privileges because of Suzie Tustman's murder, which his office was investigating. He asked her to go over the story again. She avoided his gaze by fixing hers on the picture on the wall behind them. The special investigator took notes. They interrupted her occasionally to ask her to clarify something. Ondavin didn't question her certainty that Rick March had taken Jenny, and it magnified Beth's fear. By the time she finished, her hands were plucking nervously at her slacks.

Like the city detective, Ondavin asked where and when she met Vince Norris. He said off-handedly that it was a routine question, but Beth's doubts about Vince Norris began to grow again.

"According to the veterinarian, someone tried to kill the dog," Ondavin told her.

"Kill Baron? Oh, my God—Is he all right?"

"The vet says he'll pull through." Ondavin leaned forward, his elbows on the knees of his pale gray suit. "There was enough residual sedative and poison in the dog's stomach to suspect a lethal dose. If he hadn't vomited, he'd be dead now. That means March knew about the dog."

There was no question in Beth's mind anymore that Rick March had followed her from work. She tried to think if she and Jenny passed anyone when they took Baron for his walk.

Ondavin said, "Mrs. Davies, how well did you know Rick March in Pine Lake?"

"I didn't—"

"You went to high school together."

"He was only there a few months. You know that. You brought it out at the trial."

"But you did talk to him, right?"

"Yes," she said with a touch of irritation. "He sat next to me in home room. I never saw him outside of school, if that's what you're implying."

"I'm not implying anything," Ondavin said. "I'm trying

186

to get a grasp on the connection between you and March."

"Connection!" Tears welled at her eyelids. "There *is* no connection except that he's got Jenny!" Sitting here dredging her memory like a swamp wasn't going to get her daughter back. She wondered if the police were even searching for Jenny and March.

"Why do you think he took your little girl?"

She was close to tears. "To torture me. He thinks I'm responsible for his going to prison. He thought Suzie Tustman was, too. He killed her."

"Why do you think he killed her and not you? Why would he only want to make you suffer?"

"I don't know," she said helplessly. "I don't know. All I know is he has Jenny, and while we sit here talking, God only knows where he's taken her." *Or what he's done* . . . She thought she was going to be violently ill.

"Ms. Davies, your daughter was in your husband's office that day. She may have seen March commit the murder. She's a witness, too, even though she didn't testify at the trial."

For a moment, Beth was too stunned to react. Then the impact of Ondavin's words hit her. Of course that was true! She sat in frozen silence as tears brimmed and coursed down her cheeks.

CHAPTER TWENTY-SIX

It was after one when the last car drove down the hill. Beth locked the doors and set the security system. She turned on the air conditioning, then shut it off again when she found herself jumping every time it made a noise. The silence insulated her from the world outside, as if she were in a glass cage. She was numb with fatigue and fear. She hadn't been able to put what the district attorney said about Jenny being a witness out of her mind. If he'd been trying to frighten her more than she already was, he'd definitely succeeded.

She had wanted Ondavin and his investigator gone, and now that they were, she was frightened to be alone. The wall she built around herself and Jenny had given them the privacy she craved, but now it sealed her off from everyone she knew. The only one who had glimpsed her secrets was Madelaine.

She glanced at the clock. She couldn't call Madelaine at this hour. Vince Norris was the only other person who knew about her past, but she would never call him. She hoped he was out of her life forever, but she wouldn't be that fortunate. The morning paper would carry his story about the kidnapping, and her life would be spread out like a drying canvas. Why had she ever let him into the apartment? Was it only two days ago? How naïve she'd been to think she could talk to a reporter and hide from Rick March.

She walked through the house trying the keep her terror at bay. The police and the district attorney didn't tell her how they planned to look for March. They had all but admitted they didn't have any idea where to search. They hadn't found any trace of him since Suzie's murder.

She thought again about what Ondavin had said. Jenny might have witnessed the murder. Madelaine believed Jenny had locked off a memory that was too painful to face. Beth and the therapist both assumed it was seeing her father's bloody body, but had Jenny seen March kill Gil?

Beth sank weakly onto the sofa. Oh, God, don't let that be true. A spasm of fear shook her. Vince Norris said March would be tried again if the district attorney put together a new case. But if March eliminated everyone who could testify against him, there couldn't be another trial.

She tried to block the horrible thought from her mind. Jenny was still alive. She knew it. She felt it in her heart. She had to go on believing that or her own life would disintegrate into meaningless existence. *Jenny is alive . . . Jenny is alive . . .* Beth told herself. Where had March taken her?

Something plucked at Beth's memory, tauntingly close but elusive. Was the key in her own head somewhere? Something from the past that would give her a clue to the present? The harder she tried to think, the more confused she got. She had gone over what happened so many times tonight. Surely if there was anything, she would have seen it.

Stop thinking about it. Relax. Let your thoughts float . . .

She went through the house turning off lights, then dimmed the one in the kitchen to a soft glow. In the semidarkness, she sat at the corner table where she and Jenny had eaten dinner just hours ago and willed her mind to be still as she gazed out at the night-enshrouded city below. She went through the relaxation steps of the creative meditation course she had taken in art school. She placed her hands in her lap, palms up, and began to breathe deeply and rhythmically. Gradually her pulse slowed and the tension went out of her shoulders. Thoughts drifted across her mind like clouds, and she made no effort to control them. Rick March . . . her sophomore year in Pine Lake High School . . . home room . . .

A sullen Rick March had been assigned the seat next to her. She thought he'd be nice looking if he smiled, but he was scowling as if he were mad at the world. The other kids ignored him, and he didn't try to make friends. He was late a lot, and sometimes he didn't show up at all. She wondered what his life was like living in a foster home. She didn't know the family he stayed with, but a succession of kids had come and gone from it. Everyone knew Rick March was a welfare ward. The social stigma didn't make his life easy in school, and he didn't even try to keep up with the work. He was sent to the principal's office almost daily when teachers couldn't cope with his behavior or his indifference, but it didn't have any effect. He seemed determined to get himself kicked out of school permanently.

One morning when his seat was empty at the first bell, Beth idly sketched his likeness on the cover of her notebook. He slid into his seat just as the second bell rang, and she turned over her notebook so he wouldn't see the sketch. She forgot all about it until a week later when she walked up to the teacher's desk to hand in an excuse note for her absence the day before. The note said she'd been sick. Her mother always wrote them when she kept Liz home until she was sure her husband was over his abusive, drunken rage. Anything was better than facing her husband alone when he woke.

It was the week before Christmas. The annual school Holiday Hop had everyone excitedly making plans. Girls whispered about who was taking whom and who hadn't been asked. Like Liz Davies. She stared at her desk pretending not to hear or care. When the bell rang, she got up so quickly she knocked her books to the floor. Before she could bend down, Rick March picked them up. For a moment she thought he was going to keep them, but then she realized he was looking at his sketched likeness on the cover of her notebook.

"You draw good," he said. "It looks like me." He smiled as if no one had ever really looked at him before. When she didn't answer, he handed her the books and walked away.

The scene evaporated. There was something else . . . about a drawing . . . She closed her eyes and breathed deeply again.

"That where you live?"

She looked up from her sketching. It was lunch hour, and she had taken her sandwich outside to sit in the sun and to avoid the party planning in which she had no part. Christmas break meant a lot of holiday cheer from a bottle for her father and more misery than good will for her and her mother.

Rick March was looking over her shoulder at the sketch filling her pad.

"No, it's a cabin up by the lake." She felt awkward talking about her work.

"I've been there," he said. "Up on Sullivan Road, right?"

She nodded, not looking at him. "I clean for summer people sometimes."

His mouth curled in a sneer. "Those rich city bastards let those places sit empty most of the time. They're all closed up except for a weekend once in a while and the summer. It serves them right if they get ripped off."

She concentrated on detailing the pattern of the sloped roof. She was uncomfortable with him watching her, but her pencil moved automatically to fill in a shadow here, a touch of light there. She had never seen Rick talk to anyone except two older boys who were always in trouble. Why was he talking to her? For a horrible moment, she was afraid he was going to ask her to *the Holiday Hop. Her cheeks flushed, but after a little while, she was aware that his shadow no longer stretched across the walkway. She looked up, and he was gone.*

Four months later Rick March was sent to a juvenile detention center for breaking into and looting cabins on Sullivan Road. She never told anyone what he'd said about the rich people who owned them.

The cabins . . . The story in the *Pine Lake Courier* at the time had made Rick March sound incorrigible, already a hardened criminal, but Liz only remembered the sad empty look in his eyes, the lonely pain of a kid who didn't belong and who hid out in other people's houses. She never heard how long he was in jail or wherever they sent him, but he never came back to Pine Lake. Not until the day Gil died.

Don't think about the murder.

The cabins at the lake . . . that article in the *Courier* . . . So long ago . . .

She took several deep breaths, relaxing, this time letting her mind search for the *Courier* article. It came into focus like a camera being adjusted.

Young March was defiant when questioned about the break-ins. He admitted being in the cabins but denied any vandalism except for cutting a telephone wire in a cabin where he'd stayed repeatedly. When asked why he had done it, he said, "Just to let people know I was there."

Beth's anxiety curled in a suffocating wave. He cut the bedroom phone cord so she'd know he'd been here. He wanted her to know he had Jenny. Suddenly the hazy night wrapping the house was filled with terror. Why did he want her to know? It had to be more than to torment her. He could have frightened her even more with Jenny right there, but he hadn't. Why?

Again she thought of the sad-eyed youth who had broken

into isolated lake cabins. At the murder trial, March's lawyer had painted the defendant as the victim of a broken home and an abusive mother who moved a dozen times before she abandoned him at a young age. His entire life was a shifting pattern of unhappy experiences. He had no place to call home, no place to go back to.

Beth shuddered at the thought that he might have taken Jenny to some sleazy hotel or boarding house. She put her head down on her arms and tried to tell herself he wouldn't do that. Among all the sordid details the defense and prosecution brought out at the trial, there was never a hint of March's abusing or molesting anyone. When the telephone rang, she leaped up to grab it.

"Yes?"

"Beth, it's Vince Norris. Look, don't hang up—"

"Please leave me alone."

"I'm in my car at the end of your street. Can I come up and talk to you for a few minutes?"

"No."

"Beth, listen. I've been in your apartment."

"My apartment? How did you get in?"

"I took the keys from your purse."

She was speechless. She started to hang up and heard him yelling.

"Beth, listen, damn it. I'm on your side. Hello? Are you there?" She put the receiver back to her ear without saying anything. "March was in your apartment, too."

She had already figured that out, but Norris didn't know about Sasha getting out. "What makes you say that?"

"There's a silver picture frame with a cracked glass and no picture on your dresser."

The enlargement of Jenny's school photo. Beth's knees went weak and she sank into a chair. The picture was there when she packed her suitcase.

"He must have gone through your jewelry case. There are green beads all over the floor. The cat damn near scared me when it leaped out to bat one of them around. As far as I can tell, nothing else is missing, and the place isn't trashed, but there are papers on the table in the living room that would have told him where you work. I think that's where he picked up your trail. He followed you from there."

"I know," she said wearily. "I figured that out, too."

He let out a breath as if he'd been holding it. "Does that mean we can be friends again? I want to help. I have an idea. Look, let me in and we'll talk, okay?"

She hesitated, then said, "Okay."

She heard the relief in his voice. "Two minutes." He hung up.

She turned on some lights and went into the den to watch the road below the glass wall. Moments later she saw him sprinting toward the house. She went to the front door to let him in.

CHAPTER TWENTY-SEVEN

The rush of adrenaline began wearing off by the time he reached Interstate 5. Rick leaned back and relaxed for the long drive ahead. Everything was working for him now. Better than his original plan. When he saw Liz and the guy go outside with the dog, he was just going to find the kid and wait for Liz to come back, but then he remembered the painting in her apartment of the cabin. It was perfect. Liz would remember it, and when she did, she'd follow him because of the kid. The L.A. cops couldn't help her up there, so she'd have to call that jerk sheriff, maybe even the D.A. himself.

"Hail, hail, the gang's all here," he said with a laugh. He slapped his hand against the steering wheel. Everything was going to work just fine.

He glanced at the kid. She was really gone now, not just spaced out. He wondered if one Seconal was too much for a kid that size. He pulled back the blanket and touched her to make sure she was still breathing. Her face was warm as he ran his fingers across her smooth skin. She was okay, just dead to the world.

He glanced at the fuel gauge and decided to fill the tank now while he didn't have to worry about the kid. He remembered a small, self-service station with a shelf of groceries not far from the turnoff to 99. He could pick up some stuff to eat while he was at it. He'd pulled a holdup at the station five years ago, but nobody would remember him. The station was the kind most people passed up for the cheaper, big stations, so there wouldn't be many cars around. And it didn't carry diesel, so there wouldn't be any truckers in high cabs to look down into the car and get curious about the bundle on the seat.

Twenty minutes later he saw the lights of the station and slowed for the exit. The ramp led to an underpass. He'd forgotten the station was on the southbound side of the highway. So much the better. If anyone did remember him, they wouldn't know if he'd been heading north or south. It was a pay-first deal, which meant he had to go inside twice, but it couldn't be helped. He was down to his last twenty. Maybe it was time to use the doctored credit card he'd been carrying the past few days. Night clerks in stations like this were usually dumb kids who spent most of their time reading girlie magazines.

There were no other cars in the station. He went inside and dropped the credit card on the counter, went back out and kept his back to the station while he filled the tank. As he screwed the gas cap back on, another car pulled in and stopped behind him. Rick turned his head as the driver got out and went inside. A woman and two kids trailed behind and headed for the wash rooms. Rick waited until the driver came out and started to pump gas. Still averting his face, Rick went inside.

He moved along the aisle of food, pulling out bags of chips, cookies and donuts. From the cooler, he got a six-pack of beer, then on second thought, a six-pack of Coke, too. He shoved them across the counter. With the gas, it came to more than twenty bucks. As the scrawny kid behind the counter fished for a charge slip, the woman and kids came out of the rest rooms. The kids started to run around like greyhounds after a rabbit, pulling stuff off shelves and screaming that they wanted everything in sight. The mother took stuff away from them and put it back, but she was no match for the two of them. The clerk was nervously trying to keep them all in sight. He slapped the credit card on the machine and put the slip in place for the imprint, all the while shooting worried glances at the trio.

When he filled in the amount and pushed the slip across the counter, Rick almost laughed as he scrawled "Duane Cass" by the X. Instead of wanting to choke the screaming little bastards, he ought to buy them each a candy bar. The clerk would be lucky if he remembered his own name after all this. Rick started for the door.

"Hey. Mister!"

He froze.

"You forgot your receipt."

Rick crammed the yellow slip into his pocket and went out as the man who belonged to the screaming tribe hung up the hose and turned toward the station. Rick detoured around the front of his car to avoid passing the guy. He dropped the bag onto the back seat and pulled away before the family got its act together.

Back on the highway, he got the car up to the speed limit and held it there. The breeze coming in the open window dried off the thin sheen of sweat on his face. Those damned kids had made him nervous with all their yelling. He hated noisy, crying brats.

He drew back the blanket from Liz's kid's face. She'd better not give him any trouble. But even if she did, by then he'd have a gun that would equalize things.

CHAPTER TWENTY-EIGHT

Beth took the keys Vince Norris held out to her and put them on the table where they lay like an accusation.

"One of the windows in the living room was unlocked," Norris said. "He may have gotten in that way."

"They were locked when I left," she said. "I check every morning." It was a ritual that never varied, a last tour of the apartment while Jenny got her knapsack. And Beth was sure she hadn't unlocked a window during the brief time she and Jenny were in the apartment packing to come here. Rick March had been in the apartment that day, she was sure. And now he'd been there again. She felt violated and scared. Her voice faltered. "Were either of the phone wires cut?"

Norris looked at her sharply. "No. Why do you ask?"

"Because this one was, that's all," she lied. She wasn't sure she could trust Norris, even though she accepted the fact that March had followed *her,* not him. She could hardly trust him after he stole her keys.

"Look, Beth, I'm trying to figure out March's next move," Norris said. "So far he hasn't made any demands or threats, right? We both know he's not stupid. He knows the first thing you'd do when you found the kid missing is call the cops. He's had enough experience with the law to figure they'll be all over this place. So how come he didn't leave a note or hasn't called before they can get a tap on the phone? I think it's because he thinks you know where he is or can figure it out."

The blood drained from Beth's face. That was ridiculous. How in the world was she supposed to know where he'd go? If March got in touch with her, she'd do whatever he asked. He had to know that.

Vince was talking again. "So far he's been able to move around without calling attention to himself, but now with a kid, it'll be a lot harder. He's always been a loner. I've read his file. He never changes his pattern much. He's never had any partners or belonged to a gang. He doesn't have any family to turn to. So where does he go now that he has to stay out of sight with a kid? It has to be someplace isolated or where a kid won't be out of place if she's seen."

"Stop calling her kid!" Beth exploded. "Her name is Jenny!"

Norris ignored the outburst. "I think he's headed back up north."

Beth's mouth fell open.

"It's not as crazy as it sounds," Vince said. "Think about it a minute. Where can he go in L.A.? It's easy to lose yourself in this town if you're alone. March can be invisible in the kind of places he's used to: cheap rooming houses or motels, bars and porn theaters where he can sit for hours with nobody asking questions. But he can't take an eight-year-old girl to those places without someone noticing."

Beth stammered, "North? You mean to Pine Lake? He—he can't go there, not after Suzie—"

"Yeah, but remember, he lived in half a dozen towns along the foothills. He knows that whole area. He was always running away as a kid. He probably knows a dozen places to hide."

Beth blinked. The cabin up at the lake . . . *I was there three days and no one ever knew it.*

"What is it?" Vince asked. "You remember something?"

199

She looked away from his perceptive gaze. "How in the world would you know where to look? There are hundreds of gravel roads up in the hills. You couldn't possibly check them all."

"I was hoping you'd be able to think of a place to start," he said, watching her.

She kept her face averted. She didn't even remember which cabin she'd been sketching the day Rick March said he'd been there. He had lived in lots of places longer than he had Pine Lake. And he'd gotten in trouble before and probably found dozens of places to hide. Besides, he'd know the state police would be all over that area after Suzie's murder.

"You sure you can't think of anyplace he might go?" Norris prodded.

Beth hugged her arms tightly. Why was he pushing her so hard? What could he do? He wasn't the police, only a reporter after a story. A city reporter at that. If by some crazy chance March was headed for one of those cabins at the lake, Norris would make things worse, not better, by blundering around. Suddenly she wanted him to go. He was already making things worse.

"Please leave. I can't take anymore." She pressed her fist to her mouth, close to tears again.

Norris puffed his cheeks and blew out a breath. "Okay, I'll go over the trial transcript. Maybe I can pick up a lead from it." He moved toward the door. "Look, Beth, I know you're ticked off about the keys. If it helps, I'm sorry. I'm trying to help. I needed to look around the apartment before the cops were all over the place." He took an amber plastic vial from his pocket and put it on the table. "I got these from a doctor friend. Take one. It'll help you sleep without putting you under so far you won't hear the phone if it rings."

She got up and walked to the door without answering.

"I can stay if you don't want to be alone," Vince offered.

She shook her head. He started to say something else, then changed his mind. She locked the door behind him and reset the security system, then stood with her hand on the panel. If she had set the system right after she let Baron in last night, the security people would have been alerted when March broke in. Would the armed guard have gotten here in time to keep him from taking Jenny?

Stop it! she told herself. It wasn't going to do any good to wonder what she should have done. She had to decide what she was going to do now. She couldn't sit here and wait. Norris was right: If March planned to call, he would have done it by now.

Was Norris right about March heading north, too?

The cabins on Sullivan Road flashed through her mind again. March claimed he had stayed in more than one of them when they were closed for the season. With such an early hot spell and the drought, a lot of cabins would already be open for the summer. Not all though. Some people didn't come up until the Fourth of July weekend, and every year one or two cabins stayed empty all summer.

Like the one she'd been sketching that day? Was that the cabin Rick had broken into, the one he told her he stayed in? What was the owner's name? Drew? Drake? It didn't matter. What did matter was that the couple was killed in a car crash the summer before Gil died. She remembered reading it in the *Courier*. The fiery crash ten miles out of town made headlines for two issues, and there were follow-up stories for several weeks afterward. The cabin became part of an estate fight among warring relatives. As far as she knew, it was still tied up in litigation. Empty.

Was that where he'd taken Jenny? A wave of nausea and

terror struck her. She felt in her pocket for the card Ondavin had given her and held it under the light. *His business card—with his office number.* She turned the card over, then threw it on the counter. He hadn't had time to get back there. He probably wouldn't go to his office at this hour anyhow.

She fingered the phone wire. *Just to let people know I was there.* That's what Rick March had said. And now he was telling *her* he'd been here. And where he was going!

She ran to the bedroom and grabbed a sweater for herself and a pair of jeans and a shirt for Jenny. She stuffed them into a carryall and checked to be sure the sliding glass door was locked. She checked the kitchen door and the ones in the living room, then picked up the keys Vince Norris had put on the table. She started for the door, then on second thought dropped the vial of pills into the carryall as well.

As she started to turn off the security system so she could open the door, a wave of guilt flooded her. The Fischers had entrusted their house and dog to her care. She'd failed miserably in keeping Baron safe. She couldn't abandon the house as well. She left the system set and opened the door, then went to stand in front of the bamboo plant in the dining room. She counted to ten to be sure the security people registered the alarm before she spoke.

"This is Beth Davies, the sitter at the Fischer house. I have to go away—" The password! Her mind blanked for a moment then snapped back. "Red Doberman. Red Doberman. I have to go away and the house will be empty. Please have someone check it until I get back. The dog is at the vet's. I—I'll let you know as soon as I'm back." She started to turn away, then looked back at the greenery behind which the microphone was hidden. "I'm resetting the system when I go out."

She picked up the bag and left, concentrating on punching in the correct code before she went down to the garage.

Her car veered out of its lane coming down the steep grade at Lebec. Beth was exhausted, and the dark, nearly deserted road was hypnotic. She turned the air conditioning to high and set it to blow directly on her face. When she saw the lights of an all-night service area and restaurant, she turned off at the ramp. The hot, dry air did little to revive her as she filled the tank. After she paid, she pulled the car away from the pumps and walked briskly to the restaurant a hundred yards down the road, breathing deeply to force oxygen into her lungs.

A cheerful waitress filled her coffee cup and asked if she wanted anything else.

"By any chance do you have a thermos I can buy?"

"Sorry. During the day you could get one at the shop next door, but we don't carry anything like that."

"Thanks. Just the coffee then."

The girl said, "I could fill a big Styrofoam cup to go. It'll stay hot for quite awhile."

"That would be great."

"I'll have it all set when you're ready to go. You look wrung out. You should maybe think about getting some sleep before you drive anymore." The girl sounded as if her customer's well-being was a real concern. "The motel down at the end of the strip isn't bad."

"Thanks, but I have to get somewhere."

"Well, you be careful. It's easy to fall asleep at the wheel."

The steaming coffee revived Beth, and she was glad she had stopped. When she paid her check, the girl gave her a paper sack with two large containers of coffee.

"I used double cups to hold the heat better."

Beth thanked her again, glad she'd left a good tip.

In the car, Beth propped the coffee where she could reach it easily and set out again. The dashboard clock showed four-thirty when she reached Pine Lake. Main Street was dark except for faintly glowing nightlights in the store and bank windows. A painful cramp knotted her stomach as she passed the old livery stable where Jack still had his office. She hadn't been inside since the day Gil died. The two times she'd come to see her mother, she'd gone through town by the back street so she wouldn't see anyone or be seen. Too many Pine Lake people would feel it was their duty to phone Gil's parents and report that she was in town. Glen Husby would rush to the rest home to confront her with a new attempt to take Jenny "home." He would never give up trying to take Jenny away from her legally, no matter how many times he failed. Jack had told her at Christmas that the Husbys had hired a new lawyer.

Beth had lived here since she was four, but it had never felt like "home." She'd always been an outsider. *Digger-pine savage.* She hadn't known what the mocking words meant when she first heard them as a child, but they brought tears to her mother's eyes. When Beth started school, the other kids made sure she knew the label meant she was an outsider who would never be on equal footing with the families who claimed the town by birthright. Like the Husbys.

And if that wasn't enough, her father's drinking and sporadic working habits put them into the lowest echelon of Digger-pine savages. In the South, poor white trash would have been a step up. It had made her marriage to Gil all the more difficult for the Husbys and the town to accept. At first Gil had laughed and told her she was too sensitive, but it wasn't long until she was painfully aware of the gulf between their worlds and between them. She wondered why he had married her. Plenty of guys walked out when girls got pregnant. If it weren't for Jenny, he probably would have divorced her years ago, but he didn't dare cross his parents. They'd disown him if he ever left the child they idolized. And if Beth had left, they would have tried to take Jenny, just as they were doing now.

So Pine Lake had never been, never would be, "home."

On the road northeast of town, she slowed to watch for Sullivan Road, praying she was right about this being where March was. The long drive had left her numb with fatigue and jumpy from the huge amount of coffee she'd consumed. If Rick March had hurt Jenny, she would kill him. She didn't know how, but she'd find a way. She'd never be able to beat him in a direct confrontation. He had a knife, maybe other weapons, too.

The enormity of what she was about to do made her shudder so violently that she had to grip the steering wheel. She was almost there. She needed a plan. She tried to think, but Jenny's terrified face superimposed itself on every thought.

The headlights picked out the fork where Sullivan Road cut off from the highway. She turned onto it. The car bumped and jolted on the unpaved gravel, and she slowed to a crawl. She hadn't been up here since high school. How far was it? She used to walk. A mile? More? What if she couldn't find the cabin? Everything looked different. She'd never been here at night. The heavy growth of pines that offered respite from the hot California sun in the daytime were dark sentinels holding back the faint blush of predawn. The headlights swept across several dirt tracks that led to cabins hidden among the pines. There were no mailboxes. Summer people picked up their mail at the post office in town.

She tried to remember how far in she used to come carrying her sketch pad and pencils. It had seemed a long way then. The cabin was on a bluff fifty or sixty feet above the lake. It had a long flight of wooden steps going down to the water. She used to sit in the tiny gazebo at the top of the stairs to sketch. The lake and cabin fascinated her, and she'd drawn them dozens of times.

The bluff was on the east side of the lake. She'd come northeast out of town to Sullivan Road, and then angled north-northeast from the highway. The lake was on her left. When the road began to curve, her headlights swept across a twisted, triple-trunked pine tree. Beth hit the brake. She had made dozens of sketches of that tree. She was directly below the cabin. Peering at the overgrown brush, she saw the driveway. The dry grass was crushed where a car had driven over it. Her heart pounded. She resisted the urge to race up the hill to make sure Jenny was all right. She had to be more careful now than ever. She couldn't move blindly. In the still mountain air, sound traveled easily. March would hear the car, might already have.

She took her foot off the brake and let the car roll back. Turning off the headlights, she nosed the Honda into the foot of the driveway to block it, then turned off the engine and rolled down the car window. It was so quiet, she could hear her own breathing. As her eyes got accustomed to the dark, she realized the sky had begun to gray. It would be light enough soon for March to see anyone approaching. If she wanted surprise to be on her side, she had to move now.

She took the keys from the ignition and dropped them into the pocket of her slacks. She got the dark sweater from the bag and the flashlight from the glove compartment, then shoved her purse under the seat. She opened the door quietly and got out. She eased the door shut far enough so the interior lights went off. Then, walking carefully on the uneven ground, she started up the drive.

CHAPTER TWENTY-NINE

Beth stumbled up the driveway. When her foot dislodged a stone that bounced and skidded down the hill, she held her breath until the sound died away. She didn't dare use the flashlight. The cabin couldn't be much farther.

As the slope grew steeper, she remembered there was a sharp turn just before the top. She breathed quietly through her mouth when she finally felt the ground begin to level. She was at the clearing. She hunkered down and studied the shadows until she could make out the faint outline of the cabin. Feeling like a child playing Blind Man's Bluff, she moved sideways until she reached the thick brush at the side of the drive. It used to be a hedge of honeysuckle, but now it felt like a tangle of weeds.

As the sky gradually lightened from a deep charcoal to a slate gray, she made out the outline of the gazebo at the edge of the bank. Beyond it, the surface of the lake was a sheet of smooth steel. An almost imperceptible shadow of a heron glided across it soundlessly, the bird itself invisible against the background of trees.

There was enough light to see across the clearing. The driveway ended in a carport that hadn't been there ten years ago. A car was parked in it. The chance it belonged to the legitimate owner made her nervous, but she wasn't going to leave now. March had brought Jenny here, she was sure of it. He cut her phone wire the same way he had cut the one here, counting on Beth to remember. He and Jenny were inside. She felt it as surely as dawn was breaking.

Overhead, a bird chirped a tentative greeting to the new day. It would be light soon. She had to get closer to the cabin while she could still do it without being seen. Crouched as low as possible, she circled toward the cabin, staying inside the rim of the surrounding trees. The dry, spiky ground cover crackled underfoot. She prayed March wouldn't hear or if he did, that he'd think it was a prowling animal. Every few steps she paused to quiet her breathing and check the cabin. The shades were drawn at the windows and the door was closed. The only sound was her own racing heart and the warm-up chorus of birds heralding the dawn. When she was parallel with the carport, she listened carefully before she ran across the grass and ducked behind the car.

When her breathing slowed to a manageable rate, she raised her head and looked inside the car. There was a straw hat and a magazine on the back seat, and several empty beer cans. She almost cried out when she saw Jenny's teddy bear on the floor.

She squatted until her heart stopped pounding, then raised up again to survey the cabin. The door and window facing her would be the kitchen. She remembered the layout of the cabin. The living room and dining area stretched across the front. There was a short hall, then the bath and two small bedrooms at the far end. Jenny was probably in one of them. March too? *Don't think about it!* She wouldn't be able to act rationally if she let a horrible image of Rick March touching Jenny invade her mind. She would kill him if he had touched her baby.

Her best chance was to get March outside, distract him somehow so she'd have time to grab Jenny and get away before he realized what was happening. But how? If she broke a window, the noise would alert him and he'd be waiting. A fire? It would bring him out, but the ground was so tinder dry, a fire could easily get out of control and trap them all.

What then? All her life she had hated guns and the swaggering men who bragged of their hunting prowess, but now she wished she had one. A handgun or a rifle. Anything.

She leaned against the car, breathing deeply to calm herself as she looked inside the car again. The doors weren't locked. She eased the one beside her open and slid onto the seat. She reached across to move the gearshift lever from park to neutral, then released the emergency brake. Shutting the door quietly, she went around to the front of the car and began to push. Her shoes fought for traction on the hard-packed ground and her muscles strained. She braced her feet against the log marking the front end of the carport and pushed with every ounce of strength she had. Finally the car began to move. What seemed an eternity later, she felt the back wheels drop onto the slight slope of the drive. The car's weight gave it enough momentum so it rolled across the clearing, slowly at first, then gradually picking up speed as the incline became steeper. Beth grabbed the flashlight as the car crashed through the brush where she'd been hiding a few minutes ago. It missed the curve and plowed down the bank, ripping through birch and young pines until it crashed into the gazebo.

Timing the moment of impact, Beth used the flashlight to smash the window of the kitchen door. The sound of tinkling glass was absorbed by the noise of the crash. Before it died away, she heard someone running inside. The front door was flung open, and a man uttered a startled curse. Wrapping her sweater around her arm, Beth reached through the broken pane and unlocked the door. A moment later she was inside.

She ran through the living room, checking chairs and the

sofa to be sure Jenny wasn't there. Through the open front door, she saw March racing toward the car. She looked in the first bedroom. It was empty except for a crumpled pillow on the bare mattress and a pair of men's shoes on the floor. She scooped up the shoes and rushed to the other bedroom. Her pounding heart threatened to crack her ribs when she saw the still, small hump on the bed under the blue plaid blanket from the Fischers' house. She dropped the shoes and kicked them under the bed as she lifted Jenny into her arms. Jenny's eyes were closed and her face so pale, Beth put her own to it and almost cried with relief when she felt the warm, damp skin. Cradling Jenny in her arms, she ran back through the living room and kitchen and outside.

She cut across the carport and into the woods, zigzagging until she was gasping for breath. She leaned against a tree and looked at Jenny. She was sleeping so deeply, March must have given her something. *Like Baron?* Terrified, Beth set out again and began to work her way toward the drive. She stopped abruptly and shifted Jenny to her shoulder as she realized she would be out in the open on the driveway. March was still outside and would spot her easily.

Glancing toward the cabin to orient herself, she cut off at an angle that should bring her out down by the car. To her own ears she sounded like a moose blundering through the brush. She slipped and slid down the hill, not caring about sharp sticks or rocks that stabbed at her. When she finally saw the car through the trees, she stumbled out of the brush and yanked open the passenger door. She propped Jenny on the seat and slammed the door shut. She ran around the car, reaching into her pocket for the keys. As she opened the door, something hit her hard below the ribs and pulled her to the ground.

"Bitch!"

Rick March stood over her, his fist raised. Beth lunged for his legs and wrapped her arms around them before he could kick her away. He staggered and fell. She scrambled toward the open car door, but he grabbed her foot and yanked her back, dragging her across the rough ground so it raked her palms and chin. She tried to kick, but he grabbed both her ankles and before she knew what was happening, he flipped her over onto her back and straddled her. He leaned on her shoulder and put one arm across her neck. His face was only inches from hers, his breath hot on her cheek.

"Pretty damned smart, aren't you!" He spat the words through clenched teeth. She tried to claw at him, but he shifted position and pinned her other arm with his knee. "I ought to crack your head open," he snarled. Then, so suddenly that it startled Beth more than a blow, he laughed. "Jesus, you are something. I never took you for a scrapper. You're a God-damned mother tiger!" He laughed again as he ran his hand down her body. She stiffened, then realized he was searching for her pocket. He pulled out the car keys.

"Let me go!" she demanded.

"Sure." He bounced to his feet and dived for the car. Before Beth could get up, he pulled Jenny out. She flopped like a rag doll in his arms.

"Now let's see how tough you are," he said.

Beth struggled to her feet. When she brushed her hands, they were sticky with blood from oozing scratches.

"Come on," March taunted. "Make a grab for her. See if you can get her before I hurt her."

Beth shook her head. "You win. Don't hurt her. Please."

He snorted. "That's better. Now walk up the friggin' hill nice and slow."

"Leave her here in the car," Beth pleaded. "She hasn't

done anything. I'll do whatever you say if you leave her here."

"You're really a piece of work." He bounced Jenny onto his shoulder. Her head flopped and her hair covered her face. "This kid's my insurance. Now get moving before I change my mind!"

Beth walked ahead, stumbling as she kept turning around to make sure Jenny was all right.

"Not so damned fast!" March ordered.

She realized then he was barefoot. She slowed down and tried to think of some way to gain an advantage again, but with him holding Jenny, there wasn't anything she could do. Tears of frustration ran down her cheeks, and she wiped them away furiously.

At the cabin, March ordered her into the living room. He dumped Jenny onto the sofa. When Beth tried to sit next to her, he pushed her toward a chair instead.

"You stay over there where I can keep an eye on you."

He sidled toward the bedroom and reached for something. A knife! Why hadn't she looked? He came back to the sofa and sank down beside Jenny.

He jerked his thumb toward the first bedroom. "Go get my shoes. They're under the bed."

She hesitated, then said, "They're in the other room. I hid them."

He looked surprised, then laughed again. "If you ain't something!" The laugh died abruptly, and he put his hand on Jenny's shoulder and flicked her hair with the tip of the knife. "Go get them, and make it quick!"

Beth hurried to the bedroom and got down on her hands and knees. In the dim light, she could see the shoes but couldn't reach them. She grabbed a hanger from the closet and used it to fish out the shoes. Was the hanger strong enough to stab him? She tried to undo the twisted section.

"I'm getting impatient," March yelled.

She threw the hanger onto the bed and hurried back with his shoes. He was examining the bloody heel of one foot.

"Get me something to clean the dirt out of this cut."

She went into the bathroom and opened the medicine cabinet. All that was in it was a small bottle of hydrogen peroxide and a box of Band-Aids. She checked the shelves a second time to be sure she hadn't missed a razor blade. Damn! She grabbed a washcloth from a rack and held it under the tap, but no water came out. Of course, the cabin had been shut up. It snowed occasionally at this elevation. People turned off the water in the winter so the pipes wouldn't freeze. This place had never been opened this year. She hid the small bottle of peroxide in her pocket then took the washcloth and Band-Aids back to March.

"There's no water. I'll look in the kitchen for something."

"If you're thinking of looking for knives, don't. I already took them."

She went into the kitchen and began opening cupboards noisily. Taking out the peroxide, she picked up a sharp triangle of glass and slipped it into her pocket. She went back holding out the brown bottle. March had shifted Jenny so her head was in his lap.

"It was in a cupboard," she said with difficulty.

"What is it?"

"Hydrogen peroxide. It's a good disinfectant."

"Okay, clean the cut, and no tricks, understand?" He stroked Jenny's hair as he lifted his injured foot.

Beth knelt and uncapped the bottle. Holding the washcloth under his foot, she poured peroxide onto the cut, then scrubbed at it to clean out bits of grass and dirt.

March didn't flinch. Beth dried the cut. The bleeding had slowed to an ooze. She stretched three Band-Aids across the wound.

"That's the best I can do," she told him.

He raised his foot, looked at it, then pushed it toward her again. "Put my shoes on."

Shaking, she put aside the first aid supplies and struggled to get his feet into his running shoes. When she fastened the Velcro tapes, he said, "Okay, now go over there and sit. It's time for you and me to talk."

CHAPTER THIRTY

Vince propped his elbows on the kitchen table and turned another page of the transcript Mayville had given him of March's trial. He'd been reading steadily since he got home. His eyes felt like molten lava, and he fought to keep them open as the print blurred.

He was missing something. There had to be a clue somewhere in the volume of paper. Suzie Tustman and Rick March couldn't both be telling the truth. The jury sided with Suzie, but Vince knew that justice wasn't only blind, she was sometimes deaf and dumb as well, especially when it came to someone with a record like March's. Once a bad guy, always a bad guy.

He sipped coffee from the cup in front of him, then pushed it away when he realized it was cold. How long ago had he made it? He glanced at his watch. Too damned long. He'd been reading for more than two hours. Or trying to. Guilt kept nudging his attention off track. He had screwed up royally with Beth Davies. He shouldn't have told her about the keys and being in her apartment. He should have gotten back into the house somehow and put the keys back in her purse or dropped them where she'd find them. Now all he'd managed to do was get her mad again. So much for honesty.

Was she mad enough to tell the cops what he'd done? Unlawful entry, tampering with evidence, Atkins would make something stick. Even though they'd known each other a long time, Atkins wasn't one to bend the rules very far. If he went to Macaleer at the paper, there'd be hell to pay. Macaleer's patience was already stretched like an old rubber band. He'd have Vince writing obits or on the unemployment line if he blew this story.

Vince massaged the back of his neck and shook his head like a wet puppy. He picked up the transcript and turned to Suzie Tustman's testimony again.

Q: Please state your full name for the court.

A: Suzie Marian Tustman.

Q: Are you married?

A: Yes. To Jack. Jack Tustman.

Q: How long have you resided in Pine Lake?

A: Two years. Since Jack and I got married.

Q: Where did you reside before that?

A: In Bushville.

Q: Did you go to school in Bushville, Mrs. Tustman?

A: In Pine Lake. There's no school in Bushville.

Q: Did you know the defendant, Rick March, in high school?

A: No, Sir. He was already gone by the time I started.

Q: Have you ever met him anywhere before this trial?

A: No, never.

Q: Have you ever seen him before?

A: Once. In Sheriff Mayville's office.

Q: Describe that occasion for us, please, Mrs. Tustman. What were the circumstances of that meeting?

A: It wasn't a meeting. I mean I didn't meet him. He was just there when I went to tell Sheriff Mayville about the kids knocking over the county road sign again. It was the fourth time that month. Jack was mad.

Q: Did you talk to Rick March that day in the sheriff's office?

A: No. When I went in, everybody was talking about the

murder and him (witness pointed at defendant) being a suspect. I didn't want to talk to him. Gil was Jack's partner. He and Liz were our friends. (The witness broke down.)

Q: Can you go on now, Mrs. Tustman? (The witness indicated yes.) Good. When did you next see the defendant?

A: Here, in the courtroom. Today.

Q: Are you aware, Mrs. Tustman, that the defendant claims he was with you, in your house, the afternoon of the murder?

A: He's lying. I never saw him except the time I just said.

Q: Why would he make up such a story?

D: Objection, Your Honor!

J: Sustained.

Q: Were you at home the day Gil Husby died?

A. Yes. All day until I went in to talk to the sheriff.

Q: Were you alone?

A: Most of the time. Jack came home after lunch to pick up some papers he needed. That was when he told me about the sign. I said I was going into town later and I'd tell Sheriff Mayville about it.

Q: And you went into town about quarter to four, is that right?

A: Yes.

Q: I believe you said you've lived in Pine Lake two years?

A: It was two years in January.

Q: During that time, is it safe to say you've gotten to know a lot of people?

A: Yeah, I guess so.

Q: And your husband is well known?

A: Yes.

Q: Have your name and picture ever been in the local newspaper?

A: Yes.

Q: Was it in the paper the week Rick March was arrested?

A: Yes. The Chamber of Commerce puts on the Halloween parade. Jack's president. The *Courier* did a story. Pictures, too. There was one of me throwing candy to kids.

Q: Was your name mentioned in the article?

A: Sure, right under the picture.

Q: Just a few more questions, Mrs. Tustman. What day was the parade?

A: Saturday, the day before Halloween. There's a party for the kids at the high school, you know, so they don't go out trashing stuff and getting in trouble.

Q: What day of the week does the *Courier* come out?

A: Tuesday.

Q: That would be November second, two days after Halloween and the day before the murder. Is that right?

A: Yes.

Q: Thank you, Mrs. Tustman. You've been very helpful.

Vince rubbed his eyes. March's lawyer had tried his damnedest to poke holes in Suzie Tustman's story, but she didn't budge. As it turned out, it was convincing enough for the jury. Still, March had honed in on her the minute he got out of Folsum. There had to be a link somewhere.

He turned back the page to reread what she'd said about why she went into town that day. " 'To tell Sheriff Mayville about the kids knocking over the county road sign again. It was the fourth time that month, and Jack was mad.' "

There wasn't any sign the night he'd driven out there. He'd relied on Gary Kellog's directions to find the place. It wasn't exactly in the middle of town. He flipped through pages of the transcript to Rick March's testimony and found what he was looking for. When the lawyer asked March where he'd pulled off the road with the flat, March answered, "Just past County Road Forty-two."

How had he identified the road without a sign? Remembered from ten years back when he'd lived there? Or was the sign there that day when he stopped? When had it gotten knocked down?

Vince reached for the phone, then realized it was four o'clock in the morning. Mayville wouldn't appreciate being wakened, and Vince couldn't afford to have the sheriff mad at him, too.

He got up and stretched. A few hours' sleep would help clear his head. He was going to need it. And he needed Beth Davies' cooperation, which he sure as hell didn't have now.

He went into the bedroom and managed to pull off his shoes before he fell across the bed. He was asleep in seconds.

CHAPTER THIRTY-ONE

Beth couldn't keep her gaze from sliding to Jenny's pale face. Her head was still on March's lap, and her breathing was so shallow and even, it was difficult to detect the rise and fall of her thin chest. March's arm lay across her shoulders, the blade of the knife in his hand partly covered by her hair.

Beth tried to keep the tremor from her voice. "What do you want?"

His mouth twisted. "I've got what I want. Now we're going to find out what you want."

"I—All I want is Jenny to be safe. Please don't hurt her. Let us go, and I won't tell anyone you were here."

"You already called the cops."

She trapped her lip between her teeth, not sure if he was guessing or had watched the house. "I was terrified when I discovered that Jenny was gone. I didn't know who took her." She swallowed rapidly to dislodge the lump in her throat. "I didn't know what to do."

"You told them you thought it was me took her, right?"

She nodded. If she kept him calm, she might be able to lure him away from Jenny so she could grab her. But then what? March had the car keys. The nearest cabin was half a mile away, and she had no guarantee anyone was there. *Think,* she commanded her fogged brain.

"What'd they say about me?"

Surprised by the question, she said, "Nothing. They didn't say anything."

He lifted the knife and pointed it at her. Jenny's hair fluttered across his knee. "Liar."

Keep him calm. "They asked questions."

"Like?"

"How well I knew you. Why I thought you'd take Jenny." She looked at the sleeping child. *Did I realize Jenny was the witness who could put you behind bars again . . . ?*

"They say I killed that Tustman bitch?" He tapped the knife on his knee absently, and each beat cut across Beth's view of Jenny like a windshield wiper.

She knew she was on dangerous ground. "They said they weren't sure." That wasn't quite accurate, but maybe it would keep him appeased.

"That jerk still sheriff?"

It took a moment for Beth to follow his thought leap. "Mayville? Yes. At least he was last I heard. I don't come to Pine Lake very often."

"Shame on you not visiting your momma regular. What kind of daughter are you?" His mouth curled in a mocking grin as he shifted Jenny's head and crossed his legs. When she didn't answer, he said, "I asked you, what kind of kid are you?"

She licked her dry lips. "How do you know about my mother?"

He moved so suddenly she jumped. His legs uncrossed and he leaned forward, covering Jenny's face, and stabbed the knife toward Beth.

"You don't ask me questions, hear? You answer!"

She fought for control. "I'm a good daughter. My mother had a bad stroke. She's in a nursing home. She doesn't know me when I go to see her. They take good care of her there. She's been sick a long time. If she—If anything happens, they'll call me."

He watched her with a narrow gaze. "You love her?"

"Yes, of course."

"Was she good to you when you were a kid?"

What was he getting at? Beth wanted desperately to tell him whatever he wanted to know, but his questions kept throwing her off balance. "She took good care of me."

"But was she good to you? You know, did she hold you and read to you, stuff like that?"

Sorrow filled Beth as she remembered the loneliness that had plagued her growing-up years. Her mother had become less demonstrative with each passing year as she concentrated more on surviving her husband's rages than comforting her child. Their roles had reversed, the mother becoming the child, and the child the comforter. March was still watching her.

"She did when I was small, but not much later. My father drank a lot. He made our lives miserable."

March's scowl eased, and Beth knew she had passed some kind of test he'd devised.

"The kids at school used to talk about your old man," he said. "He was the town drunk. He wouldn't let you go anywhere. You always had to go home right after school to help your ma."

Her cheeks warmed. Even after all this time, the hurt wanted to surface, but Madelaine had taught her to fight it. *You can't remember pain, Beth. You can only remember that it hurt. And like all memories, even that will fade with time. You don't have to be angry anymore unless you choose to. When you forgive yourself for your anger at your parents, you'll be able to forgive them too.*

Beth's glance fell to the knife, still much too close to Jenny. She raised her eyes and met March's. "My mother had all she could do to survive," she told him. "She was never a strong person, and she didn't get any stronger as the years went by. I pretty much took care of her from the time I was eight or nine."

"Yeah?" Something changed in his expression, but it was undefinable. She nodded. "You must have thrown a party when your old man croaked," he said.

She wasn't shocked. "I was relieved," she admitted. She hadn't cried at the funeral. She hadn't felt anything, no pain, no joy, only a lightness of being at knowing her life had changed finally. She had wished him gone so many times, the actuality was almost too good to be true.

Like Jenny? The thought popped into her head so suddenly, she glanced at her sleeping child. Madelaine thought Jenny felt guilty because she had wished her daddy gone. *So natural for a child*—She wanted to take Jenny in her arms and hold her tight. The sky outside the open door had paled, and light reflected off the surface of the lake like a sheet of glass. In the easing gloom, she saw again how pale Jenny was.

"What did you give her?" she asked March, nodding toward the sleeping child.

"She's okay."

"Please, tell me what you gave her. I've never seen her sleep like this. I'm worried."

"Just one Red. It won't hurt her."

A red? Street talk for a sleeping pill. She prayed he was right, but she couldn't help thinking what the vet had said about Baron.

"You tell anyone you were coming here?" he asked.

The impulse to pretend help wasn't far away was overwhelming, but she shook her head. If he thought the police were coming, he might decide to run. Here she was on familiar ground and might have a chance to escape. March hadn't spent as much time up here as she had. He knew the cabin, but she was sure she knew the woods and roads better than he did. It was a slight advantage. He was looking at her so intently, she wondered what he was thinking.

"No," she said honestly. "I didn't remember the cabin until after the district attorney left." She wished she had told them. Or even Vince Norris. Instead, no one had a clue that she was here.

A flicker of surprise crossed March's face. "Ondavin? The bastard himself is checking me out?" He laughed as if she'd told him a great joke.

She'd been too upset to think of anything but Jenny at the time, but now she realized it was unusual for the D.A. of another county to question her personally. Obviously volunteering the information had gained her a bit of March's trust.

March looked out the open door. "It's getting light. I'm hungry. There's a bag of stuff in the bedroom. Get it."

Her knees were wobbly when she stood, but she was glad to move. With a quick glance at Jenny, she hurried into the bedroom where she found a paper sack on the chair in the corner. An empty beer can sat beside it. She looked around for something she could use as a weapon. Nothing in sight. The closet? The hinges squeaked faintly when she opened the door.

"Get away from there!" he yelled.

She gave the dark, empty interior a quick glance, then backed away and carried the bag to him. The piece of glass in her pocket would have to do. She'd have to pick her time carefully. She wouldn't get a second chance.

"That wasn't smart, Liz. You try anything again, and I'll hurt the kid. I don't want to, but I will. Don't push me."

"I'm sorry."

"Put it down. Over here." He patted the cushion beside him.

She put the bag down and reached out to touch Jenny's face, but March slapped her hand away. She stepped back.

"I told you, don't push me. You don't do nothing unless I say it's okay, you got that?" When she nodded mutely, he said, "Go sit down."

She backed to the chair. The sharp point of glass in her pocket pricked her thigh as she sat down. She gave a startled wince, but March seemed not to notice. She had to remember she was dealing with a killer, not the rebellious high school kid she'd known years ago. She couldn't afford to forget again.

He reached into the sack and took out a can of beer. When he popped the pull tab, foam bubbled out and ran down the side of the can and across his hand. Some dripped onto Jenny's hair as he took a long swallow and licked his lips. He balanced the can on the arm of the sofa so he could reach into the bag again without putting down the knife. He brought out a box of sugar-covered donuts and tore it open. He took one and left the box in his lap. Taking almost half the donut in one bite, he alternated chewing with swallows of beer. Powdered sugar sprinkled his shirt front.

His mouth full, he said, "Want some?"

Beth shook her head. Her throat was so tight she'd never be able to swallow. She hoped eating would settle him down again. It had been a mistake to reach for Jenny the way she did. If she didn't make any unexpected moves, maybe he'd stay calm. If she could keep him talking, maybe she could figure out what his plan was. If he was going to kill her the way he had Suzie, wouldn't he have done it already? He said Jenny was his insurance. For what? Flight? Was she a hostage to insure his safe passage to wherever he wanted to go? But why was he sitting here? Why hadn't he run as soon as he had Jenny? Why not take the Honda and make a run for it now?

He demolished two more donuts and started on a second can of beer, all the while never relaxing his grip on the knife. So close to Jenny, it was a powerful threat that kept Beth from doing anything. In a peculiar way, she was almost glad. He was forcing her to think rationally.

Did anyone else know about the cabin? People in Pine Lake, or at least they did years ago when Rick March was caught here and arrested. After all this time, would anyone make the connection? Vince Norris had, but he had no idea this cabin existed. Everyone else would figure March to run as fast and as far as possible.

The only one who might start adding up the past and present was Sheriff Mayville. He'd been a hero when March was caught and arrested before he got out of town after Gil's murder. The popularity had made him a sure bet for re-election this year until now, but heroes played second string to scapegoats. She was sure people in Pine Lake blamed him now for March being out of prison and, no matter how indirectly, for Suzie's death. Mayville would search the past, present and future for connections. He might remember the cabins on Sullivan Road and check them. For a moment, her hopes climbed, then fell. Mayville probably had checked the cabins right after Suzie's murder, but he wouldn't think of it now when everyone believed March was in L.A.

Dawn crested the ridge behind the cabin and poured light across the stretch of yard leading to the bank. Through the open doorway, Beth saw the dark hulk of March's car under the collapsed gazebo. It was tilted at an odd angle with the back wheels over the bank. If it had gone all the way over, she might have gotten away if March had gone down to check it.

March tore open a bag of potato chips. Her stomach heaved uncomfortably at the thought of his junk food diet. It seemed to be all he had, and she wondered if he had planned to feed Jenny the same stuff. Maybe she should offer to fix coffee. She'd seen a jar of instant when she pretended to look for the peroxide. The propane would be turned off at the tank, but she knew how to turn it on.

Maybe it would be better to let him keep drinking beer. Alcohol would make him sleepy. Even on a beer binge, her father used to fall into a dead stupor eventually. It might take a lot to produce a reaction in March, and there was always the possibility he'd get mean first, like her father always had.

She cleared her throat nervously. "I could make coffee. There's some instant in the kitchen."

He shoved a handful of chips in his mouth and chewed noisily. "You said there's no water."

"Oh. I forgot."

"You lying? Or maybe you want to go borrow some from a neighbor?"

"No. I forgot, really I did. I'm sorry."

"Go get some from the lake."

"The lake?"

"Sure. You boil it, it ain't going to kill you. Find a pot in the kitchen."

She was sorry she'd mentioned it. She was afraid to leave Jenny alone with him.

"Go on," he ordered.

She got up and went to the kitchen. She found a teakettle and carried it back through the living room. March watched her go out. She ran down the slope and around the crushed gazebo to the stairs leading down to the lake.

The car hung precariously over the edge of the bank, the front end caught in the foundation of the gazebo, and the rear end suspended over the steps. Clutching the handrail, she went down as fast as she dared. The wooden steps were old and dry. If one snapped, she could break a leg. Her heart thumped nervously as she squeezed past the wheel of the car.

The narrow, rocky beach was tangled with saw grass, and a dilapidated dock stuck out from the shore like a broken Tinker Toy construction. She made her way onto it and knelt to scoop water into the kettle. Her reflection wavered in the widening ripples she created, giving her a grotesque, misshapen body as she got to her feet. She made her way back to the steps and started up. Cold water sloshed from the kettle and soaked her sandal.

She was halfway up when she heard the whine and cough of a car engine as it hummed to life. The Honda! Dropping the kettle, she leaped the stairs two at a time, pushing past the car so fast it teetered dangerously. Her breath came out as a ragged scream.

"Jenny!"

CHAPTER THIRTY-TWO

Vince woke with a crick in his neck. Glancing at the clock, he reached for the phone so he could catch Mayville before he left home. The sheriff wasn't happy.

"What is it now, Norris?"

"March grabbed Beth Davies' kid last night."

"I heard."

"Any idea why?"

Mayville snorted. "To get to Liz Husby, or Beth Davies as you call her. Why else?"

"She was right there in the house. He could have gotten her just as easily as the kid." Vince gave a brief account of the events of the previous night. "So you tell me why he didn't wait for her to come inside, kill her and take off for parts unknown. He would have had a hell of a head start. It was an hour before I got back from the vet's."

"You knew all along where she was," Mayville said with an edge in his voice. "Why didn't you tell me you're on such good terms with her?"

"I'm not. She blames me for leading March to her."

"Did you?"

"Hell, no. March found her on his own. Somebody in Pine Lake must have told him she was in L.A."

The sheriff was quiet a moment, then said, "Could be Jack mentioned it to Suzie. March could have gotten the information from her."

Vince plunged on. "I read the trial transcript last night, Sheriff."

"So?"

"Suzie said she went to your office the day of the murder to report a road sign that had been knocked down."

"I don't rightly recall. I was pretty busy."

"*The County Road 42 sign.* That's the road the Tustmans live on, isn't it?"

"Yeah. Jack persuaded the county to cut it through when he bought the Jepson farm and began subdividing."

Vince felt a surge of excitement. "When was that, Sheriff?"

"Oh, 'bout four, five years ago. Around the time he set his sights on Suzie and decided to remodel the old farmhouse out there for himself."

"Where was the sign? I don't remember seeing one the night I drove out there."

"It's not there anymore. Damned kids swiped them as fast as we put them up. It started as an initiation prank at one of the clubs in the high school. Caught on. The damned things got more popular than Elvis sightings. The county billed us for them, so we quit putting them up. Ain't but three houses out there."

"When was that?"

"Year ago."

"After Gil Husby's murder?"

"Yeah. You getting at something, Norris?"

"Rick March testified he pulled off the road just past County Road 42. How'd he know that without a sign? You say the road didn't exist when he lived there as a kid. Suzie testified that Jack told her the sign was gone when he came home after lunch that day. What time would that be? One? Two? Husby was killed a little after three. When was the sign there and when wasn't it?"

The silence lengthened. Finally the sheriff said, "I don't

know, but I'm going to find out. I always thought Suzie's story was a little bit too smooth."

"Could March have been with her?"

"I'm not ready to say that, but he killed Gil Husby, sign or no sign."

"Sure, but why, Sheriff?"

"Keep in touch, Norris."

Vince was listening to an empty line. He glanced at the clock and decided to shower and shave before he called Beth.

Ted Fischer's voice on the answering machine asked him to leave a message after the beep. Vince waited, then said, "Beth, if you're monitoring calls, please pick up. It's Vince Norris." There was no response. "Beth? I need to talk to you. Come on, pick up." Still nothing. "I called the vet and Baron is doing okay. He's still groggy, but he's going to be all right."

When that didn't bring her to the phone, he hung up, wondering where the hell she was. Could the cops have taken her in? Was there a break in the story he didn't know about? If March had been caught, Mayville would have heard. Still . . .

He dialed the paper. The day shift was just coming on, and he had to wait for someone to locate the managing editor.

"Vince Norris, Ed. The Rick March story. Someone snatched the little Davies girl last night. March is the number one suspect."

"I saw the story you called in last night. Good work."

Norris allowed himself a grin. "The D.A. from Kings County has taken over the case and the F.B.I. may be in it by now too. I'm going to Pine Lake. I've got an inside track with the sheriff and a new lead."

"We've got an exclusive so far. Let's keep it that way. Be in touch before the early edition."

"You got it. Listen, the mother isn't answering her phone. I'm going to check it out. Have someone keep an eye on the wire. If anything breaks, make sure I'm called, okay?"

"Yeah. And don't forget, the early edition."

"Right. Thanks, Ed."

He hung up and tried Beth Davies again, but she still didn't pick up. He decided to drive up there. The worst she could do was tell him to beat it.

When he rang the bell, there was no sound to indicate she was inside. The red light glowed on the security panel showing it was set. Not satisfied, Vince drove to the top of the hill and parked in the turn-around. Pocketing his keys, he walked past Amos Westerland's place and down the steps to Fischers' side gate, which was still standing open. He made his way along the back of the house and peered through the glass at the empty living room and kitchen. The door was locked. So was the one in the bedroom, but the drape was still hooked back over the chair the way it was last night. The bedroom was empty. He could see a slice of the den opposite the open door, but there was no sign of her there either. He rapped on the glass. Where the hell was she? Uneasy, he went back to the car and drove down to the house, where he copied down the name of the security company from the sign pounded into the bank of ivy.

Down the hill, he drove to the apartment complex where Beth lived. She didn't answer the bell, and as far as he could tell, the drapes were still drawn at the windows. His next stop was the Hollywood Police Division. Detective

Atkins was at his desk. He looked as if he hadn't slept.

"Hi, Steve. Where's Beth Davies?"

"You the new police commissioner, Norris?"

"She's not at the house or her apartment."

"Tell me something I don't know."

Vince heard the weariness in his voice. "Didn't you put a man up there to keep an eye on her?"

"Last I heard, the Kings County D.A. and the state police were in charge. You working for them?"

"I was just up at the house. There's no sign of her. Who's got her hidden and where?"

Atkins leaned back and stretched his shoulders. "The state boys think you do. They want to talk to you."

"Didn't they have anyone watching her?"

Atkins flashed a tired grin. Someone had goofed, but he was clear of the fallout. "They parked a man at the bottom of the road. He wasn't expecting her to drive down."

Vince swore. "She drove off alone?"

"It looks that way. The guy called in when the car went by, but by the time they had a make on the plate, she was long gone. The guy tried to follow her, but he made a few zigs when he should have zagged and got lost in the maze. Dumb ass should have left himself a trail of bread crumbs. They've got a bulletin out."

Vince slapped his hand on the desk and turned away.

"Hold it, Norris. They want to talk to you."

"Tell them I'll be at the paper or my apartment." He kept walking, and Atkins didn't stop him. Unbelievable, bloody unbelievable screw-up. Talk about too many badges on the scene. The jerk stationed up there last night probably had ten pictures of March lined up on his dashboard but had no idea what Beth looked like. Great. It was a small consolation to know she'd taken off under her own power, but what made her bolt? And where the hell had she gone?

He used his cell phone to dial the number he copied from the security sign. The woman who answered the phone was polite but firm, and she wouldn't give him the time of day about a customer. Frustrated, he called the police division he'd just left and asked for Atkins.

"Thanks for not holding me, Steve."

"Don't push your luck, Norris. Where are you?"

"A pay phone. Listen, Beth set the security system on the house before she left. That means she still feels responsible for the place. She's the type to honor her promise to the letter if she can. I have a hunch she called the security outfit to let them know she was leaving. They told me to get lost when I called. You've got clout. They'd tell you."

"And I'll tell you, right?"

"I'd appreciate it."

After a moment, Atkins said, "What the hell, give me their number and call me back in ten minutes."

Vince called back in ten minutes. Beth had told the security operator the dog was at the vet's, and she was leaving. She didn't say where she was going.

"Has the FBI come into the picture yet?"

"On the way."

Time was running out. "Is her phone tapped yet?"

Atkins didn't answer.

"Okay, Steve, thanks. Look, I'm going to check out a couple of things. I'll call you later."

"I want to know where you are."

"I'm headed for the office if anyone asks."

"Why do I have the feeling you're cooperating too easily?"

"Cops get paid to be suspicious. Trust me."

"The last time I swallowed that line, I wound up paying alimony."

"How is Laura?"

"Richer than I am."

Vince laughed. "I'll be in touch. Thanks, Steve."

"Yeah."

Vince headed for Creative Color Graphics on Sunset Boulevard. The girl behind the counter upstairs was the one he had asked about Beth three days ago. She recognized him.

"Did you ever introduce yourself to Beth?" she asked with frank curiosity.

"Matter of fact, I did." He put out his hand. "I'm Vince Norris."

"Kim Hartman." Her smile vanished. "You're the reporter who wrote the story about Jenny in this morning's paper. Is it true?"

"Yeah."

"God, how awful!"

"Is Beth here?"

"No. She didn't come in. I tried calling her, but I get someone's machine. Do you have the number at the place where she's staying?" She looked so worried, Vince felt sorry for her.

"Her calls are being forwarded."

"She must be frantic."

"Listen, does she have a boyfriend or someone she'd go to?"

"She doesn't have a guy. I'm always telling her to get out more. I don't know about any of her other friends."

"Anyone she talks about a lot?"

Kim frowned. "Why are you asking? She's not—She's not gone too?"

236

"No, nothing like that. I just need to talk to her as soon as possible. Can you think of anyone?"

Kim shook her head, then said, "The only person she mentions is her therapist."

"Know the name?"

"Madelaine."

"That's all?"

"I'm afraid so."

Even if he could track down a therapist named Madelaine, she'd hit him with that patient confidentiality crap.

"Look, if she calls, tell her to get in touch with me, will you? Tell her to call the paper. They'll put her through to me.

"You see her, tell her how sorry I am—we all are. If there's anything I can do—"

Back in the car, Vince drummed his fingers on the steering wheel. Where would Beth Davies go at two in the morning? He should have asked Atkins when the tap went on her phone. He wanted to eliminate the possibility she'd gotten a call from March and gone to meet him. Somehow he didn't think she'd be dumb enough to do that without backup. He should have camped out up there and kept an eye on her himself.

Where did she go? Her world was pretty limited. The apartment, the studio, the Fischer house, Pine Lake . . . No relatives and only a handful of friends. He reviewed the list, discarded it, then retrieved it when he realized the only possibility he hadn't checked: Pine Lake. She knew it better than Los Angeles when it came right down to it. He himself had proposed the theory that March would head that way. But where up there would she go?

It was time to talk to Mayville again, but Beth had a hell of a head start going north. Vince started the car and headed for the airport.

CHAPTER THIRTY-THREE

She raced up the steps, hitting the car wheel as she tried to veer past it. The motion made the car tilt against the stair rail, and the dry wood creaked and split with a loud crack. Off balance, she stumbled and sprawled headlong over the top step. Slivers pierced her palms as her chin slammed against the ground. The shard of glass in her pocket shattered, and a piece stabbed into her groin. She stumbled to her feet as the car shifted again, and the stair rail creaked ominously. She raced in blind panic toward the driveway, screaming.

"Jenny! Jenny!"

She saw the Honda coming up around the curve. *Toward* her, not away! For a moment, her momentum carried her directly at it until she realized that March wasn't going to stop. She leaped out of the car's path, but not fast enough. The fender hit her hip. A stunning pain shot through her back. She fell against the passenger side window and pounded it with her fists. March laughed. Too late, she realized Jenny wasn't in the car.

She wheeled and raced for the cabin. March gunned the engine, and the car jumped forward. The wheels sent up a cloud of dust that blinded her. She coughed and rubbed her eyes without slowing down, but when she reached the clearing, the car was already parked. March was loping toward the front door of the cabin, jangling her keys and laughing. Why hadn't she checked the house first? She could have grabbed Jenny and run into the woods. By the time March got back, they could have hidden or gone to the next cabin for help.

Beth realized she was crying. He had outsmarted her. He was counting on her reacting from gut level panic if she thought he was leaving with Jenny. She had played right into his hands. Now he still had Jenny, and all she had were bloody hands and smarting eyes.

I won't underestimate him again, she vowed as she climbed the two steps to the front door. He was sitting on the sofa with Jenny's head in his lap as if he had never stirred.

"Where's the water for the coffee?" he asked with a grin.

Not trusting her voice, she turned and walked back toward the lake. It took her several minutes to spot where the kettle had landed. It was too far to reach from the steps. For a moment she considered going back for another pan, but she didn't trust herself to face March yet. She had to be thinking clearly and be alert in case another opportunity to escape presented itself or she could create one.

She emptied the broken glass out of her pocket. Blood had seeped through her slacks, but she barely felt the cut. With an apprehensive glance at the car which had settled on the broken railing, she moved past cautiously until she was across from the kettle. She sat down, slid under the railing and dropped to the bank. Her sandals skidded on the dry, loose soil. To keep from plummeting down the bank, she grabbed a post that was split to a dangerous bow. Overhead, the car teetered like a sword of Damocles. She prayed it wouldn't break loose. She sat, still clinging to the post, and moved sideways until she could grab the kettle. The post creaked with an ominous sound as her weight pulled at it. The car rocked dangerously. Afraid the dry wood was giving way, Beth let go and slid the rest of the way down the bank. She landed with a soft thud on the narrow strip of sand behind the rocky shoreline. The car settled on the groaning rail again like a huge vulture.

Beth ran to the end of the dock and looked along the shore. The cabins she remembered had vanished behind the thick growth of trees. The placid lake was empty, no boats or early fishermen. Across the two-mile stretch of water, the opposite shore was a dark, impenetrable blur.

Too frightened for Jenny to delay any longer, Beth knelt on the weathered wood to wash the grime and blood from her hands before she rinsed and filled the kettle. As long as March was holding Jenny, there wasn't any way to escape. He was dangerous and unpredictable. The very thought of him and Jenny alone in the cabin gave her chills.

She went back up the stairs and held her breath as she edged past the hovering car. Her pulse raced as she hurried across the clearing and up the front steps. He must have been listening for her return. He came out of the bedroom as she came in. He was holding a rifle and two boxes of ammunition! Where had they come from? Beth's heart locked in a painful spasm.

March looked cocky. "Can you imagine that stupid jerk not taking his gun when he closed the place up? It was still up in the attic crawl space where he kept it ten years ago. Jerk." He sat on the sofa and opened the box of ammunition to load the gun. Then raising it, he sighted along the barrel at her.

"You going to stand there all day, or are you going to make that coffee?"

She moved numbly toward the kitchen. "I'll have to go out and turn on the propane tank."

"You know how to do that?" He sounded suspicious.

She nodded. "I used to open up and clean cabins for summer people."

"Yeah, that's right. I forgot you used to work for these jerks. Okay, but no funny stuff." He motioned with the gun.

In the kitchen, she put the kettle on a burner and opened a cupboard. March appeared in the doorway instantly, the gun in his hands. "What are you looking for?" he demanded.

"Matches," she said. She picked up a book to show him.

His eyes narrowed. "Don't you think you ought to turn on the gas first?"

She nodded and went out, noticing another large shard as she stepped over the broken glass. The weather and long disuse had frozen the shut-off valve on the tank. She found a tattered rag stuck behind the gauge and wrapped it around the handle, then picked up a rock from the edge of the carport and banged the valve until it loosened. When she had it open all the way, she shoved the rag into her pocket.

Inside, she turned on the gas and waited for the propane to come through the line before she struck a match. The jet flared, and she put the kettle over it. March was still watching her from the doorway, and she pretended complete concentration in getting down two mugs and spooning instant coffee into them.

She'd always been afraid of guns, and the one March was holding terrified her. Why had he gone for it now? Steam poured from the kettle spout. She turned off the burner, filled the cups and asked March if he wanted sugar.

"Yeah. Two spoons. See if they have any of that cream stuff."

She opened another cupboard and found some. She stirred some into his mug and turned to hand it to him. He backed up two steps.

"Put it there on the counter," he told her. "I don't trust

241

you." She did, and he picked it up. "Now you pick yours up nice and slow and go sit in that chair over there." He pointed to a chair too far from the sofa for her to throw the cup and scald him with the hot coffee.

She did as she was told. March settled beside Jenny again. The child stirred restlessly, and Beth tensed. March glanced at the sleeping child lying in the path of light spilling through the open doorway.

"I told you she was okay," he said. "It's probably the best night's sleep she's had since her old man croaked."

His casual reference to the man he'd murdered caught Beth by surprise. She held the mug in front of her face to disguise the contempt she felt for March. She fastened her gaze on Jenny. Was she waking up? Her eyes fluttered but stayed shut as March settled back with his coffee and another donut. He didn't offer Beth one this time.

"Why did you come here?" Beth asked in what she hoped was a normal, conversational tone.

March glanced around. "I like it here. Don't you remember we talked about this place? You still got that picture you were drawing of it that day back in school?"

Surprised that he remembered, she said, "No. My father burned all my drawings one night when he was drunk."

"Christ, what a jerk. What'd you do about it?"

"Nothing. I was used to it."

He snorted. "No wonder he got away with so much crap." He was angry, even though he'd never known her father. "You have to show people they can't get away with stuff like that."

Like Suzie? Beth swallowed. "What could I do? I was only a kid."

He snorted again. "When I was ten, the guy in the foster home I was in was a drunk like your old man. He used to

242

beat the crap out of me just for exercise. I got pretty sick of it, so I started pouring his booze into pop bottles and selling it to the kids at school. I filled up his bottles with tea and wood alcohol." He gave a nasty laugh. "He never knew the difference. Drank the stuff like it was bottled in bond. The scum bag never even wondered why his bottle was always full."

"What happened to him?" she asked to keep him talking.

"He got too sick to hit me anymore. He croaked a few weeks later."

Beth stiffened. Wood alcohol was poisonous. March had killed someone at the age of *ten*. He shifted the rifle on his knees.

"Another place, the lazy slut used to lock me in the closet so she wouldn't have to watch me. I was five. Can you beat it? Five, and too much for her to bother with. She had a bit part in a movie once and thought she was a star. All she did all day was dress up in clothes she was too fat for and sit in front of the mirror or outside in the back yard. Working on her tan, she called it. Her two kids were a couple of scared rabbits who wouldn't say boo. She hated us all. She took foster kids for the dough. Her own two must have been accidents. I set fire to her closet one day when she was stretched out in the sun." He laughed. "You should have seen old tubby trying to stomp out the flames and bawling and screaming while all that crap went up in smoke."

Beth stared. He was a monster. Revenge was his solution to any injustice. There was a time when she would have felt sorry for him, but now his revenge was directed at her. He had killed Gil and Suzie. She was next, but he hadn't finished tormenting her yet. He'd found her most vulnerable spot the same way he had with those foster parents.

Jenny flung out an arm and stirred again. March looked down as she turned her head. Her damp hair clung to her cheek. Her eyes opened and seemed to be looking right at Beth, but there was no recognition in them. The stare was vacant, the terrible empty look she'd retreated behind after Gil's death. Frightened, Beth put down her coffee mug and started to get up. March swung the rifle around toward her.

"Let me hold her," Beth pleaded.

"Sit down."

She sank back into the chair. Jenny lay silent and withdrawn. Lost. Beth summoned all her willpower to fight the tears that warmed her eyes lest they goad March into further cruelty.

When she finally had control of herself again, she said, "How long are we going to stay here?"

"You should know."

"I don't."

"I've got a score to settle with that S.O.B. sheriff. I should shoot up the whole damned town. They were all against me. Not one of them ever gave me a chance." He looked at her. "Except maybe you. You were the only one who talked to me and wasn't after something. I sure as hell was surprised when that guy turned out to be your husband. Too bad. You never would have gotten mixed up in this."

She had trouble following him. Their high school days and the time of Gil's death seemed to have merged in his mind. The only glimmer of hope was that he wasn't lumping her together with the townspeople.

She said, "I had to testify; the district attorney subpoenaed me. I didn't have a choice. I only told the truth."

His face twisted. "None of the others did," he said. "Lying didn't bother them any. How come you were different?"

She didn't know what to say. He went on, as if he hadn't expected an answer.

"I thought about it a lot in prison. You got plenty of time to think when you're doing time." He finished his coffee and put the cup on the end table. "Truth is what I say it is. Evidence is something they make up for court."

"That's not so."

He laughed. "You don't get it, do you?"

"Get what? I don't know what you mean. I told the truth in court. You never denied being in Gil's office or running down those stairs the way you did. That's all I testified to."

His expression was a curious mix of scorn and amusement. "Two people tell the truth, and what they say makes all the other lies true. That's justice for you, huh?"

She was confused again, but talking seemed to be relaxing him. The rifle lay across his knees, the butt end toward Jenny, the barrel pointed toward the kitchen. Dust motes floated in the light from the two open doors. Jenny's eyes were open, but her face was as blank as a wax mold. March had plunged Jenny back into the twilight world from which she had just begun to emerge. Rage began to build in Beth's heart again.

CHAPTER THIRTY-FOUR

Vince's hopes were higher than his expectations when he walked into the sheriff's office. During the flight to Bakersfield and the drive from the car rental place, he hadn't been able to come up with anything other than his gut feeling that the answer to the riddle of March's behavior lay in this town where so much of his trouble had started. Miriam looked up from the file drawer she was bending over.

"You're here early," she commented.

"Sheriff in?"

She glanced toward his closed office door. "He's on the phone. Has been since he got here."

"He's expecting me," Vince said and headed for the sheriff's office. Miriam's expression was full of curiosity, but she didn't ask questions.

The sheriff had the phone propped between his ear and his shoulder, his neck bent like a puppet with a broken string. He glanced at Vince without interrupting his conversation.

"Handle it quietly, Jerry. Last thing we need is people getting stirred up." He hung up and looked at Vince. "You didn't waste any time getting here."

"What did you find out about the sign?"

Mayville moved some papers around on his desk as if looking for something. "Sam Porter who lives at the end of the road says the sign was there at two o'clock. He came back from town about then and says he would have noticed if it was gone.

"Betty Hoffman, lives between Porter and Tustman,

246

didn't go out that day, so she can't say. Her husband was on the road and one of the kids was sick. She canceled her volunteer day at the library. Heard about the murder on the five o'clock news."

"Sam Porter—how sure is he?"

Mayville shrugged. "As sure as he can be after eighteen months, which is to say it would never stand up in court. We talked to him and Betty both right after the murder, but the question of the sign never came up then." He shifted the papers in front of him again and looked at Vince as though he was deciding how much he could trust him. "My deputy Jerry's boy is a senior at the high school. Jerry's asking him to check around, see if maybe that sign is in someone's Hall of Fame. If one of the kids took it the day of the murder, it had to be during lunch hour or after three, unless he was playing hooky."

Vince hadn't thought of that angle. The sheriff went up a notch in his estimation.

"Suzie Tustman's funeral is at one o'clock," Mayville said. He got to his feet and reached for his hat but didn't put it on. "According to Marian, Jack's sister's got him talked into going back to Illinois with her for a while. Thought maybe I'd have a few words with him first."

"Okay if I tag along?"

"I can't invite you into Jack's house if he doesn't want you."

"Why should he object?"

"I didn't say he would, but the man just lost his wife. He's entitled to some privacy."

"Sure. I'll drive my car over, just in case," Vince said and followed the sheriff out.

Jack Tustman's sister had taken on the role of mother

hen. She told Mayville in no uncertain terms that Jack was in no condition to talk about the murder or anything else. The sheriff was on the verge of making it official when Jack appeared behind his sister and told her it was all right. She gave in grudgingly and disappeared down the hall.

"Come in and sit. I don't have much time. We're leaving for the mortuary soon. It doesn't seem possible—" His voice broke, and he cleared his throat noisily. "You're coming to the service, aren't you, Sheriff?"

Mayville nodded and sat in a green print chair that made him look like a sapling smothered by foliage. He put the hat he'd taken off after the ten-step walk from the car to the front door on his lap.

"This is Vince Norris, works for the *L.A. Times*," Mayville said. "He's been following the case down there."

Tustman shook his head. "I have nothing to say for publication. This has all been too much. Sheriff—"

Vince hurried to reassure him. "Strictly off the record, Mr. Tustman. I'm only interested in seeing March caught."

Jack looked back at the sheriff. "Any news yet?"

"No sign of him in these parts, Jack."

"He's probably halfway across the country and still running, the bastard."

"I doubt that. He was in L.A. last night. Mr. Norris thinks he may be headed back this way."

Tustman's head came up sharply. "What the hell are you talking about? He'd be crazy to come back here. I swear, I'll blow his head off if I see him first."

"He's got Jenny Husby," the sheriff said quietly.

"What!" Tustman came halfway out of his chair then fell back with a confused look. "Got her? You mean kidnapped?"

"That's about the size of it," the sheriff said. "The Kings

248

County D.A. has taken over the case. Between him and the FBI, they should catch up with March soon."

Tustman looked from one to the other of them. "How did it happen?"

The sheriff bounced the ball into Vince's court with a nod.

"Somehow he found out Liz was living in L.A. as Beth Davies. He tracked her down and grabbed Jenny out of bed last night. He left the door open behind him and cut a telephone wire so there'd be no mistake about what happened, but no note with ransom demands or threats of any kind."

Tustman fingered the air nervously. "He cut phone wires when he broke into cabins around here. Remember, Sheriff? He bragged about it. Cocky little bastard."

The sheriff scowled at Vince. "You didn't tell me about the phone wire."

"I didn't know it meant anything until now. I'd say it ties all this together, wouldn't you?"

Tustman had been nervous and distraught since they got there, but now he seemed to be unraveling at the seams. "My God. Poor Liz. Is she okay? I'd better call her. She's been through so much." He shook his head. "But if he's got Jenny, like you say, why would he come back here? It'd be the last place on earth—I mean, everyone here would recognize him, especially if they saw him with Jenny. He'd be crazy—" He shifted his gaze from the sheriff to Vince.

"My theory is he needs a place to hole up," Vince said. "He knows this area better than any place else. He grew up in these parts. It makes sense to head somewhere he knows. He probably spent a lot of time in prison planning this. He's smart enough to figure once the Feds come into it, there'll be roadblocks and checkpoints if he tries to make a run for it. These foothills are only a couple of hours driving time from L.A. and he's tucked away before the manhunt begins. The idea would make a lot of sense to someone as crazy as March."

"I don't know," Tustman said, shaking his head as if it were too much to understand. "It would make more sense for him to head for the Mexican border and lose himself down there. But I appreciate your coming to tell me, Sheriff. If there's anything I can do, just let me know. March can't go back to prison fast enough to suit me, or better still, get himself gunned down in a shootout with the F.B.I. My sister wants me to go back to Illinois with her and Joe, but now with this—" He shook his head again. "I'm going to stay. Liz needs her friends more than ever."

"A couple more questions, Jack, and we'll get out of your hair. The day Gil died, what time was it you stopped home to pick up those papers?"

Tustman seemed to have trouble following the change of course before he said, "After lunch."

"What time would that have been, near as you can remember?"

Tustman smiled and frowned in the same expression. "I usually go to lunch at twelve-thirty, except for Rotary days it's noon. You know that, Bill." It was the first time Vince had heard anyone call the sheriff by his given name. It suited him almost as poorly as his hat. "Why do you ask?"

"Just trying to set things in order in my head," Mayville said. He flipped his hand as if it didn't matter. "One more. I know for a fact you kept in touch with Liz when she moved to L.A., what with her momma in the nursing home and all. Did Suzie know the address?"

"No. What are you getting at?"

"Now don't get me wrong, Jack. I'm just trying to put things in place. Somehow March found out where Liz and

Jenny were. If Suzie knew, he could have forced her to tell him."

Tustman's face twisted in an agonized expression. He stared at the floor. "When Liz moved away, I kept in touch so we could handle the house sale, signing papers and depositing checks and that sort of thing. I have her address and phone number in my Rolodex at the office. Not her name, mind you, only initials. Liz wanted to cut all her ties with folks here. I can't blame her for that." He looked up. "Suzie comes—came to the office a lot. She could have figured out who B.D. was."

The sheriff nodded.

"That bastard must have forced her to tell." Tustman's voice cracked. He buried his face in his hands.

"That's the way we figure it, Jack. Nobody's blaming Suzie, though, so set your mind to rest on that."

Tustman wiped his eyes before he lifted his head. "Thanks, Bill. I loved that woman. I don't know how I'm going to go on." He looked away.

"We'll be leaving now, Jack. I appreciate your time. Get some rest."

Jack walked them to the door and shook hands with both of them. When Vince glanced at the rearview mirror as he pulled away, the front door was closed. At the bottom of the drive, Vince motioned the sheriff over and pulled up beside him. He rolled down the window and leaned out.

"I've got to check in with my paper, Sheriff. I'll be at the Sunset Motel if you need to get in touch. I'll see you at the funeral. Maybe your deputy will have something on the sign by then."

The sheriff nodded, rolled up his window and left a faint trail of blue exhaust as he pulled away. Vince waited for his car to be out of sight before he turned in the opposite direction. He drove a couple of hundred yards and pulled off the road to watch the intersection where Tustman would have to come out. Despite the temperature that was climbing as the morning sun crested the tops of the tree line, he opened the window and turned off the engine. He settled down to wait.

CHAPTER THIRTY-FIVE

Ten minutes later, the blue Oldsmobile that had been in Tustman's garage came down the drive and turned on the highway toward Vince. He slid down in the seat until it passed, then started the engine as the Olds disappeared on the highway ahead of him. Jack Tustman was alone. Not headed for the funeral home either, that was clear.

Vince pulled out to follow. A warning buzz had gone off in his head while he and the sheriff were talking to Tustman. He still wasn't sure what it was, but the expression on Tustman's face when they told him Jenny had been kidnapped was startling. Tustman had looked terrified. For Jenny? Possible, Vince supposed, but he remembered the stricken look on Beth's face when her child vanished. Somehow the two didn't equate.

Following the Oldsmobile became a game of tag on the curving mountain road. Vince sped up each time the Olds vanished around a curve, then fell back on the straight stretches. He thought he had lost the other car when it wasn't in sight when he came out of a sharp S-turn. He slowed to look for a turn-off, then hit the brake when he saw a faint haze of dust fanning the trees on the right where a narrow gravel road wound through the trees. Vince cut the wheel sharply.

A sign nailed to a tree said *SULLIVAN ROAD*. It climbed gradually, curving toward the west as it reached higher ground. The air was so still, the dust from Tustman's car settled slowly and left an easy trail to follow.

Vince kept his speed down so he wouldn't come upon the Oldsmobile unexpectedly.

Despite his precautions, he came upon the Olds parked at the side of the road so suddenly he swore as he hit the brake. The car was empty, and Tustman wasn't in sight. The only place he could have gone unless he cut off into the woods was a narrow driveway on the left side of the road. Vince backed around the curve and parked, then went to check out the driveway.

It was overgrown with weeds that had recently been crushed in parallel tracks by a car. There were some other scuffed places including one at the side where it looked as if someone had plowed through the brush.

Vince ran back to the car for the binoculars he'd put in the glove compartment, then he started up the drive. He walked cautiously and stopped to listen frequently, but all he heard were occasional birds and the shrill drone of cicadas announcing the heat. The drive rose steeply from the road, the kind that wasn't expected to be shoveled in winter. Higher in the mountains above the snow line, it would be a toboggan run.

When the drive angled sharply, he saw blue sky of a clearing ahead. The air was faintly cooler and had the fresh smell of water. A lake. There were dozens of them around here, summer havens for city people who could afford to get away. And small town folks like Tustman, too? A few hours before his wife's funeral?

Vince stepped off the rutted trail into the cover of trees. The cabin would be there in the clearing. He didn't want to come upon it suddenly as he had the Olds. What would bring Tustman up here only a few hours before his wife's funeral? A mistress? The need to be alone for awhile? Business? He could have a perfectly valid reason for being here, but Vince was betting it was more than that.

He looked around for someplace where he could have a look at the clearing. A few feet ahead of him, a swath of felled saplings and brush cut toward the lake. Tire tracks came from the clearing as if someone had driven a vehicle right through the foliage. He examined the tracks. They were spaced like car tires, not a tractor or all terrain vehicle. Curious, he moved cautiously up the drive until he could see the cabin, then stepped behind a towering pine and lifted the binoculars.

The cabin was a dark color that blended with the thick stand of pines it was nestled in. All the shades were drawn, but the front door was standing open. There was no sign of Tustman.

The driveway ended at a carport. There was a blue car parked at an angle so he couldn't see the plates, but he recognized the lines of a Honda Civic. *Beth drove a blue Civic,* but then, so did thousands of other people in California. He trained the glasses on the license plate and turned the fine adjustment until he could make out the letters and numbers. It *was* Beth's car!

A movement behind the carport caught Vince's attention. He adjusted the glasses as he saw it again. Someone was hiding in the trees back there, watching the house the same way he was. Tustman? Was he spying or eavesdropping? The only way to find out what was going on was to get closer.

The ground underfoot was covered with tinder-dry pine needles and leaves that crunched at every step he took. He darted past several trees, then stopped to lift the binoculars again. There was no sign of life from the house, but Tustman, or whoever the other watcher was, was on the move, too. Vince saw him emerge from the woods and duck into the carport. He ran doubled over, but the light colored seersucker suit was a dead giveaway. It was Jack Tustman.

Vince tried to see what he was doing, but Tustman had ducked behind the Honda. Was Beth in there waiting for Tustman? If so, why didn't he go in? Wait a minute! What had Tustman said when Vince mentioned the cut phone wires—It was Rick March's trademark "when he broke into cabins around here." *This* cabin? Excitement made the blood ring in Vince's ears. Hot damn! This story was about to break! He stumbled back to the driveway and ran down to his car. He dialed the sheriff's number on his cell phone and told Miriam to connect him fast.

When Mayville came on the line, Vince blurted, "Listen, I haven't got much time. I followed Tustman to a cabin up on Sullivan Road."

"Norris, what the hell—"

"I don't have time to explain. Just get up here fast. I think March is here. Beth Davies too."

"Where are you?"

"I don't know. Maybe half, three-quarters of a mile in from the highway. You'll see my car. Tustman's, too. Right near the driveway to the cabin."

"Did you see the little girl?"

"No. Tustman is slinking around outside. I think he's going to try to go in there."

"Jesus! You wait there for me, understand?"

"Sure, Sheriff. I'm no hero. Make it snappy!"

Vince hung up and unlocked the trunk. Grabbing the Nikon he kept handy for emergencies, he ran back up the drive.

CHAPTER THIRTY-SIX

March caught his mind drifting and pulled it back sharply. He had to stay awake. Things were going to be happening fast before long. It would take that dim-witted sheriff a while to add up the score, but he'd do it eventually and head this way. And Liz was sitting there watching and waiting for the chance to try something. That trick she pulled with the car was pretty clever. Her spunk surprised him. She'd changed. Was it because she was a mother, or had getting away from this jerk-water town done it?

The warmth of the kid's head on his lap was relaxing. Her eyes were open, but she still seemed pretty much out of it. She was probably still feeling the effects of the downer, or maybe she was hiding inside her head, shutting the world out like he used to do when he was a kid. She hadn't made a peep since he took her out of her bed. The rifle slid on his knees, and he shifted it so it wouldn't fall against her.

He looked at Liz. He felt sorry for her. She wanted to hold the kid so bad, she was having trouble sitting still. He was tempted to talk to her again, but talking took his attention away from listening. He couldn't take the chance. Not now.

He reached for a donut, then realized the box was empty. He was still hungry. He had polished off everything he bought last night. He wondered if there was any canned stuff in the cupboards, but he didn't want to watch Liz fix anything now, and he sure as hell couldn't trust her in there alone. He'd been hungry before. He'd live. There would be plenty of time to eat when this was over.

He studied Liz through half-closed eyes. She was prettier now than she used to be. He remembered the day he stopped to talk to her when she was drawing a picture of this cabin. She had looked scared to death, like he was accusing her of stealing something. He figured she was afraid he was going to ask her to that stupid dance everyone was excited about. Fat chance. Her old man would never let her go. Rick wasn't going either. He didn't know how to dance, and the only clothes he had were the ratty jeans he wore to school. Besides, he didn't want any attachments. He liked Liz well enough, but he already knew he wasn't going to hang around Pine Lake long.

Liz's gaze darted to the kitchen so suddenly, he tensed. His hand tightened around the rifle as he looked at the part of the front yard he could see outside the open door. Nothing moved in the baking sun, and all he heard was the racket of those damned bugs.

The doorway to the kitchen was on his left about two feet past the end of the sofa. He couldn't see the side door, but Liz could. She must have spotted something. She was watching him so intently now, it was a dead giveaway. He kept his face blank so she wouldn't know she had already tipped him off. He fine-tuned his hearing to catch any new sound. It wouldn't be long now. He slipped his finger onto the trigger.

There. He heard it that time. A faint crackle . . . A footstep on the dry ground. She heard it too. In spite of herself, her glance flicked toward the kitchen. It darted back to the hands in her lap so fast, he almost laughed.

His finger stroked the trigger of the rifle as he slipped his hand under the butt.

CHAPTER THIRTY-SEVEN

When March shifted the gun, Beth realized he'd heard the sound. He was on guard, but he didn't get up to look outside. It was almost as if he was expecting someone. An accomplice? Could he have contacted someone before he got here, maybe to bring a safe car or money for his flight? Or was he expecting someone else? He said he had a score to settle with "that stupid sheriff." Was he waiting for Mayville? My God, was he crazy enough to try to kill the sheriff?

Tension pulled at her jaw like a tightening wire. She shifted slightly in the chair so she could watch the kitchen more easily. She prayed that whoever was there had come to help her, not March. Did the person know March had a gun? There'd be shooting—She had to warn him that March had Jenny. She tried to coax saliva to her dry mouth.

The patch of light falling through the open kitchen door wasn't as bright as the one from the front because of the carport, but compared to the rest of the closed-up house, it was a beacon. Another faint noise made her stiffen, then a shadow fell across the path of light. She looked quickly at March and tried to distract him.

"Do you want more coffee?" She was astonished at how normal her voice sounded.

He shook his head and raised the gun slightly. Below the steel barrel, Jenny's blue eyes didn't blink.

"Let me hold Jenny, please—"

"Shut up!" He spat the words, and they quivered in the

259

quiet air. March looked toward the kitchen. Beth's gaze darted to the open door as a figure appeared suddenly. It was Jack Tustman! He had a gun. A pistol or revolver, she didn't know the difference, only that it looked huge and deadly. Jack put a finger to his lips. She looked back at March. He moved so quickly, Beth screamed.

"No—"

He scooped Jenny under his arm and ducked behind the end of the sofa. Jenny fell to the floor like a rag doll. March raised the rifle and sighted down the barrel toward the kitchen.

"No!" Beth screamed again, half in protest, half in warning as Jack flung himself into the archway and fired a shot in March's direction, then ducked back into the kitchen. The bullet tore into the arm of the sofa and sprayed up a spume of white plastic foam.

"No, for God's sake, don't! He's got Jenny!" Beth screamed as the deafening roar of the shot died. She lunged at March, pulling the shard of glass from her pocket. She stabbed wildly. The point of glass plunged into his shoulder as he swung the rifle butt and hit Beth in the stomach.

She doubled over in agony as air whooshed from her lungs. March gave her a push that sent her reeling as another shot rang out. She collapsed behind the chair near the door, clutching her stomach and struggling for breath. When she saw the blood on her slacks and blouse, she realized her hand was bleeding. The piece of glass had fallen when March hit her. It lay smeared with his blood and hers on the gray carpet between them. A bloodstain was spreading on March's shirt, but he seemed unaware of it. He had the rifle balanced on the arm of the sofa, again aimed toward the kitchen. Behind him, Jenny was slumped against the wall. She hadn't made a sound, and her empty expression was more than Beth could bear. Her fear and fury fused. Wasn't it enough he had murdered Gil and destroyed their lives? She wouldn't let him have Jenny, too!

She breathed in shallow gasps until the pain in her midsection eased. She wiped her bloody hand on her slacks and looked around the side of the chair toward the kitchen. She didn't see Jack. March hadn't fired at him, but maybe Jack had seen the rifle. How in the world had Jack known where to find them? She prayed he hadn't come alone, that the sheriff was with him or on his way.

She straightened up slowly and leaned against the high-backed chair, still breathing gingerly. She was only a few feet from the open front door. She could be outside before March could grab her, but it didn't seem to worry him. Why should it when he had the gun and Jenny? He knew she'd never leave without Jenny. He'd been toying with her, playing the way a cat teases a mouse before the kill.

Jack, where are you? March was volatile. She couldn't risk waiting to see what he'd do next. He could kill them or get them killed in the crossfire when the sheriff got here. Their lives meant nothing to him.

Think, Beth, think! A movement behind March's crouched figure caught her attention. Jenny was looking around as if the noise had snapped her back to reality. She looked scared to death as she glanced from March to her mother. Beth put her finger to her lips, praying that Jenny wouldn't cry out and startle March.

CHAPTER THIRTY-EIGHT

Vince had just started up the drive when a shot blasted the quiet. He broke into a run, clutching the binoculars when they thumped against his ribs.

As he came to the curve near the clearing, another shot rang out. He dove into the trees. No way he wanted to be a clear target if March was blowing off heads. Leaning against a pine trunk to catch his breath, he raised the binoculars. He couldn't spot Tustman. Had he ducked back into the woods or gone inside? Christ, he could be lying somewhere with a bullet in his heart. And what about Beth and Jenny? Sweat trickled down Vince's sideburns. What the hell was going on in there?

Raising the Nikon, he focused and snapped a few shots of the cabin before he began to work his way around to where he'd last seen Tustman. It was slow going. He skidded and slipped on the dry ground as he tried to stay low and out of sight. He muffled a surprised yelp and swore silently when a tree branch slapped him. For all he knew, March could have a bead on him right now. He wiped away another trickle of sweat.

He stopped again to check things out. Both doors of the cabin were open, but he didn't see anyone moving around inside. He should wait for the sheriff, but it would take Mayville a good ten minutes to drive from town. If Tustman was planning to storm the place, it could be all over by then. Okay, so go for it. Vince got down on his hands and knees and scrambled up the incline near the carport. The noise sounded loud enough to raise the dead, but there were no shots from inside the cabin. He lay flat to catch his breath and study the house.

The door behind the car led to a kitchen. He could make out the corner of a table and the refrigerator. And there was a figure outlined against the white enamel. Unless Rick March had gained forty pounds in the joint, it was Jack Tustman, and he was holding a gun. Jesus . . . Had he fired the shots or had March? Where were Beth and the kid?

Staying low, Vince crept around the carport to the back of the house. It was built on the edge of the clearing with only a foot or so between it and the woods. A wild tangle of weeds had grown right up to the foundation in places. Vince picked his way carefully and ducked as he passed the first window, which he figured was still the kitchen. The other two would probably be bedrooms. On the first one, the shade was pulled down right to the windowsill, and he couldn't see in. At the next one, the shade only came to within four inches of the sill. He leaned close. The curtains were pulled, but there was a narrow slit where they didn't quite meet. He pressed his face to the glass and shielded his eyes. He could see part of a bed. A plaid blanket was heaped on the bare mattress. Beyond it, a faint spill of light came through a doorway. In it he could make out something against the wall. It was the kid.

A shot blasted so close, Vince flattened himself against the siding, his heart pounding. Another shot followed on its heels, louder and sharper. Someone started to scream, but it cut off almost instantly.

He was no expert, but he'd swear both shots didn't come from the same gun. The second one sounded like a rifle. If March had a rifle, no wonder Tustman was being cautious.

Vince peered between the curtains again to study the

kid. Was she the one who screamed? He wished he could see her face. Where was Beth? If she wasn't holding the kid, it was a pretty sure bet March and the gun were between her and the kid, but where in the room?

Holding the camera and binoculars so they wouldn't bang together, he made his way around the corner and along the side of the cabin. There was another window in the room he'd just looked into, but the shade was down all the way. The next small, high window would be the bathroom.

At the front corner, he stopped and lifted the binoculars to check the driveway for any sign of Mayville. Damn it, where was he? He couldn't be more than a few minutes away. Vince swung the glasses to the trail of crushed grass, brush and saplings he'd examined on his way up. It ended in a deck or pavilion of some kind. Upended in it, nose in the air and the roof of the structure clamped to its hood like jaws, was a car. He raised the camera and snapped a picture before he turned back to the cabin. The open front door had two concrete steps up to a three-foot-square landing. If he could get closer, he might be able to spot Beth and March.

He slipped the binoculars from around his neck and put them on the grass. Checking the focus on the Nikon, he held it ready for a quick shot as he ducked around the corner and crept to the steps. Hardly daring to breathe, he raised his head to look inside, then stifled his surprise when he found Beth Davies looking right at him. She was sitting on the floor behind a high-backed chair, her face dead white except for a mean-looking scrape on her chin. Her blouse and slacks were smeared with blood. Her mouth opened in astonishment, then shut as Vince put his finger to his lips. Without turning her head, she glanced sidelong toward the doorway where he'd seen the kid. Did that mean March was there?

Jack Tustman's voice boomed. "Throw down the gun, March."

"Come and get it," March yelled. His voice came from across the room.

"You won't get away," Tustman said. "The sheriff has the place surrounded."

Beth looked at Vince. He shook his head. Tustman was a lousy bluffer. March had been in enough confrontations with lawmen to know they didn't send citizens into gunfights.

"Let the little girl go," Tustman said. "You don't want her to get hurt."

"She's fine where she is," March said. "I'm taking good care of her."

"Let her go," Tustman said again.

"You'd like that, wouldn't you? How far would she get? Halfway across the room?"

"Let her go, damn it!"

Vince was watching the kitchen doorway, but he was astonished at how fast the big man moved. Tustman spun around the corner and crouched in firing position, the pistol held straight out in both hands. He squeezed off a shot and leaped back in a single motion. But not fast enough. March's gun blasted. Tustman grabbed his shoulder as he disappeared into the kitchen.

"I was aiming for the shoulder, Tustman," March called. "Figured maybe to chip the collarbone a little. How'd I do?" Tustman didn't answer.

Vince cursed silently. If he'd been in position when he saw Tustman, he could have gotten a picture, but at least the exchange had pinpointed March for him. He was right across from the open door, maybe ten feet. Vince gauged the dimensions of the cabin. That probably put March next to the kid near the bedroom doorway.

He craned his neck to look past Beth. There was a sofa against the wall between the kitchen and the bedroom. March must be using it for cover. It gave him time to aim, but it was still damned good shooting. If March was that good, why hadn't he finished off Tustman? Maybe he was bluffing, claiming a bull's eye after the fact.

Vince weighed his chances of popping out into the open long enough to get a picture of March through the open doorway. The light was pretty lousy in there, but he had Tri-X film. Still, it wasn't worth the risk. Not when he didn't know for sure what was going on. So far March didn't know he was here. Vince wanted to keep it that way, but he wanted that picture, too.

He worried that Beth might give him away, but her attention was focused on March and the kid across from her. She sure as hell didn't look like the scared worrier he'd talked to in her apartment. She looked mad enough to kill. God, what a picture. He raised the camera and clicked the shutter. Her head came around fast, and he got off another shot before he ducked, keeping his fingers crossed that the whir of the automatic film advance wasn't loud enough for March to pick up.

March yelled again. "Where's the sheriff, Tustman? He's moving mighty slow out there, don't you think? Tell him to come in. I've been waiting for him. You're a surprise bonus. I feel like I won the lottery."

March sounded so cocky, Vince wondered if he knew Tustman was bluffing. The sheriff had to be as high on March's Most Wanted list as March was on Mayville's. Maybe March was waiting for him. It was going to make a hell of a story.

The real puzzler was why March hadn't killed anyone so far. He didn't seem worried about Beth. Maybe she'd already tried to grab the kid and gotten those cuts and bruises for her efforts. Or maybe he had the kid tied up. Vince wished he could see.

Tustman didn't answer March's last taunt. How badly was he hurt? Vince considered going around to the kitchen to check, but discarded the idea quickly. Things weren't going to be quiet much longer.

CHAPTER THIRTY-NINE

Beth's breathing hadn't caught up with her racing heart since she saw Vince Norris outside. Did he come with Jack? She had almost cried out when he raised a camera and took a picture of her. Was he crazy? She didn't think March had heard the click and whir of the camera, or if he had, he wasn't letting on. He was sighting down the barrel of the rifle again, waiting.

She glanced toward the kitchen where Jack had disappeared. Something at the end of the living room caught her eye, and she realized with horror that any movement in the kitchen was reflected by the glass of a picture hanging on the wall. It wasn't a clear image, but the blur of Jack's light-colored suit moved toward the doorway like a miniature spotlight. March was watching his every move—

She jumped when March fired. Jack screamed, and his gun fell to the carpet several feet from the doorway. His reflection disappeared from the glass. Behind March, Jenny covered her ears and began to cry. March backhanded her without taking his eyes off the doorway. Beth started to crawl toward Jenny, but March raised his hand toward Jenny again, ready to swing.

"Stay where you are!" he warned.

Beth backed down. Jenny gave her a terrified look, then cringed into a tight ball as she stared at March. Beth tried to decide if he was bluffing. He'd had plenty of chances to kill her but didn't. If she went for Jenny, would he shoot? Maybe not, but his threatening hand over Jenny reminded her he had other ways to stop her.

She glanced toward the kitchen. How badly was Jack hurt? He should have gone for help while he had the chance. He was crazy to try to rescue her and Jenny by himself. Was he stalling for time because the sheriff was on the way? She looked at Jenny, wanting to reassure her, but the child was staring at March. Beth prayed she wouldn't do anything to startle him. She jumped when he yelled.

"That was a stupid move, Tustman, but then I figured out some time ago you're not as smart as you think you are. Come out where I can see you." There was no answer from the kitchen. "Come out before I forget about talking and come in after you."

There was a scuffle of sound, and Beth looked around as Jack staggered into the doorway, his coat and shirt front bloody. He was holding his shoulder, and his right hand was covered with blood.

"That's far enough," March said. Jack stopped at the end of the sofa like an obedient dog. He eyed the gun several feet away.

"Kick it over here," March ordered.

Jack moved toward the gun and nudged it with his foot. It skidded halfway down the room but not close enough for March to reach. Jack moved toward it tentatively.

"Leave it there, jerk!" March said. He pointed with the rifle. "Sit." He indicated the chair Beth had sat in earlier.

Jack moved without taking his eyes from March. March got up off his knees and flexed his legs like a runner before a race. Jenny made a soft mewling sound, and March reached back and pulled her to her feet. Every muscle in Beth's body tensed.

Suddenly, Jack dove for the gun on the floor. March

fired and pumped a new shell into the chamber in a single motion. The bullet smacked the floor beside Jack as he rolled, grabbed the gun and fired. March shoved Jenny and dropped back behind the sofa. A trickle of blood appeared across his temple as he raised the rifle. Jack fired two more shots in rapid succession. One shattered a window somewhere behind March; the other thudded into the sofa arm close to his head. March shoved Jenny to the floor and flattened himself beside her. At floor level, he edged the rifle barrel around the sofa and fired. Jack rolled again, toward the kitchen, but the bullet caught him in the thigh. He screamed, and the gun flew from his hand as he grabbed his leg. March sprang like a cat and kicked it away before Tustman could recover. He jabbed the rifle in Tustman's ribs. Beth started to scramble toward Jenny, but March stepped back and blocked her way.

"Sit there." He pointed to the chair she'd been hiding behind. He poked the rifle at Jack again. "You, on the sofa."

Jack whimpered. "I'm hurt bad. I need a doctor."

March grabbed his arm and dragged him to the sofa, leaving a trail of blood across the carpet. Jack moaned, still clutching his leg. "I need a doctor."

"Shut up!" March told him. He brushed his hand across his bleeding temple as Jack's gaze moved nervously to the gun on the floor. It was only inches from Beth's feet. He looked at her and gave an almost imperceptible nod toward it.

Beth licked her lips. How many shots did March have left without reloading? Time was running out. Jenny was crumpled where March had pushed her. Her face was hidden, but her tightly clenched fists showed how frightened she was. As March looked at his bloody hand, Beth lunged for the gun. March shot out his foot to kick it away, but he was an instant too late. She grabbed the gun and pointed it at him. She had to steady it with both hands.

"Shoot!" Jack yelled.

CHAPTER FORTY

RELEASED SLAYER KILLS AGAIN! Well, maybe Tustman wasn't dead, but it was still a hell of a picture.

Vince scuttled back to retrieve the binoculars and made a fast retreat around the house. He crouched as he went by the windows, even though he was sure March was too busy now to notice anything but his targets.

As he reached the carport, a volley of shots rang out. Vince dove into the woods as he heard a window shatter. It was turning into a God damned bloodbath in there. Where the hell was the sheriff? He looked at his watch and was astonished to see only ten minutes had elapsed since he phoned.

He heard voices inside the cabin but not clearly enough to understand what they were saying. Sounded like March and Tustman. Something was going down in there. He was torn between finding out what and checking on the sheriff. Finally he scrambled to his feet and circled through the trees along the trampled trail he'd made earlier. He skidded and slid down the bank until he came out below the cabin where he wouldn't be seen.

He broke through the brush and stopped dead in his tracks when he found two guns pointed at him. He raised a hand to wipe his face.

"Jeez, take it easy, Sheriff. We're on the same side."

Mayville motioned to the deputy and lowered his gun. "I thought I told you to wait at the car."

"Hell, they're shooting up there. Let's not waste time arguing."

"Are they all inside the cabin?" Mayville glanced up the drive.

"Yeah. March has a rifle and the kid. Tustman has a pistol. Looks like a thirty-eight. One of March's shots got him, but I think he's still in there fighting. There were some more shots as I was coming down. Everything's happening so damned fast, it's hard to keep score."

"Where's Liz?"

Vince described the cabin and where the four people were.

"Are Liz and Jenny okay?"

"I didn't get a good look at the kid. March is sticking to her like a linebacker. Liz has some cuts and bruises. Looks like March may have knocked her around a little."

"What about March?"

"I only saw him for a second. There's blood on his shirt. I don't know if it's his." Vince glanced at the deputy who seemed to be the only help Mayville had brought. "You two going to try to take him?" The sheriff and one deputy against March with two or three hostages weren't great odds.

Mayville squinted up the drive as if he were sorting mental pictures. "The D.A. made it clear that this is his case. I called Miriam when we turned off the highway. Asked her to phone over to the State Police so they can notify Ondavin about the tip that March might be up here." Mayville looked at Vince. "You say both doors are wide open?"

"Yeah."

Mayville turned to the deputy. "Jerry, take the driveway. Stay out of sight when you get near the clearing. Cover the front door. I'll go around to the kitchen and see if I can get inside without tipping off March." The sheriff glanced at

273

his watch. "I should be in place in the short side of five minutes. Don't do anything until I give the word. Just keep that damned door covered and remember, it's March we want. Make sure who you're shooting at."

"Right, Sheriff." The deputy stepped into the brush and vanished like a cat into the thicket of trees.

"You stay put this time, Norris," the sheriff said.

"Forget it. We're in this together, Mayville. I called you, didn't I?"

The sheriff squinted. "Not until you were damned good and ready."

Vince said, "I'll follow orders. Come on, we're wasting time. They've fired enough shots up there to make a hell of a mess."

The sheriff motioned Vince behind him as he started up the bank, following the path of scattered leaves and debris Vince had left in his wake.

CHAPTER FORTY-ONE

The gun was so heavy, Beth had trouble steadying her hands.

"Put the gun down," she told March.

"Shoot!" Jack shouted again.

March reached into his pocket for shells and dropped them into the magazine.

"Shoot now, damn it!" Jack yelled. He lunged toward her, but his leg buckled, and he fell writhing to the floor. "For God's sake, shoot the bastard. He murdered your husband and my wife!"

Beth's finger tightened on the trigger.

March looked at her. "You want your husband's murderer? There he is." He pointed the rifle barrel at Tustman.

Jack's face was twisted with pain, and sweat beaded on his temples. "Don't listen to him," he said. "He's trying to save his own neck."

March was still between Beth and Jenny. He watched her but didn't move. She was afraid to fire because Jenny was so close. There had been plenty of chances for March to kill her, but he hadn't.

March said, "Did you know your husband was having an affair with his wife?"

The gun wavered in Beth's hands.

"You didn't know, did you?" He looked at Jack. "But Jack here did, right, Tustman? Suzie knew you were slipping home spying on her. She was afraid you found out about Gil, but she figured she'd be able to talk her way out of it. She'd done it plenty of times before."

Jack's face mottled with rage. "For God's sake, Liz, shoot the bastard! Don't you see what he's trying to do?"

March poked him in the gut with the rifle barrel. Jack cowered. "What happened that day when Husby got back to the office?" March said. "Did he accuse you of diddling the company books? Suzie told Husby about that, just like she told me. It was her insurance, her hold over you when you came down too hard on her about her catting around. I was going to try using it to squeeze a couple of hundred bucks out of old Gil, but you got there before me."

Beth looked from one to the other of them. What was March saying? He seemed so sure of himself.

"Don't listen to him, Liz," Jack urged. "He's a liar and a cold-blooded killer!"

"He was shooting at Jenny, not me," March said. "It was okay if he took me out, too, but Jenny was the one he had to get rid of."

Stunned, Beth looked at Jack. His face was smeared with blood where he had wiped away the sweat. Under it, he was deathly pale. She had warned him Jenny was behind the sofa with March, and he'd shot anyhow. But *at* Jenny? A fragment of breath escaped from her lungs.

"He wants Jenny out of the way. She's the witness he's scared of. She came in the back way and saw him hitting her daddy with the pipe he managed to ditch," March said. "Ask her. I dropped the tire iron and got the hell out of there. Jack here saw his chance to frame me. He probably would have killed the kid on the spot, too, if you hadn't come along."

Beth's hands were damp with sweat and shaking so badly she didn't have the strength to hold up the gun. She let it drop to her side. Jack reached for it, but March jabbed him in the wounded shoulder with the point of the rifle. Jack let out a howl of pain.

Jenny whimpered, and Beth started toward her, but March flung out his arm to stop her. She sank to her knees, still watching her child.

"Jenny? Please, honey, talk to me."

Jenny raised her head slowly. She looked so frightened. Beth remembered the gun in her hand. She put it down on the floor beside her and leaned toward Jenny, holding out her arms.

"Don't cry. It's going to be okay. Mommy's here."

"Ask her," March said.

"Liz, for God's sake—"

"Shut up, Tustman, or I'll blow a hole through you!" March said. Jenny cringed and squeezed her eyes shut. "You're not going to get the chance to frame me for Suzie's murder. She was alive when I left. What did she do, call you and tell you she paid me off, or were you spying at the windows again? Did she tell you how much she enjoyed it?"

Beth rocked back and forth. "Jenny?"

Jenny opened her eyes. "Mommy?"

"It's okay, honey. We're going to be okay."

Rick March made an impatient sound and took a step toward Jenny. "Tell your mother, kid. Tell her!"

Jenny hid her face. March grabbed her arm and shook her. "Tell her!"

Beth forgot the gun, forgot March's threats, and forgot everything but her child. She leaped at March.

"Leave her alone! Can't you see she's terrified?"

March shoved Beth aside and stood over her with the rifle. Beth realized she had pushed him too far. Then suddenly March lowered the gun and wiped his mouth with the back of his hand.

For a moment, he wasn't a crazed killer but the lonely teenager whose face she had drawn on the back of her notebook, wanting something he never had, anger and defiance his only weapons against his own vulnerability.

Beth said, "Please, give her a little time."

March let the rifle slide to the crook of his arm. Relief flooded Beth, and she looked back at her daughter.

"Jenny, darling—"

There was a noise in the kitchen. They all had heard it. Jack seemed to be holding his breath expectantly. March's eyes narrowed as he moved quickly toward Jenny. Beth sprang before he could reach her and gathered Jenny into her arms. March sank beside them. When Beth skittered crab-like into the tiny hall, he didn't try to stop her. He balanced the rifle on the sofa arm and aimed toward the kitchen. Jack threw himself sideways and rolled away from the sofa.

"Behind the sofa, Sheriff," he yelled. "He's got a rifle!"

The cabin was so quiet, Beth heard her heart beat and March's ragged breathing. Was the sheriff there? Someone was. She remembered Vince Norris.

"Come out with your hands up, March!" It was Mayville. "You can't get away. We've got the cabin surrounded."

March didn't shoot. Again Beth thought about how many times he could have killed her in the past hours and hadn't, or Jenny either. He had bragged about deliberately only wounding Jack.

The sheriff called again. "This is your last chance, March. Throw down the gun and come out."

"Shoot!" Jack yelled.

"No!" Beth didn't realize she screamed until March turned to look at her. In that instant, Jack grabbed the gun

278

Beth had forgotten on the floor. "Look out!" Beth cried.

March whirled and flung himself across the doorway as Jack's shot exploded with a deafening roar. Air whooshed from March's lungs in a huge breath as he sprawled in front of Beth and Jenny.

Blood began to seep across the back of his shirt.

Jenny gave a muffled cry, and Beth realized she was hugging her so tight the child couldn't breathe. She loosened her grip and looked up in time to see Jack aim again at her and Jenny. Instinctively she fell back and rolled, hugging Jenny, bumping over her small body as she dragged herself behind the protection of the wall. Jack's shot came so close she heard the hiss of air before it slammed into plasterboard.

"Don't shoot," she screamed. "Don't shoot."

There was a scuffle of noise, and moments later the sheriff was beside her. "You okay?"

She tried to sit up and was grateful when Mayville helped her. Behind him, Vince Norris' camera clicked and whirred. Jenny was crying with huge, gulping sobs. Beth rocked her. This time she meant it when she said, "Shh, it's all over, honey."

They were safe, but nothing would ever be all right again. She buried her face in Jenny's tousled hair as Norris' camera clicked away.

CHAPTER FORTY-TWO

"Put down that damned camera and get out of the way," Mayville ordered Norris as he leaned over Beth and Jenny. "Are you okay, Liz?"

She nodded. She hadn't been hit by any bullets, but she felt critically wounded in her emotions. Jack . . . the one person she had trusted . . . It was hard to believe.

The sheriff turned to examine March. Hugging Jenny, Beth scooted back to get her slacks out of the pool of blood collecting on the floor. March's eyes were open. His breathing rattled.

"Call for an ambulance," Mayville ordered over his shoulder. The deputy ran out the front door.

"Is he going to live?" Beth asked shakily. The sheriff shrugged.

In the living room, Jack Tustman moaned. "Never mind that scum bag, Sheriff. Get me a doctor before I bleed to death!"

Mayville picked up March's rifle and retreated to the living room. Beth rocked Jenny who had stopped crying and lay in her arms, looking very pale and wide-eyed as she watched the activity around her. Beth met March's slightly unfocused stare. His accusation of Jack hung between them like an impending storm. She didn't want it to be true. Not Jack, who had helped her and Jenny survive the trauma of Gil's death. Not the one person she had trusted and believed her friend.

She heard Rick March's voice in her mind. *Your husband*

was having an affair with his wife . . . Did he accuse you of did-dling the company books . . . He's shooting at Jenny, not me . . .

March had saved Jenny's life and perhaps hers as well, by throwing himself in front of them when Jack fired. What March said was true: Jack wanted to kill them. Tears rolled down Beth's cheeks.

"You okay?"

She looked up. Vince Norris was watching her with a concerned expression. She looked away.

"I was in the kitchen with the sheriff," he said. "You think March was telling the truth about your husband's murder?"

She didn't answer. All Norris wanted was a story. From start to finish, it had been his only interest. She would never forget his camera clicking away while March and Jack held her life and Jenny's in jeopardy. She wanted to hate Norris, but her anger had drained, and she felt sorry for him. He lived in a world of truth and lies that were too similar to tell apart easily. Right now she needed to be alone, to let time heal her wounds so she could forget this horror and start over. She pressed her face to Jenny's hair.

"Mommy?"

Beth hugged her. "Yes, honey?"

"I was scared."

Beth shifted the child in her arms so she wouldn't see Rick March on the floor. "I was scared, too, but it's over now. No more. No more . . ."

Jenny clutched her hand as if trying to make herself be-lieve it. "I'm still scared, Mommy."

"I know, honey." Did she really? How could anyone know the trauma Jenny had suffered?

"Is Uncle Jack mad at me like he was at Daddy?"

281

Beth's gaze caught March's. His face mirrored pain. A trickle of blood ran from the corner of his mouth.

"No, honey," Beth said. "No one is mad at you, I promise."

"I went up the back way so I could surprise Daddy."

The back way . . . The stairs Jack would have used . . . Jenny had seen, if not the murder, enough to incriminate Jack if March hadn't been there, too. Beth suppressed a shudder. Jack must have decided on the spot that it would be easy enough to frame the town's former bad boy. And later when he found out Suzie had been entertaining March as well as Gil, he forced her to lie and seal March's fate.

Beth glanced at March's pale face. His eyes were those of the boy she'd sketched on her notebook. Suddenly she prayed with her whole heart that he would live. His mouth twitched and very slowly, as if each muscle movement caused him pain, March smiled. His eyes closed.

Beyond the open front door, a mockingbird fenced off its feeding territory with a song. As the sound died in the quiet morning, an ambulance siren wailed in the distance.

CHAPTER FORTY-THREE

The morning newspaper was on the apron in front of the garage. Beth retrieved it, and as she picked it up, saw the envelope sticking out of the open mailbox. She took it out and shut the box before she went back up the steps of the Fischer house.

In the bright kitchen, she poured herself a cup of coffee from the electric maker and put it on the table where she could look out over the city. Before she sat down, she walked down the hall to the bedroom to be sure Jenny was still asleep. She stood a moment gazing at her sleeping child. She was exhausted, poor thing, but the drawn, pained look was gone while she slept.

Yesterday she and Jenny had spent hours going over their stories and answering questions for the sheriff, the district attorney and the state police. Sheriff Mayville had offered to put them up for the night, but Beth refused. She and Jenny needed to get away from Pine Lake, to be alone. They hadn't stopped for dinner until they were almost home.

She fortified herself with several swallows of coffee before she took a deep breath and finally opened the paper. The headline spanned four columns.

KIDNAPPED GIRL FOUND SAFE

Beneath it was a wide-angle shot of the living room of the cabin on Sullivan Road. Jack Tustman lay twisted on the floor, his light-colored suit stained darkly with blood. Sheriff Mayville stood over him, pistol still in hand. At the other side of the picture Rick March was at an angle to the lens so the top of his head eclipsed his face, and his body faded into a blur. She and Jenny, cradled in her arms, were invisible in the deeply blurred shadow of the hall beyond him.

She let out her breath, remembering the whir and click of the camera, the snap of the shutter that had caught her by surprise when she first saw him outside the open cabin door. Relief flooded her. Had Norris spared her, or had he used this photo because blood and gore sold papers?

She scanned the story quickly. She needed no reminding of what had happened. Norris' account of the shoot-out between Tustman and March was vivid and compelling, but he skimmed over Jenny and Beth's ordeal other than saying March had apparently kidnapped the child in order to prove his innocence and force a showdown with Tustman. He left it to the reader's imagination as to how Beth had gotten there, but that was fine with her. The sooner the whole thing died from the news the better.

She folded the paper and put it aside, then picked up the envelope she'd taken from the mailbox. Her name was written on the front. When she tore it open, a roll of film fell out. There was no note. She turned the envelope over. There was no return address.

She sat for a long time holding the canister of film. With only a brief mention of her and Jenny in the paper, the furor would die out quickly. They could get on with their lives. Honestly now. No more lies or half-truths, no more hiding. She would face her past and future squarely so Jenny could too. Neither of them had to be scared anymore.

She jumped to grab the phone when it rang. She had left

a message on Madelaine's machine asking her for an emergency appointment. She wasn't going to send Jenny back to school until the psychologist helped them both sort out things.

But it wasn't Madelaine; it was Vince Norris. He didn't say so, but she recognized his voice.

"There's a lonesome Doberman tied to your mailbox. The vet says he's as good as new."

She didn't know what to say, so she said nothing.

"Good luck, Beth."

She hung up when the dial tone hummed. Was that an apology, that and the film?

She hurried to the front door and ran down the stairs. Baron gave a delighted wiggle when he saw her. She had to fend off his tongue as she untied the piece of rope attached to the mailbox post.

"Come on, boy. I know a little girl who is going to be very happy to see you."

Inside, she undid the rope and let him run. He headed straight for the bedroom, and a moment later she heard Jenny's happy squeals.